THE MAN WHO COULD NOT LOSE

They found Dromedary in the paddock, and thanked him, and Carter left Dolly with him.

THE NOVELS AND STORIES OF
RICHARD HARDING DAVIS

THE MAN WHO COULD NOT LOSE

BY

RICHARD HARDING DAVIS

WITH AN INTRODUCTION BY
LEONARD WOOD

ILLUSTRATED

NEW YORK
CHARLES SCRIBNER'S SONS
1927

The first seven stories in this volume from "The Man Who Could Not Lose," copyright, 1911, by CHARLES SCRIBNER'S SONS.

"The Log of the 'Jolly Polly,'" copyright, 1915, by THE METROPOLITAN MAGAZINE COMPANY.

COPYRIGHT, 1916, BY
CHARLES SCRIBNER'S SONS

Printed in the United States of America

RICHARD HARDING DAVIS

The death of Richard Harding Davis was a real loss to the movement for preparedness. Mr. Davis had an extensive experience as a military observer, and thoroughly appreciated the need of a general training system like that of Australia or Switzerland and of thorough organization of our industrial resources in order to establish a condition of reasonable preparedness in this country. A few days before his death he came to Governors Island for the purpose of ascertaining in what line of work he could be most useful in building up sound public opinion in favor of such preparedness as would give us a real peace insurance. His mind was bent on devoting his energies and abilities to the work of public education on this vitally important subject, and few men were better qualified to do so, for he had served as a military observer in many campaigns.

Throughout the Cuban campaign he was attached to the headquarters of my regiment in Cuba as a military observer. He was with the advanced party at the opening of the fight at Las Guasimas, and was distinguished throughout the fight by coolness and good conduct. He also participated in the battle of San Juan and the siege of Santiago, and as an observer was always where duty called him. He was a delightful companion, cheerful, resourceful, and thoughtful of the interests and wishes of others. His reports of the campaign were valuable and among the best and most accurate.

The Plattsburg movement took very strong hold of him. He saw in this a great instrument for building up a sound knowledge concerning our military history and policy, also a very practical way of training men for the duties of junior officers. He realized fully that we should need in case of war tens of thousands of officers with our newly raised troops, and that it would be utterly impossible to prepare them in the hurry and confusion of the onrush of modern war. His heart was filled with a desire to serve his country to the best of his ability. His recent experience in Europe pointed out to him the absolute madness of longer disregarding the need of doing those things which reasonable preparedness dictates, the things which cannot be accomplished after trouble is upon us. He had in mind at the time of his death a series of articles to be written especially to build up interest in universal military training through conveying to our people an understanding of what organization as it exists to-day means, and how vitally important it is for our people to do in time of peace those things which modern war does not permit done once it is under way.

Davis was a loyal friend, a thorough-going American devoted to the best interests of his country, courageous, sympathetic, and true. His loss has

RICHARD HARDING DAVIS

been a very real one to all of us who knew and appreciated him, and in his death the cause of preparedness has lost an able worker and the country a devoted and loyal citizen.

LEONARD WOOD.

CONTENTS

Richard Harding Davis . . . . . . *Leonard Wood*

	PAGE
THE MAN WHO COULD NOT LOSE	1
MY BURIED TREASURE	62
THE CONSUL	93
THE NATURE FAKER	128
BILLY AND THE BIG STICK	149
THE FRAME-UP	186
THE LOST HOUSE	223
"THE LOG OF THE 'JOLLY POLLY'"	312

ILLUSTRATIONS

THEY FOUND DROMEDARY IN THE PADDOCK, AND THANKED HIM, AND CARTER LEFT DOLLY WITH HIM . . . . *Frontispiece*

FACING PAGE

AS THOUGH GIVING A SIGNAL, HE SHOT HIS FREE HAND INTO THE AIR 28

IN HIS HANDS HE CLUTCHED THE TWO SUIT-CASES. . . . "GET OUT!" HE SHOUTED . . 88

"THEN I AM TO UNDERSTAND," HE EXCLAIMED, "THAT YOU REFUSE TO CARRY OUT THE WISHES OF A UNITED STATES SENATOR AND OF THE PRESIDENT OF THE UNITED STATES?" 120

IN A COCKNEY ACCENT THAT MADE EVEN THE ACCOMPANIST GRIN, FORD LIFTED HIS VOICE 244

THE MAN WHO COULD NOT LOSE

THE Carters had married in haste and refused to repent at leisure. So blindly were they in love, that they considered their marriage their greatest asset. The rest of the world, as represented by mutual friends, considered it the only thing that could be urged against either of them. While single, each had been popular. As a bachelor, young "Champ" Carter had filled his modest place acceptably. Hostesses sought him for dinners and week-end parties, men of his own years, for golf and tennis, and young girls liked him because when he talked to one of them he never talked of himself, or let his eyes wander toward any other girl. He had been brought up by a rich father in an expensive way, and the rich father had then died leaving Champneys alone in the world, with no money, and with even a few of his father's debts. These debts of honor the son, ever since leaving Yale, had been paying off. It had kept him very poor, for Carter had elected to live by his pen, and, though he wrote very carefully and slowly, the editors of the magazines had been equally careful and slow in accepting what he wrote.

THE MAN WHO COULD NOT LOSE

With an income so uncertain that the only thing that could be said of it with certainty was that it was too small to support even himself, Carter should not have thought of matrimony. Nor, must it be said to his credit, did he think of it until the girl came along that he wanted to marry.

The trouble with Dolly Ingram was her mother. Her mother was a really terrible person. She was quite impossible. She was a social leader, and of such importance that visiting princes and society reporters, even among themselves, did not laugh at her. Her visiting list was so small that she did not keep a social secretary, but, it was said, wrote her invitations herself. Stylites on his pillar was less exclusive. Nor did he take his exalted but lonely position with less sense of humor. When Ingram died and left her many millions to dispose of absolutely as she pleased, even to the allowance she should give their daughter, he left her with but one ambition unfulfilled. That was to marry her Dolly to an English duke. Hungarian princes, French marquises, Italian counts, German barons, Mrs. Ingram could not see. Her son-in-law must be a duke. She had her eyes on two, one somewhat shopworn, and the other a bankrupt; and in training, she had one just coming of age. Already she saw her-

THE MAN WHO COULD NOT LOSE

self a sort of a dowager duchess by marriage, discussing with real dowager duchesses the way to bring up teething earls and viscounts. For three years in Europe Mrs. Ingram had been drilling her daughter for the part she intended her to play. But, on returning to her native land, Dolly, who possessed all the feelings, thrills, and heart-throbs of which her mother was ignorant, ungratefully fell deeply in love with Champneys Carter, and he with her.

It was always a question of controversy between them as to which had first fallen in love with the other. As a matter of history, honors were even.

He first saw her during a thunder storm, in the paddock at the races, wearing a rain-coat with the collar turned up and a Panama hat with the brim turned down. She was talking, in terms of affectionate familiarity, with Cuthbert's two-year-old, The Scout. The Scout had just lost a race by a nose, and Dolly was holding the nose against her cheek and comforting him. The two made a charming picture, and, as Carter stumbled upon it and halted, the race-horse lowered his eyes and seemed to say: "Wouldn't *you* throw a race for this?" And the girl raised her eyes and seemed to say: "What a nice-looking, bright-looking young man! Why don't I know who you are?"

THE MAN WHO COULD NOT LOSE

So, Carter ran to find Cuthbert, and told him. The Scout had gone lame. When, on their return, Miss Ingram refused to loosen her hold on The Scout's nose, Cuthbert apologetically mumbled Carter's name, and in some awe Miss Ingram's name, and then, to his surprise, both young people lost interest in The Scout, and wandered away together into the rain.

After an hour, when they parted at the club stand, for which Carter could not afford a ticket, he asked wistfully: "Do you often come racing?" and Miss Ingram said: "Do you mean, am I coming to-morrow?"

"I do!" said Carter.

"Then, why didn't you say that?" inquired Miss Ingram. "Otherwise I mightn't have come. I have the Holland House coach for to-morrow, and, if you'll join us, I'll save a place for you, and you can sit in our box.

"I've lived so long abroad," she explained, "that I'm afraid of not being simple and direct like other American girls. Do you think I'll get on here at home?"

"If you get on with every one else as well as you've got on with me," said Carter morosely, "I will shoot myself."

Miss Ingram smiled thoughtfully.

"At eleven, then," she said, "in front of the Holland House."

THE MAN WHO COULD NOT LOSE

Carter walked away with a flurried, heated suffocation around his heart and a joyous lightness in his feet. Of the first man he met he demanded, who was the beautiful girl in the rain-coat? And when the man told him, Carter left him without speaking. For she was quite the richest girl in America. But the next day that fault seemed to distress her so little that Carter, also, refused to allow it to rest on his conscience, and they were very happy. *And* each saw that they were happy because they were together.

The ridiculous mother was not present at the races, but after Carter began to call at their house and was invited to dinner, Mrs. Ingram received him with her habitual rudeness. As an impediment in the success of her ambition she never considered him. As a boy friend of her daughter's, she classed him with "her" lawyer and "her" architect and a little higher than the "person" who arranged the flowers. Nor, in her turn, did Dolly consider her mother; for within two months another matter of controversy between Dolly and Carter was as to who had first proposed to the other. Carter protested there never had been any formal proposal, that from the first they had both taken it for granted that married they would be. But Dolly insisted that because he had been afraid

THE MAN WHO COULD NOT LOSE

of her money, or her mother, he had forced her to propose to him.

"You could not have loved me very much," she complained, "if you'd let a little thing like money make you hesitate."

"It's not a little thing," suggested Carter. "They say it's several millions, and it happens to be *yours*. If it were *mine*, now!"

"Money," said Dolly sententiously, "is given people to make them happy, not to make them miserable."

"Wait until I sell my stories to the magazines," said Carter, "and then I will be independent and can support you."

The plan did not strike Dolly as one likely to lead to a hasty marriage. But he was sensitive about his stories, and she did not wish to hurt his feelings.

"Let's get married first," she suggested, "and then I can *buy* you a magazine. We'll call it *Carter's Magazine* and we will print nothing in it but your stories. Then we can laugh at the editors!"

"Not half as loud as they will," said Carter.

With three thousand dollars in bank and three stories accepted and seventeen still to hear from, and with Dolly daily telling him that it was evident he did not love her, Carter decided they were ready, hand in hand, to leap into the sea

THE MAN WHO COULD NOT LOSE

of matrimony. His interview on the subject with Mrs. Ingram was most painful. It lasted during the time it took her to walk out of her drawing-room to the foot of her staircase. She spoke to herself, and the only words of which Carter was sure were "preposterous" and "intolerable insolence." Later in the morning she sent a note to his flat, forbidding him not only her daughter, but the house in which her daughter lived, and even the use of the United States mails and the New York telephone wires. She described his conduct in words that, had they come from a man, would have afforded Carter every excuse for violent exercise.

Immediately in the wake of the note arrived Dolly, in tears, and carrying a dressing-case.

"I have left mother!" she announced. "And I have her car downstairs, and a clergyman in it, unless he has run away. He doesn't want to marry us, because he's afraid mother will stop supporting his flower mission. You get your hat and take me where he can marry us. No mother can talk about the man I love the way mother talked about you, and think I won't marry him the same day!"

Carter, with her mother's handwriting still red before his eyes, and his self-love shaken with rage, flourished the letter.

"And no mother," he shouted, "can call *me*

THE MAN WHO COULD NOT LOSE

a 'fortune-hunter' and a 'cradle-robber' and think I'll make good by marrying her daughter! Not until she BEGS me to!"

Dolly swept toward him like a summer storm. Her eyes were wet and flashing.

"Until *who* begs you to?" she demanded. "*Who* are you marrying; mother or me?"

"If I marry you," cried Carter, frightened but also greatly excited, "your mother won't give you a penny!"

"And that," taunted Dolly, perfectly aware that she was ridiculous, "is why you won't marry me!"

For an instant, long enough to make her blush with shame and happiness, Carter grinned at her. "Now, just for that," he said, "I won't kiss you, and I *will* marry you!"

But, as a matter of fact, he *did* kiss her.

Then he gazed happily around his small sitting-room.

"Make yourself at home here," he directed, "while I pack my bag."

"I *mean* to make myself very much at home here," said Dolly joyfully, "for the rest of my life."

From the recesses of the flat Carter called: "The rent's paid only till September. After that we live in a hall bedroom and cook on a gas-stove. And that's no idle jest, either."

THE MAN WHO COULD NOT LOSE

Fearing the publicity of the City Hall license bureau, they released the clergyman, much to the relief of that gentleman, and told the chauffeur to drive across the State line into Connecticut.

"It's the last time we can borrow your mother's car," said Carter, "and we'd better make it go as far as we can."

It was one of those days in May. Blue was the sky and sunshine was in the air, and in the park little girls from the tenements, in white, were playing they were queens. Dolly wanted to kidnap two of them for bridesmaids. In Harlem they stopped at a jeweller's shop, and Carter got out and bought a wedding-ring.

In the Bronx were dogwood blossoms and leaves of tender green and beds of tulips, and along the Boston Post Road, on their right, the Sound flashed in the sunlight; and on their left, gardens, lawns, and orchards ran with the road, and the apple trees were masses of pink and white.

Whenever a car approached from the rear, Carter pretended it was Mrs. Ingram coming to prevent the elopement, and Dolly clung to him. When the car had passed, she forgot to stop clinging to him.

In Greenwich Village they procured a license, and a magistrate married them, and they were

THE MAN WHO COULD NOT LOSE

a little frightened and greatly happy and, they both discovered simultaneously, outrageously hungry. So they drove through Bedford Village to South Salem, and lunched at the Horse and Hounds Inn, on blue and white china, in the same room where Major André was once a prisoner. And they felt very sorry for Major André, and for everybody who had not been just married that morning. And after lunch they sat outside in the garden and fed lumps of sugar to a charming collie and cream to a fat gray cat.

They decided to start housekeeping in Carter's flat, and so turned back to New York, this time following the old coach road through North Castle to White Plains, across to Tarrytown, and along the bank of the Hudson into Riverside Drive. Millions and millions of friendly folk, chiefly nurse-maids and traffic policemen, waved to them, and for some reason smiled.

"The joke of it is," declared Carter, "they don't know! The most wonderful event of the century has just passed into history. We are married, and nobody knows!"

But when the car drove away from in front of Carter's door, they saw on top of it two old shoes and a sign reading: "We have just been married." While they had been at luncheon, the chauffeur had risen to the occasion.

THE MAN WHO COULD NOT LOSE

"After all," said Carter soothingly, "he meant no harm. And it's the only thing about our wedding yet that seems legal."

Three months later two very unhappy young people faced starvation in the sitting-room of Carter's flat. Gloom was written upon the countenance of each, and the heat and the care that comes when one desires to live, and lacks the wherewithal to fulfil that desire, had made them pallid and had drawn black lines under Dolly's eyes.

Mrs. Ingram had played her part exactly as her dearest friends had said she would. She had sent to Carter's flat, seven trunks filled with Dolly's clothes, eighteen hats, and another most unpleasant letter. In this, on the sole condition that Dolly would at once leave her husband, she offered to forgive and to support her.

To this Dolly composed eleven scornful answers, but finally decided that no answer at all was the most scornful.

She and Carter then proceeded joyfully to waste his three thousand dollars with that contempt for money with which on a honey-moon it should always be regarded. When there was no more, Dolly called upon her mother's lawyers and inquired if her father had left her anything in her own right. The lawyers regretted he had not, but having loved Dolly since she was

THE MAN WHO COULD NOT LOSE

born, offered to advance her any money she wanted. They said they felt sure her mother would "relent."

"SHE may," said Dolly haughtily. "*I* won't! And my husband can give me all I need. I only wanted something of my own, because I'm going to make him a surprise present of a new motor-car. The one we are using now does not suit us."

This was quite true, as the one they were then using ran through the subway.

As summer approached, Carter had suddenly awakened to the fact that he soon would be a pauper, and cut short the honey-moon. They returned to the flat, and he set forth to look for a position. Later, while still looking for it, he spoke of it as a "job." He first thought he would like to be an assistant editor of a magazine. But he found editors of magazines anxious to employ new and untried assistants, especially in June, were very few. On the contrary, they explained they were retrenching and cutting down expenses—they meant they had discharged all office boys who received more than three dollars a week. They further "retrenched," by taking a mean advantage of Carter's having called upon them in person, by handing him three or four of his stories—but by this he saved his postage-stamps.

THE MAN WHO COULD NOT LOSE

Each day, when he returned to the flat, Dolly, who always expected each editor would hastily dust off his chair and offer it to her brilliant husband, would smile excitedly and gasp, "Well?" and Carter would throw the rejected manuscripts on the table and say: "At least, I have not returned empty-handed." Then they would discover a magazine that neither they nor any one else knew existed, and they would hurriedly readdress the manuscripts to that periodical, and run to post them at the letter-box on the corner.

"Any one of them, *if accepted*," Carter would point out, "might bring us in twenty-five dollars. A story of mine once sold for forty; so to-night we can afford to dine at a restaurant where wine is *not* 'included.'"

Fortunately, they never lost their sense of humor. Otherwise the narrow confines of the flat, the evil smells that rose from the baked streets, the greasy food of Italian and Hungarian restaurants, and the ever-haunting need of money might have crushed their youthful spirits. But in time even they found that one, still less two, cannot exist exclusively on love and the power to see the bright side of things—especially when there is no bright side. They had come to the point where they must borrow money from their friends, and that, though there were

THE MAN WHO COULD NOT LOSE

many who would have opened their safes to them, they had agreed was the one thing they would not do, or they must starve. The alternative was equally distasteful.

Carter had struggled earnestly to find a job. But his inexperience and the season of the year were against him. No newspaper wanted a dramatic critic when the only shows in town had been running three months, and on roof gardens; nor did they want a "cub" reporter when veterans were being "laid off" by the dozens. Nor were his services desired as a private secretary, a taxicab driver, an agent to sell real estate or automobiles or stocks. As no one gave him a chance to prove his unfitness for any of these callings, the fact that he knew nothing of any of them did not greatly matter. At these rebuffs Dolly was distinctly pleased. She argued they proved he was intended to pursue his natural career as an author.

That their friends might know they were poor did not affect her, but she did not want them to think by his taking up any outside "job" that they were poor because as a literary genius he was a failure. She believed in his stories. She wanted every one else to believe in them. Meanwhile, she assisted him in so far as she could by pawning the contents of five of the seven trunks, by learning to cook on a "Kitchen-

THE MAN WHO COULD NOT LOSE

ette," and to laundry her handkerchiefs and iron them on the looking-glass.

They faced each other across the breakfast-table. It was only nine o'clock, but the sun beat into the flat with the breath of a furnace, and the air was foul and humid.

"I tell you," Carter was saying fiercely, "you look ill. You *are* ill. You must go to the sea-shore. You must visit some of your proud friends at East Hampton or Newport. Then I'll know you're happy and I won't worry, and I'll find a job. *I* don't mind the heat—and I'll write you love letters"—he was talking very fast and not looking at Dolly—"like those I used to write you, before——"

Dolly raised her hand. "Listen!" she said. "Suppose I leave you. What will happen? I'll wake up in a cool, beautiful brass bed, won't I?—with cretonne window-curtains, and salt air blowing them about, and a maid to bring me coffee. And instead of a bathroom like yours, next to an elevator shaft and a fire-escape, I'll have one as big as a church, and the whole blue ocean to swim in. And I'll sit on the rocks in the sunshine and watch the waves and the yachts——"

"And grow well again!" cried Carter. "But you'll write to me," he added wistfully, "every day, won't you?"

THE MAN WHO COULD NOT LOSE

In her wrath, Dolly rose, and from across the table confronted him.

"And what will I be doing on those rocks?" she cried. "You *know* what I'll be doing! I'll be sobbing, and sobbing, and calling out to the waves: 'Why did he send me away? Why doesn't he want me? Because he doesn't love me. That's why! He doesn't *love* me!' And you DON'T!" cried Dolly. "You DON'T!"

It took him all of three minutes to persuade her she was mistaken.

"Very well, then," sobbed Dolly, "that's settled. And there'll be no more talk of sending me away!"

"There will *not!*" said Champneys hastily. "We will now," he announced, "go into committee of the whole and decide how we are to face financial failure. Our assets consist of two stories, accepted, but not paid for, and fifteen stories *not* accepted. In cash"—he spread upon the table a meagre collection of soiled bills and coins—"we have twenty-seven dollars and fourteen cents. That is every penny we possess in the world."

Dolly regarded him fixedly and shook her head.

"Is it wicked," she asked, "to love you *so?*"

"Haven't you been listening to me?" demanded Carter.

THE MAN WHO COULD NOT LOSE

Again Dolly shook her head.

"I was watching the way you talk. When your lips move fast they do such charming things."

"Do you know," roared Carter, "that we haven't a penny in the world, that we have nothing in this flat to eat?"

"I still have five hats," said Dolly.

"We can't eat hats," protested Champneys.

"We can *sell* hats!" returned Dolly. "They cost eighty dollars apiece!"

"When you need money," explained Carter, "I find it's just as hard to sell a hat as to eat it."

"Twenty-seven dollars and fourteen cents," repeated Dolly. She exclaimed remorsefully: "And you started with three thousand! What did I do with it?"

"We both had the time of our lives with it!" said Carter stoutly. "And that's all there is to that. Post-mortems," he pointed out, "are useful only as guides to the future, and as our future will never hold a second three thousand dollars, we needn't worry about how we spent the first one. No! What we must consider now is how we can grow rich quick, and the quicker and richer, the better. Pawning our clothes, or what's left of them, is bad economics. There's no use considering how to live from meal to meal. We must evolve something big,

THE MAN WHO COULD NOT LOSE

picturesque, that will bring a fortune. You have imagination; I'm supposed to have imagination; we must think of a plan to get money, much money. I do not insist on our plan being dignified, or even outwardly respectable; so long as it keeps you alive, it may be as desperate as——"

"I see!" cried Dolly; "like sending mother Black Hand letters!"

"Blackmail——" began that lady's son-in-law doubtfully.

"Or!" cried Dolly, "we might kidnap Mr. Carnegie when he's walking in the park alone, and hold him for ransom. Or"—she rushed on—"we might forge a codicil to father's will, and make it say if mother shouldn't like the man I want to marry, all of father's fortune must go to my husband!"

"Forgery," exclaimed Champneys, "is going further than I——"

"And another plan," interrupted Dolly, "that I have always had in mind, is to issue a cheaper edition of your book, 'The Dead Heat.' The reason the first edition of 'The Dead Heat' didn't sell——"

"Don't tell ME why it didn't sell," said Champneys. "I wrote it!"

"That book," declared Dolly loyally, "was never properly advertised. No one knew about it, so no one bought it!"

THE MAN WHO COULD NOT LOSE

"Eleven people bought it!" corrected the author.

"We will put it in a paper cover and sell it for fifty cents," cried Dolly. "It's the best detective story I ever read, and people have got to know it is the best. So we'll advertise it like a breakfast food."

"The idea," interrupted Champneys, "is to make money, not throw it away. Besides, we haven't any to throw away."

Dolly sighed bitterly.

"If only," she exclaimed, "we had that three thousand dollars back again! I'd save *so* carefully. It was all my fault. The races took it, but it was *I* took you to the races."

"No one ever had to drag *me* to the races," said Carter. "It was the way we went that was extravagant. Automobiles by the hour standing idle, and a box each day, and——"

"And always backing Dromedary," suggested Dolly.

Carter was touched on a sensitive spot.

"That horse," he protested loudly, "is a mighty good horse. Some day——"

"That's what you always said," remarked Dolly, "but he never seems to have his day."

"It's strange," said Champneys consciously. "I dreamed of Dromedary only last night. Same dream over and over again."

Hastily he changed the subject.

THE MAN WHO COULD NOT LOSE

"For some reason I don't sleep well. I don't know why."

Dolly looked at him with all the love in her eyes of a mother over her ailing infant.

"It's worrying over me, and the heat," she said. "And the garage next door, and the skyscraper going up across the street, might have something to do with it. And YOU," she mocked tenderly, "wanted to send *me* to the sea-shore."

Carter was frowning. As though about to speak, he opened his lips, and then laughed embarrassedly.

"Out with it," said Dolly, with an encouraging smile. "Did he win?"

Seeing she had read what was in his mind, Carter leaned forward eagerly. The ruling passion and a touch of superstition held him in their grip.

"He 'win' each time," he whispered. "I saw it as plain as I see you. Each time he came up with a rush just at the same place, just as they entered the stretch, and each time he won!" He slapped his hand disdainfully upon the dirty bills before him. "If I had a hundred dollars!"

There was a knock at the door, and Carter opened it to the elevator boy with the morning mail. The letters, save one, Carter dropped upon the table. That one, with clumsy fingers,

THE MAN WHO COULD NOT LOSE

he tore open. He exclaimed breathlessly: "It's from *Plympton's Magazine!* Maybe—I've sold a story!" He gave a cry almost of alarm. His voice was as solemn as though the letter had announced a death.

"Dolly," he whispered, "it's a check—a check for a *hundred dollars!*"

Guiltily, the two young people looked at each other.

"We've *got* to!" breathed Dolly. "*Got* to! If we let TWO signs like that pass, we'd be flying in the face of Providence."

With her hands gripping the arms of her chair, she leaned forward, her eyes staring into space, her lips moving.

"*Come on*, you Dromedary!" she whispered.

They changed the check into five and ten dollar bills, and, as Carter was far too excited to work, made an absurdly early start for the race-track.

"We might as well get all the fresh air we can," said Dolly. "That's all we will get!"

From their reserve fund of twenty-seven dollars which each had solemnly agreed with the other would not be risked on race-horses, Dolly subtracted a two-dollar bill. This she stuck conspicuously across the face of the clock on the mantel.

"Why?" asked Carter.

THE MAN WHO COULD NOT LOSE

"When we get back this evening," Dolly explained, "that will be the first thing we'll see. It's going to look awfully good!"

This day there was no scarlet car to rush them with refreshing swiftness through Brooklyn's parkways and along the Ocean Avenue. Instead, they hung to a strap in a cross-town car, changed to the ferry, and again to the Long Island Railroad. When Carter halted at the special car of the Turf Club, Dolly took his arm and led him forward to the day coach.

"But," protested Carter, "when you're spending a hundred dollars with one hand, why grudge fifty cents for a parlor-car seat? If you're going to be a sport, be a sport."

"And if you've got to be a piker," said Dolly, "don't be ashamed to be a piker. We're not spending a hundred dollars because we can afford it, but because you dreamt a dream. You didn't dream you were riding in parlor-cars! If you did, it's time I woke you."

This day there was for them no box overlooking the finish, no club-house luncheon. With the other pikers, they sat in the free seats, with those who sat coatless and tucked their handkerchiefs inside their collars, and with those who mopped their perspiring countenances with rice-paper and marked their cards with a hat-pin. Their lunch consisted of a massive ham sandwich with a top dressing of mustard.

THE MAN WHO COULD NOT LOSE

Dromedary did not run until the fifth race, and the long wait, before they could learn their fate, was intolerable. They knew most of the horses, and, to pass the time, on each of the first races Dolly made imaginary bets. Of these mental wagers, she lost every one.

"If you turn out to be as bad a guesser when you're asleep as I am when I'm awake," said Dolly, "we're going to lose our fortune."

"I'm weakening!" declared Carter. "A hundred dollars is beginning to look to me like an awful lot of money. Twenty-seven dollars—and there's only twenty of *that* left now—is mighty small capital, but twenty dollars *plus* a hundred could keep us alive for a month!"

"Did you, or did you not, dream that Dromedary would win?" demanded Dolly sternly.

"I certainly did, several times," said Carter. "But it may be I was thinking of the horse. I've lost such a lot on him, my mind may have——"

"Did you," interrupted Dolly, "say if you had a hundred dollars you'd bet it, *and* did a hundred dollars walk in through the door instantly?"

Carter, reassured, breathed again.

"It certainly did!" he repeated.

Even in his proud days, Carter had never been able to bet heavily, and instead of troubling the club-house commissioners with his

THE MAN WHO COULD NOT LOSE

small wagers, he had, in the ring, bet ready money. Moreover, he believed in the ring he obtained more favorable odds, and, when he won, it pleased him, instead of waiting until settling day for a check, to stand in a line and feel the real money thrust into his hand. So, when the fourth race started he rose and raised his hat.

"The time has come," he said.

Without looking at him, Dolly nodded. She was far too tremulous to speak.

For several weeks Dromedary had not been placed, and Carter hoped for odds of at least ten to one. But, when he pushed his way into the arena, he found so little was thought of his choice that as high as twenty to one was being offered, and with few takers. The fact shattered his confidence. Here were two hundred book-makers, trained to their calling, anxious at absurd odds to back their opinion that the horse he liked could not win. In the face of such unanimous contempt, his dream became fantastic, fatuous. He decided he would risk only half of his fortune. Then, should the horse win, he still would be passing rich, and should he lose, he would, at least, have all of fifty dollars.

With a book-maker he wagered that sum, and then, in unhappy indecision, stood, in one hand

THE MAN WHO COULD NOT LOSE

clutching his ticket that called for a potential thousand and fifty dollars, and in the other an actual fifty. It was not a place for meditation. From every side men, more or less sane, swept upon him, jostled him, and stamped upon him, and still, struggling for a foothold, he swayed, hesitating. Then he became conscious that the ring was nearly empty, that only a few shrieking individuals still ran down the line. The horses were going to the post. He must decide quickly. In front of him the book-maker cleaned his board, and, as a final appeal, opposite the names of three horses chalked thirty to one. Dromedary was among them. Such odds could not be resisted. Carter shoved his fifty at the man, and to that sum added the twenty dollars still in his pocket. They were the last dollars he owned in the world. And though he knew they were his last, he was fearful lest the book-maker would refuse them. But, mechanically, the man passed them over his shoulder.

"And twenty-one hundred to seventy," he chanted.

When Carter took his seat beside Dolly, he was quite cold. Still, Dolly did not speak. Out of the corner of her eyes she questioned him.

"I got fifty at twenty to one," replied Carter, "and seventy at thirty!"

THE MAN WHO COULD NOT LOSE

In alarm, Dolly turned upon him.

"Seventy!" she gasped.

Carter nodded. "All we have," he said. "We have sixty cents left, to start life over again!"

As though to encourage him, Dolly placed her finger on her race-card.

"His colors," she said, "are 'green cap, green jacket, green and white hoops.'"

Through a maze of heat, a half-mile distant, at the starting-gate, little spots of color moved in impatient circles. The big, good-natured crowd had grown silent, so silent that from the high, sun-warmed grass in the infield one could hear the lazy chirp of the crickets. As though repeating a prayer, or an incantation, Dolly's lips were moving quickly.

"Green cap," she whispered, "green jacket, green and white hoops!"

With a sharp sigh the crowd broke the silence. "They're off!" it cried, and leaned forward expectant.

The horses came so fast. To Carter their conduct seemed outrageous. It was incredible that in so short a time, at a pace so reckless, they would decide a question of such moment. They came bunched together, shifting and changing, with, through the dust, flashes of blue and gold and scarlet. A jacket of yellow

THE MAN WHO COULD NOT LOSE

shot out of the dust and showed in front; a jacket of crimson followed. So they were at the half; so they were at the three-quarters.

The good-natured crowd began to sway, to grumble and murmur, then to shout in sharp staccato.

"Can you see him?" begged Dolly.

"No," said Carter. "You *don't* see him until they reach the stretch."

One could hear their hoofs, could see the crimson jockey draw his whip. At the sight, for he rode the favorite, the crowd gave a great gasp of concern.

"Oh, you Gold Heels!" it implored.

Under the whip, Gold Heels drew even with the yellow jacket; stride by stride, they fought it out alone.

"Gold Heels!" cried the crowd.

Behind them, in a curtain of dust, pounded the field. It charged in a flying wedge, like a troop of cavalry. Dolly, searching for a green jacket, saw, instead, a rainbow wave of color that, as it rose and fell, sprang toward her in great leaps, swallowing the track.

"Gold Heels!" yelled the crowd.

The field swept into the stretch. Without moving his eyes, Carter caught Dolly by the wrist and pointed. As though giving a signal, he shot his free hand into the air.

THE MAN WHO COULD NOT LOSE

"Now!" he shouted.

From the curtain of dust, as lightning strikes through a cloud, darted a great, raw-boned, ugly chestnut. Like the Empire Express, he came rocking, thundering, spurning the ground. At his coming, Gold Heels, to the eyes of the crowd, seemed to falter, to slacken, to stand still. The crowd gave a great cry of amazement, a yell of disgust. The chestnut drew even with Gold Heels, passed him, and swept under the wire. Clinging to his neck was a little jockey in a green cap, green jacket, and hoops of green and white.

Dolly's hand was at her side, clutching the bench. Carter's hand still clasped it. Neither spoke or looked at the other. For an instant, while the crowd, no longer so good-natured, mocked and jeered at itself, the two young people sat quite still, staring at the green field, at the white clouds rolling from the ocean. Dolly drew a long breath.

"Let's go!" she gasped. "Let's thank him first, and then—*take me home!*"

They found Dromedary in the paddock, and thanked him, and Carter left Dolly with him, while he ran to collect his winnings. When he returned, he showed her a sheaf of yellow bills, and as they ran down the covered board walk to the gate, they skipped and danced.

As though giving a signal, he shot his free hand into the air.

THE MAN WHO COULD NOT LOSE

Dolly turned toward the train drawn up at the entrance.

"Not with me!" shouted Carter. "We're going home in the reddest, most expensive, fastest automobile I can hire!"

In the "hack" line of motor-cars was one that answered those requirements, and they fell into it as though it were their own.

"To the Night and Day Bank!" commanded Carter.

With the genial democracy of the race-track, the chauffeur lifted his head to grin appreciatively.

"That listens good to me!" he said.

"I like him!" whispered Dolly. "Let's buy him and the car."

On the way home, they bought many cars; every car they saw, that they liked, they bought. They bought, also, several houses, and a yacht that they saw from the ferry-boat. And as soon as they had deposited the most of their money in the bank, they went to a pawnshop in Sixth Avenue and bought back many possessions that they had feared they never would see again.

When they entered the flat, the thing they first beheld was Dolly's two-dollar bill.

"What," demanded Carter, with repugnance, "is that strange piece of paper?"

THE MAN WHO COULD NOT LOSE

Dolly examined it carefully.

"I think it is a kind of money," she said, "used by the lower classes."

They dined on the roof at Delmonico's. Dolly wore the largest of the five hats still unsold, and Carter selected the dishes entirely according to which was the most expensive. Every now and again they would look anxiously down across the street at the bank that held their money. They were nervous lest it should take fire.

"We can be extravagant to-night," said Dolly, "because we owe it to Dromedary to celebrate. But from to-night on we must save. We've had an awful lesson. What happened to us last month must never happen again. We were down to a two-dollar bill. Now we have twenty-five hundred across the street, and you have several hundreds in your pocket. On that we can live easily for a year. Meanwhile, you can write 'the' great American novel without having to worry about money, or to look for a 'steady job.' And then your book will come out, and you will be famous, and rich, and——"

"Passing on from that," interrupted Carter, "the thing of first importance is to get you out of that hot, beastly flat. I propose we start to-morrow for Cape Cod. I know a lot of fishing villages there where we could board and

THE MAN WHO COULD NOT LOSE

lodge for twelve dollars a week, and row and play tennis and live in our bathing suits."

Dolly assented with enthusiasm, and during the courses of the dinner they happily discussed Cape Cod from Pocasset to Yarmouth, and from Sandwich to Provincetown. So eager were they to escape, that Carter telephoned the hallman at his club to secure a cabin for the next afternoon on the Fall River boat.

As they sat over their coffee in the cool breeze, with, in the air, the scent of flowers and the swing of music, and with, at their feet, the lights of the great city, the world seemed very bright.

"It has been a great day," sighed Carter. "And if I hadn't had nervous prostration I would have enjoyed it. That race-course is always cool, and there were some fine finishes. I noticed two horses that would bear watching, Her Highness and Glowworm. If we weren't leaving to-morrow, I'd be inclined——"

Dolly regarded him with eyes of horror.

"Champneys Carter!" she exclaimed. As she said it, it sounded like "Great Jehoshaphat!"

Carter protested indignantly. "I only said," he explained, "*if* I *were* following the races, I'd watch those horses. Don't worry!" he exclaimed. "I know when to stop."

The next morning they took breakfast on the

THE MAN WHO COULD NOT LOSE

tiny terrace of a restaurant overlooking Bryant Park, where, during the first days of their honeymoon, they had always breakfasted. For sentimental reasons they now revisited it. But Dolly was eager to return at once to the flat and pack, and Carter seemed distrait. He explained that he had had a bad night.

"I'm *so* sorry," sympathized Dolly, "but to-night you will have a fine sleep going up the Sound. Any more nightmares?" she asked.

"Nightmares!" exploded Carter fiercely. "Nightmares they certainly were! I dreamt two of the nightmares won! I saw them, all night, just as I saw Dromedary—Her Highness and Glowworm, winning, winning, winning!"

"Those were the horses you spoke about last night," said Dolly severely. "After so wonderful a day, of course you dreamt of racing, and those two horses were in your mind. That's the explanation."

They returned to the flat and began, industriously, to pack. About twelve o'clock Carter, coming suddenly into the bedroom where Dolly was alone, found her reading the *Morning Telegraph*. It was open at the racing page of "past performances."

She dropped the paper guiltily. Carter kicked a hat-box out of his way and sat down on a trunk.

THE MAN WHO COULD NOT LOSE

"I don't see," he began, "why we can't wait one more day. We'd be just as near the ocean at Sheepshead Bay race-track as on a Fall River boat, and——"

He halted and frowned unhappily. "We needn't bet more than ten dollars," he begged.

"Of course," declared Dolly, "if they *should* win, you'll always blame *me!*"

Carter's eyes shone hopefully.

"And," continued Dolly, "I can't bear to have you blame me. So——"

"Get your hat!" shouted Carter, "or we'll miss the first race."

Carter telephoned for a cab, and as they were entering it said guiltily: "I've got to stop at the bank."

"You have *not!*" announced Dolly. "That money is to keep us alive while you write the great American novel. I'm glad to spend another day at the races, and I'm willing to back your dreams as far as ten dollars, but for no more."

"If my dreams come true," warned Carter, "you'll be awfully sorry."

"Not I," said Dolly. "I'll merely send you to bed, and you can go on dreaming."

When Her Highness romped home, an easy winner, the look Dolly turned upon her husband was one both of fear and dismay.

THE MAN WHO COULD NOT LOSE

"I don't like it!" she gasped. "It's—it's *uncanny*. It gives me a creepy feeling. It makes you seem sort of supernatural. And oh," she cried, "if only I had let you bet all you had with you!"

"I did," stammered Carter, in extreme agitation. "I bet four hundred. I got five to one, Dolly," he gasped, in awe; "we've won two thousand dollars."

Dolly exclaimed rapturously:

"We'll put it all in bank," she cried.

"We'll put it all on Glowworm!" said her husband.

"Champ!" begged Dolly. "Don't push your luck. Stop while——"

Carter shook his head.

"It's NOT luck!" he growled. "It's a gift, it's second sight, it's prophecy. I've been a full-fledged clairvoyant all my life, and didn't know it. Anyway, I'm a sport, and after two of my dreams breaking right, I've got to back the third one!"

Glowworm was at ten to one, and at those odds the book-makers to whom he first applied did not care to take so large a sum as he offered. Carter found a book-maker named "Sol" Burbank who, at those odds, accepted his two thousand.

When Carter returned to collect his twenty-

THE MAN WHO COULD NOT LOSE

two thousand, there was some little delay while Burbank borrowed a portion of it. He looked at Carter curiously and none too genially.

"Wasn't it you," he asked, "that had that thirty-to-one shot yesterday on Dromedary?"

Carter nodded somewhat guiltily. A man in the crowd volunteered: "And he had Her Highness in the second, too, for four hundred."

"You've made a good day," said Burbank. "Give me a chance to get my money back to-morrow."

"I'm sorry," said Carter. "I'm leaving New York to-morrow."

The same scarlet car bore them back triumphant to the bank.

"Twenty-two thousand dollars?" gasped Carter, "*in cash!* How in the name of all that's honest can we celebrate winning twenty-two thousand dollars? We can't eat more than one dinner; we can't drink more than two quarts of champagne—not without serious results."

"I'll tell you what we *can* do!" cried Dolly excitedly. "We can sail to-morrow on the *Campania!*"

"Hurrah!" shouted Carter. "We'll have a second honey-moon. We'll 'shoot up' London and Paris. We'll tear slices out of the map of Europe. You'll ride in one motor-car, I'll ride in another, we'll have a maid and a valet in a

THE MAN WHO COULD NOT LOSE

third, and we'll race each other all the way to Monte Carlo. And, there, I'll dream of the winning numbers, and we'll break the bank. When does the *Campania* sail?"

"At noon," said Dolly.

"At eight we will be on board," said Carter.

But that night in his dreams he saw King Pepper, Confederate, and Red Wing each win a race. And in the morning neither the engines of the *Campania* nor the entreaties of Dolly could keep him from the race-track.

"I want only six thousand," he protested. "You can do what you like with the rest, but I am going to bet six thousand on the first one of those three to start. If he loses, I give you my word I'll not bet another cent, and we'll sail on Saturday. If he wins out, I'll put all I make on the two others."

"Can't you see," begged Dolly, "that your dreams are just a rehash of what you think during the day? You have been playing in wonderful luck, that's all. Each of those horses is likely to win his race. When he does you will have more faith than ever in your silly dreams——"

"My silly dreams," said Carter grinning, "are carrying you to Europe, first class, by the next steamer."

They had been talking while on their way to

THE MAN WHO COULD NOT LOSE

the bank. When Dolly saw she could not alter his purpose, she made him place the nineteen thousand that remained, after he had taken out the six thousand, in her name. She then drew out the entire amount.

"You told me," said Dolly, smiling anxiously, "I could do what I liked with it. Maybe I have dreams also. Maybe I mean to back them."

She drove away, mysteriously refusing to tell him what she intended to do. When they met at luncheon, she was still much excited, still bristling with a concealed secret.

"Did you back your dream?" asked Carter.

Dolly nodded happily.

"And when am I to know?"

"You will read of it," said Dolly, "to-morrow, in the morning papers. It's all quite correct. My lawyers arranged it."

"Lawyers!" gasped her husband. "You're not arranging to lock me in a private madhouse, are you?"

"No," laughed Dolly; "but when I told them how I intended to invest the money they came near putting *me* there."

"Didn't they want to know how you suddenly got so rich?" asked Carter.

"They did. I told them it came from my husband's 'books'! It was a very 'near' falsehood."

THE MAN WHO COULD NOT LOSE

"It was worse," said Carter. "It was a very poor pun."

As in their honey-moon days they drove proudly to the track, and when Carter had placed Dolly in a box large enough for twenty, he pushed his way into the crowd around the stand of "Sol" Burbank. That veteran of the turf welcomed him gladly.

"Coming to give me my money back?" he called.

"No, to take some away," said Carter, handing him his six thousand.

Without apparently looking at it, Burbank passed it to his cashier. "King Pepper, twelve to six thousand," he called.

When King Pepper won, and Carter moved around the ring with eighteen thousand dollars in thousand and five hundred dollar bills in his fist, he found himself beset by a crowd of curious, eager "pikers." They both impeded his operations and acted as a body-guard. Confederate was an almost prohibitive favorite at one to three, and in placing eighteen thousand that he might win six, Carter found little difficulty. When Confederate won, and he started with his twenty-four thousand to back Red Wing, the crowd now engulfed him. Men and boys who when they wagered five and ten dollars were risking their all, found in the sight of a young man offering bets in hundreds and

THE MAN WHO COULD NOT LOSE

thousands a thrilling and fascinating spectacle. To learn what horse he was playing and at what odds, racing touts and runners for other book-makers and individual speculators leaped into the mob that surrounded him, and then, squirming their way out, ran shrieking down the line. In ten minutes, through the bets of Carter and those that backed his luck, the odds against Red Wing were forced down from fifteen to one to even money. His approach was hailed by the book-makers either with jeers or with shouts of welcome. Those who had lost demanded a chance to regain their money. Those with whom he had not bet, found in that fact consolation, and chaffed the losers. Some curtly refused even the smallest part of his money. "Not with me!" they laughed. From stand to stand the layers of odds taunted him, or each other. "Don't touch it, it's tainted!" they shouted. "Look out, Joe, he's the Jonah man!" Or, "Come at me again!" they called. "And, once more!" they challenged as they reached for a thousand-dollar bill.

And, when in time, each shook his head and grumbled: "That's all I want," or looked the other way, the mob around Carter jeered. "He's fought 'em to a stand-still!" they shouted jubilantly. In their eyes a man who alone was able and willing to wipe the name of a horse off the blackboards was a hero.

THE MAN WHO COULD NOT LOSE

To the horror of Dolly, instead of watching the horses parade past, the crowd gathered in front of her box and pointed and stared at her. From the club-house her men friends and acquaintances invaded it.

"Has Carter gone mad?" they demanded. "He's dealing out thousand-dollar bills like cigarettes. He's turned the ring into a wheat pit!"

When he reached the box a sun-burned man in a sombrero blocked his way.

"I'm the owner of Red Wing," he explained, "bred him and trained him myself. I know he'll be lucky if he gets the place. You're backing him in thousands to *win*. What do you know about him?"

"Know he will win," said Carter.

The veteran commissioner of the club stand buttonholed him. "Mr. Carter," he begged, "why don't you bet through me? I'll give you as good odds as they will in that ring. You don't want your clothes torn off you and your money taken from you."

"They haven't taken such a lot of it yet," said Carter.

When Red Wing won, the crowd beneath the box, the men in the box, and the people standing around it, most of whom had followed Carter's plunge, cheered and fell over him, to shake hands and pound him on the back. From every side

THE MAN WHO COULD NOT LOSE

excited photographers pointed cameras, and Lander's band played: "Every Little Bit Added to What You've Got Makes Just a Little Bit More." As he left the box to collect his money, a big man with a brown mustache and two smooth-shaven giants closed in around him, as tackles interfere for the man who has the ball. The big man took him by the arm. Carter shook himself free.

"What's the idea?" he demanded.

"I'm Pinkerton," said the big man genially. "You need a body-guard. If you've got an empty seat in your car, I'll drive home with you."

From Cavanaugh they borrowed a book-maker's hand-bag and stuffed it with thousand-dollar bills. When they stepped into the car the crowd still surrounded them.

"He's taking it home in a trunk!" they yelled.

That night the "sporting extras" of the afternoon papers gave prominence to the luck at the races of Champneys Carter. From Cavanaugh and the book-makers, the racing reporters had gathered accounts of his winnings. They stated that in three successive days, starting with one hundred dollars, he had at the end of the third day not lost a single bet, and that afternoon, on the last race alone, he had won sixty to seventy thousand dollars. With the text, they "ran" pictures of Carter

THE MAN WHO COULD NOT LOSE

at the track, of Dolly in her box, and of Mrs. Ingram in a tiara and ball-dress.

"Mother-in-law *will* be pleased!" cried Carter.

In some alarm as to what the newspapers might say on the morrow, he ordered that in the morning a copy of each be sent to his room. That night in his dreams he saw clouds of dust-covered jackets and horses with sweating flanks, and one of them named Ambitious led all the rest. When he woke, he said to Dolly: "That horse Ambitious will win to-day."

"He can do just as he likes about *that!*" replied Dolly. "I have something on my mind much more important than horse-racing. To-day you are to learn how I spent your money. It's to be in the morning papers."

When he came to breakfast, Dolly was on her knees. For his inspection she had spread the newspapers on the floor, opened at an advertisement that appeared in each. In the centre of a half-page of white paper were the lines:

SOLD OUT IN ONE DAY!

Entire First Edition

THE DEAD HEAT
BY
CHAMPNEYS CARTER

SECOND EDITION ONE HUNDRED THOUSAND

THE MAN WHO COULD NOT LOSE

"In Heaven's name!" roared Carter. "What does this mean?"

"It means," cried Dolly tremulously, "I'm backing my dream. I've always believed in your book. Now, I'm backing it. Our lawyers sent me to an advertising agent. His name is Spink, and he is awfully clever. I asked him if he could advertise a book so as to make it sell. He said with my money and his ideas he could sell last year's telephone book to people who did not own a telephone, and who had never learned to read. He is proud of his ideas. One of them was buying out the first edition. Your publishers told him your book was 'waste paper,' and that he could have every copy in stock for the cost of the plates. So he bought the whole edition. That's how it was sold out in one day. Then we ordered a second edition of one hundred thousand, and they're printing it now.

"The presses have been working all night to meet the demand!"

"But," cried Carter, "there *isn't* any demand!"

"There will be," said Dolly, "when five million people read our advertisements."

She dragged him to the window and pointed triumphantly into the street.

"See that!" she said. "Mr. Spink sent them here for me to inspect."

THE MAN WHO COULD NOT LOSE

Drawn up in a line that stretched from Fifth Avenue to Broadway were an army of sandwich men. On the boards they carried were the words: "Read 'The Dead Heat.' Second Edition. One Hundred Thousand!" On the fence in front of the building going up across the street, in letters a foot high, Carter again read the name of his novel. In letters in size more modest, but in colors more defiant, it glared at him from ash-cans and barrels.

"How much does this cost?" he gasped.

"It cost every dollar you had in bank," said Dolly, "and before we are through it will cost you twice as much more. Mr. Spink is only waiting to hear from me before he starts spending fifty thousand dollars; that's only half of what you won on Red Wing. I'm only waiting for you to make me out a check before I tell Spink to start spending it."

In a dazed state Carter drew a check for fifty thousand dollars and meekly handed it to his wife. They carried it themselves to the office of Mr. Spink. On their way, on every side they saw evidences of his handiwork. On walls, on scaffolding, on bill-boards were advertisements of "The Dead Heat." Over Madison Square a huge kite as large as a Zeppelin air-ship painted the name of the book against the sky, on "dodgers" it floated in the air, on handbills it stared up from the gutters.

THE MAN WHO COULD NOT LOSE

Mr. Spink was a nervous young man with a bald head and eye-glasses. He grasped the check as a general might welcome fifty thousand fresh troops.

"Reinforcements!" he cried. "Now, watch me. Now I can do things that are big, national, Napoleonic. We can't get those books bound inside of a week, but meanwhile orders will be pouring in, people will be growing crazy for it. Every man, woman, and child in Greater New York will want a copy. I've sent out fifty boys dressed as jockeys on horseback to ride neck and neck up and down every avenue. 'The Dead Heat' is printed on the saddle-cloth. Half of them have been arrested already. It's a little idea of my own."

"But," protested Carter, "it's not a racing story, it's a detective story!"

"The devil it is!" gasped Spink. "But what's the difference!" he exclaimed. "They've got to buy it anyway. They'd buy it if it was a cook-book. And, I say," he cried delightedly, "that's great press work you're doing for the book at the races! The papers are full of you this morning, and every man who reads about your luck at the track will see your name as the author of 'The Dead Heat,' and will rush to buy the book. He'll think 'The Dead Heat' is a guide to the turf!"

When Carter reached the track he found his

THE MAN WHO COULD NOT LOSE

notoriety had preceded him. Ambitious did not run until the fourth race, and until then, as he sat in his box, an eager crowd surged below. He had never known such popularity. The crowd had read the newspapers, and such head-lines as "He Cannot Lose!" "Young Carter Wins $70,000!" "Boy Plunger Wins Again!" "Carter Makes Big Killing!" "The Ring Hit Hard!" "The Man Who Cannot Lose!" "Carter Beats Book-makers!" had whetted their curiosity and filled many with absolute faith in his luck. Men he had not seen in years grasped him by the hand and carelessly asked if he could tell of something good. Friends old and new begged him to dine with them, to immediately have a drink with them, at least to "try" a cigar. Men who protested they had lost their all begged for just a hint which would help them to come out even, and every one, without exception, assured him he was going to buy his latest book.

"I tried to get it last night at a dozen news-stands," many of them said, "but they told me the entire edition was exhausted."

The crowd of hungry-eyed race-goers waiting below the box, and watching Carter's every movement, distressed Dolly.

"I hate it!" she cried. "They look at you like a lot of starved dogs begging for a bone. Let's go home; we don't want to make any

THE MAN WHO COULD NOT LOSE

more money, and we may lose what we have. And I want it all to advertise the book."

"If you're not careful," said Carter, "some one will buy that book and read it, and then you and Spink will have to take shelter in a cyclone cellar."

When he arose to make his bet on Ambitious, his friends from the club stand and a half-dozen of Pinkerton's men closed in around him and in a flying wedge pushed into the ring. The newspapers had done their work, and he was instantly surrounded by a hungry, howling mob. In comparison with the one of the previous day, it was as a foot-ball scrimmage to a run on a bank. When he made his first wager and the crowd learned the name of the horse, it broke with a yell into hundreds of flying missiles which hurled themselves at the book-makers. Under their attack, as on the day before, Ambitious receded to even money. There was hardly a person at the track who did not back the luck of the man who "could not lose." And when Ambitious won easily, it was not the horse or the jockey that was cheered, but the young man in the box.

In New York the extras had already announced that he was again lucky, and when Dolly and Carter reached the bank they found the entire staff on hand to receive him and his winnings. They amounted to a sum so magnifi-

THE MAN WHO COULD NOT LOSE

cent that Carter found for the rest of their lives the interest would furnish Dolly and himself an income upon which they could live modestly and well.

A distinguished-looking, white-haired official of the bank congratulated Carter warmly. "Should you wish to invest some of this," he said, "I should be glad to advise you. My knowledge in that direction may be wider than your own."

Carter murmured his thanks. The white-haired gentleman lowered his voice.

"On certain other subjects," he continued, "you know many things of which I am totally ignorant. Could you tell me," he asked carelessly, "who will win the Suburban to-morrow?"

Carter frowned mysteriously. "I can tell you better in the morning," he said. "It looks like Beldame, with Proper and First Mason within call."

The white-haired man showed his surprise and also that his ignorance was not as profound as he suggested.

"I thought the Keene entry—" he ventured.

"I know," said Carter doubtfully. "If it were for a mile, I would say Delhi, but I don't think he can last the distance. In the morning I'll wire you."

As they settled back in their car, Carter took

THE MAN WHO COULD NOT LOSE

both of Dolly's hands in his. "So far as money goes," he said, "we are independent of your mother—independent of my books; and I want to make you a promise. I want to promise you that, no matter what I dream in the future, I'll never back another horse."

Dolly gave a gasp of satisfaction.

"And what's more," added Carter hastily, "not another dollar can you risk in backing my books. After this, they've got to stand or fall on their legs!"

"Agreed!" cried Dolly. "Our plunging days are over."

When they reached the flat they found waiting for Carter the junior partner of a real publishing house. He had a blank contract, and he wanted to secure the right to publish Carter's next book.

"I have a few short stories—" suggested Carter.

"Collections of short stories," protested the visitor truthfully, "do not sell. We would prefer another novel on the same lines as 'The Dead Heat.'"

"Have you read 'The Dead Heat'?" asked Carter.

"I have not," admitted the publisher, "but the next book by the same author is sure to— We will pay in advance of royalties fifteen thousand dollars."

THE MAN WHO COULD NOT LOSE

"Could you put that in writing?" asked Carter. When the publisher was leaving he said:

"I see your success in literature is equalled by your success at the races. Could you tell me what will win the Suburban?"

"I will send you a wire in the *morning*," said Carter.

They had arranged to dine with some friends and later to visit a musical comedy. Carter had changed his clothes, and, while he was waiting for Dolly to dress, was reclining in a huge armchair. The heat of the day, the excitement, and the wear on his nerves caused his head to sink back, his eyes to close, and his limbs to relax.

When, by her entrance, Dolly woke him, he jumped up in some confusion.

"You've been asleep," she mocked.

"Worse!" said Carter. "I've been dreaming! Shall I tell you who is going to win the Suburban?"

"Champneys!" cried Dolly in alarm.

"My dear Dolly," protested her husband, "I promised to stop betting. I did not promise to stop sleeping."

"Well," sighed Dolly, with relief, "as long as it stops at that. Delhi will win," she added.

"Delhi will not," said Carter. "This is how

THE MAN WHO COULD NOT LOSE

they will finish." He scribbled three names on a piece of paper which Dolly read.

"But that," she said, "is what you told the gentleman at the bank."

Carter stared at her blankly and in some embarrassment.

"You see!" cried Dolly, "what you think when you're awake, you dream when you're asleep. And you had a run of luck that never happened before and could never happen again."

Carter received her explanation with reluctance. "I wonder," he said.

On arriving at the theatre they found their host had reserved a stage-box, and as there were but four in their party, and as, when they entered, the house lights were up, their arrival drew upon them the attention both of those in the audience and of those on the stage. The theatre was crowded to its capacity, and in every part were people who were habitual race-goers, as well as many racing men who had come to town for the Suburban. By these, as well as by many others who for three days had seen innumerable pictures of him, Carter was instantly recognized. To the audience and to the performers the man who always won was of far greater interest than what for the three-hundredth night was going forward on the stage. And when the leading woman, Blanche Winter,

THE MAN WHO COULD NOT LOSE

asked the comedian which he would rather be, "the Man Who Broke the Bank at Monte Carlo or the Man Who Can Not Lose?" she gained from the audience an easy laugh and from the chorus an excited giggle.

When, at the end of the act, Carter went into the lobby to smoke, he was so quickly surrounded that he sought refuge on Broadway. From there, the crowd still following him, he was driven back into his box. Meanwhile, the interest shown in him had not been lost upon the press agent of the theatre, and he at once telephoned to the newspaper offices that Plunger Carter, the book-maker breaker, was at that theatre, and if that the newspapers wanted a chance to interview him on the probable outcome of the classic handicap to be run on the morrow, he, the press agent, would unselfishly assist them. In answer to these hurry calls, reporters of the Ten o'Clock Club assembled in the foyer. How far what later followed was due to their presence and to the efforts of the press agent only that gentleman can tell. It was in the second act that Miss Blanche Winter sang her topical song. In it she advised the audience when anxious to settle any question of personal or national interest to "Put it up to the Man in the Moon." This night she introduced a verse in which she told of her desire to know which

THE MAN WHO COULD NOT LOSE

horse on the morrow would win the Suburban, and, in the chorus, expressed her determination to "Put it up to the Man in the Moon."

Instantly from the back of the house a voice called: "Why don't you put it up to the Man in the Box?" Miss Winter laughed—the audience laughed; all eyes were turned toward Carter. As though the idea pleased them, from different parts of the house people applauded heartily. In embarrassment, Carter shoved back his chair and pulled the curtain of the box between him and the audience. But he was not so easily to escape. Leaving the orchestra to continue unheeded with the prelude to the next verse, Miss Winter walked slowly and deliberately toward him, smiling mischievously. In burlesque entreaty, she held out her arms. She made a most appealing and charming picture, and of that fact she was well aware. In a voice loud enough to reach every part of the house, she addressed herself to Carter:

"Won't you tell ME?" she begged.

Carter, blushing unhappily, shrugged his shoulders in apology.

With a wave of her hand Miss Winter designated the audience. "Then," she coaxed, reproachfully, "won't you tell *them?*"

Again, instantly, with a promptness and una-

THE MAN WHO COULD NOT LOSE

nimity that sounded suspiciously as though it came from ushers well rehearsed, several voices echoed her petition: "Give us all a chance!" shouted one. "Don't keep the good things to yourself!" reproached another. "*I* want to get rich, TOO!" wailed a third. In his heart, Carter prayed they would choke. But the audience, so far from resenting the interruptions, encouraged them, and Carter's obvious discomfort added to its amusement. It proceeded to assail him with applause, with appeals, with commands to "speak up."

The hand-clapping became general—insistent. The audience would not be denied. Carter turned to Dolly. In the recesses of the box she was enjoying his predicament. His friends also were laughing at him. Indignant at their desertion, Carter grinned vindictively. "All right," he muttered over his shoulder. "Since you think it's funny, I'll show you!" He pulled his pencil from his watch-chain and, spreading his programme on the ledge of the box, began to write.

From the audience there rose a murmur of incredulity, of surprise, of excited interest. In the rear of the house the press agent, after one startled look, doubled up in an ecstasy of joy. "We've landed him!" he gasped. "We've landed him! He's going to fall for it!"

THE MAN WHO COULD NOT LOSE

Dolly frantically clasped her husband by the coat-tail.

"Champ!" she implored, "what *are* you doing?"

Quite calmly, quite confidently, Carter rose. Leaning forward with a nod and a smile, he presented the programme to the beautiful Miss Winter. That lady all but snatched at it. The spot-light was full in her eyes. Turning her back that she might the more easily read, she stood for a moment, her pretty figure trembling with eagerness, her pretty eyes bent upon the programme. The house had grown suddenly still, and with an excited gesture, the leader of the orchestra commanded the music to silence. A man, bursting with impatience, broke the tense quiet. "Read it!" he shouted.

In a frightened voice that in the sudden hush held none of its usual confidence, Miss Winter read slowly: "The favorite cannot last the distance. Will lead for the mile and give way to Beldame. Proper takes the place. First Mason will show. Beldame will win by a length."

Before she had ceased reading, a dozen men had struggled to their feet and a hundred voices were roaring at her. "Read that again!" they chorused. Once more Miss Winter read the message, but before she had finished half of

THE MAN WHO COULD NOT LOSE

those in the front rows were scrambling from their seats and racing up the aisles. Already the reporters were ahead of them, and in the neighborhood not one telephone booth was empty. Within five minutes, in those hotels along the White Way where sporting men are wont to meet, betting commissioners and handbook men were suddenly assaulted by breathless gentlemen, some in evening dress, some without collars, and some without hats, but all with money to bet against the favorite. And, an hour later, men, bent under stacks of newspaper "extras," were vomited from the subway stations into the heart of Broadway, and in raucous tones were shrieking, "Winner of the Suburban," sixteen hours before that race was run. That night to every big newspaper office from Maine to California, was flashed the news that Plunger Carter, in a Broadway theatre, had announced that the favorite for the Suburban would be beaten, and, in order, had named the three horses that would first finish.

Up and down Broadway, from rathskellers to roof-gardens, in cafés and lobster palaces, on the corners of the cross-roads, in clubs and all-night restaurants, Carter's tip was as a red rag to a bull.

Was the boy drunk, they demanded, or had his miraculous luck turned his head? Other-

THE MAN WHO COULD NOT LOSE

wise, why would he so publicly utter a prophecy that on the morrow must certainly smother him with ridicule. The explanations were varied. The men in the clubs held he was driven by a desire for notoriety, the men in the street that he was more clever than they guessed, and had made the move to suit his own book, to alter the odds to his own advantage. Others frowned mysteriously. With superstitious faith in his luck, they pointed to his record. "Has he ever lost a bet? How do *we* know what *he* knows?" they demanded. "Perhaps it's fixed and he knows it!"

The "wise" ones howled in derision. "A Suburban FIXED!" they retorted. "You can fix *one* jockey, you can fix *two;* but you can't fix sixteen jockeys! You can't fix Belmont, you can't fix Keene. There's nothing in his picking Beldame, but only a crazy man would pick the horse for the place and to show, and shut out the favorite! The boy ought to be in Matteawan."

Still undisturbed, still confident to those to whom he had promised them, Carter sent a wire. Nor did he forget his old enemy, "Sol" Burbank. "If you want to get some of the money I took," he telegraphed, "wipe out the Belmont entry and take all they offer on Delhi. He cannot win."

THE MAN WHO COULD NOT LOSE

And that night, when each newspaper called him up at his flat, he made the same answer. "The three horses will finish as I said. You can state that I gave the information as I did as a sort of present to the people of New York City."

In the papers the next morning "Carter's Tip" was the front-page feature. Even those who never in the racing of horses felt any concern could not help but take in the outcome of this one a curious interest. The audacity of the prophecy, the very absurdity of it, presupposing, as it did, occult power, was in itself amusing. And when the curtain rose on the Suburban it was evident that to thousands what the Man Who Could Not Lose had foretold was a serious and inspired utterance.

This time his friends gathered around him, not to benefit by his advice, but to protect him. "They'll mob you!" they warned. "They'll tear the clothes off your back. Better make your getaway now."

Dolly, with tears in her eyes, sat beside him. Every now and again she touched his hand. Below his box, as around a newspaper office on the night when a president is elected, the people crushed in a turbulent mob. Some mocked and jeered, some who on his tip had risked their every dollar hailed him hopefully. On every

THE MAN WHO COULD NOT LOSE

side policemen, fearful of coming trouble, hemmed him in. Carter was bored extremely, heartily sorry he had on the night before given way to what he now saw as a perverse impulse. But he still was confident, still undismayed.

To all eyes, except those of Dolly, he was of all those at the track the least concerned. To her he turned and, in a low tone, spoke swiftly. "I am so sorry," he begged. "But, indeed, indeed, I can't lose. You must have faith in me."

"In you, yes," returned Dolly in a whisper, "but in your dreams, no!"

The horses were passing on their way to the post. Carter brought his face close to hers. "I'm going to break my promise," he said, "and make one more bet, this one with you. I bet you a kiss that I'm right."

Dolly, holding back her tears, smiled mournfully.

"Make it a hundred," she said.

Half of the forty thousand at the track had backed Delhi, the other half, following Carter's luck and his confidence in proclaiming his convictions, had backed Beldame. Many hundred had gone so far as to bet that the three horses he had named would finish as he had foretold. But, in spite of Carter's tip, Delhi still was the favorite, and when the thousands saw the Keene

THE MAN WHO COULD NOT LOSE

polka-dots leap to the front, and by two lengths stay there, for the quarter, the half, and for the three-quarters, the air was shattered with jubilant, triumphant yells. And then suddenly, with the swiftness of a moving picture, in the very moment of his victory, Beldame crept up on the favorite, drew alongside, drew ahead, passed him, and left him beaten.

It was at the mile.

The night before a man had risen in a theatre and said to two thousand people: "The favorite will lead for the mile, and give way to Beldame." Could they have believed him, the men who now cursed themselves might for the rest of their lives have lived upon their winnings. Those who had followed his prophecy faithfully, superstitiously, now shrieked in happy, riotous self-congratulation. "At the MILE!" they yelled. "He TOLD you, at the MILE!" They turned toward Carter and shook Panama hats at him. "Oh, you Carter!" they shrieked lovingly.

It was more than a race the crowd was watching now, it was the working out of a promise. And when Beldame stood off Proper's rush, and Proper fell to second, and First Mason followed three lengths in the rear, and in that order they flashed under the wire, the yells were not that a race had been won, but that a prophecy had been fulfilled.

THE MAN WHO COULD NOT LOSE

Of the thousands that cheered Carter and fell upon him and indeed did tear his clothes off his back, one of his friends alone was sufficiently unselfish to think of what it might mean to Carter.

"Champ!" roared his friend, pounding him on both shoulders. "You old wizard! I win ten thousand! How much do you win?"

Carter cast a swift glance at Dolly. "Oh!" he said, "I win much more than that."

And Dolly, raising her eyes to his, nodded and smiled contentedly.

MY BURIED TREASURE

This is a true story of a search for buried treasure. The only part that is not true is the name of the man with whom I searched for the treasure. Unless I keep his name out of it he will not let me write the story, and, as it was his expedition and as my share of the treasure is only what I can make by writing the story, I must write as he dictates. I think the story should be told, because our experience was unique, and might be of benefit to others.

And, besides, I need the money.

There is, however, no agreement preventing me from describing him as I think he is, or reporting, as accurately as I can, what he said and did as he said and did it.

For purposes of identification I shall call him Edgar Powell. The last name has no significance; but the first name is not chosen at random. The leader of our expedition, the head and brains of it, was and is the sort of man one would address as Edgar. No one would think of calling him "Ed," or "Eddie," any more than he would consider slapping him on the back.

MY BURIED TREASURE

We were together at college; but, as six hundred other boys were there at the same time, that gives no clew to his identity. Since those days, until he came to see me about the treasure, we had not met. All I knew of him was that he had succeeded his father in manufacturing unshrinkable flannels. Of course, the reader understands that is not the article of commerce he manufactures; but it is near enough, and it suggests the line of business to which he gives his life's blood. It is not similar to my own line of work, and in consequence, when he wrote me, on the unshrinkable flannels official writing-paper, that he wished to see me in reference to a matter of business of "mutual benefit," I was considerably puzzled.

A few days later, at nine in the morning, an hour of his own choosing, he came to my rooms in New York City.

Except that he had grown a beard, he was as I remembered him, thin and tall, but with no chest, and stooping shoulders. He wore eye-glasses, and as of old through these he regarded you disapprovingly and warily as though he suspected you might try to borrow money, or even joke with him. As with Edgar I had never felt any temptation to do either, this was irritating.

But from force of former habit we greeted each

other by our first names, and he suspiciously accepted a cigar. Then, after fixing me both with his eyes and with his eye-glasses and swearing me to secrecy, he began abruptly.

"Our mills," he said, "are in New Bedford; and I own several small cottages there and in Fairhaven. I rent them out at a moderate rate. The other day one of my tenants, a Portuguese sailor, was taken suddenly ill and sent for me. He had made many voyages in and out of Bedford to the South Seas, whaling, and he told me on his last voyage he had touched at his former home at Teneriffe. There his grandfather had given him a document that had been left him by *his* father. His grandfather said it contained an important secret, but one that was of value only in America, and that when he returned to that continent he must be very careful to whom he showed it. He told me it was written in a kind of English he could not understand, and that he had been afraid to let any one see it. He wanted me to accept the document in payment of the rent he owed me, with the understanding that I was not to look at it, and that if he got well I was to give it back. If he pulled through, he was to pay me in some other way; but if he died I was to keep the document. About a month ago he died, and I examined the paper. It purports

MY BURIED TREASURE

to tell where there is buried a pirate's treasure. And," added Edgar, gazing at me severely and as though he challenged me to contradict him, "I intend to dig for it!"

Had he told me he contemplated crossing the Rocky Mountains in a Baby Wright, or leading a cotillon, I could not have been more astonished. I am afraid I laughed aloud.

"You!" I exclaimed. "Search for buried treasure?"

My tone visibly annoyed him. Even the eye-glasses radiated disapproval.

"I see nothing amusing in the idea," Edgar protested coldly. "It is a plain business proposition. I find the outlay will be small, and if I am successful the returns should be large; at a rough estimate about one million dollars."

Even to-day, no true American, at the thought of one million dollars, can remain covered. His letter to me had said, "for our mutual benefit." I became respectful and polite, I might even say abject. After all, the ties that bind us in those dear old college days are not lightly to be disregarded.

"If I can be of any service to you, Edgar, old man," I assured him heartily, "if I can help you find it, you know I shall be only too happy."

With regret I observed that my generous offer did not seem to deeply move him.

MY BURIED TREASURE

"I came to you in this matter," he continued stiffly, "because you seemed to be the sort of person who would be interested in a search for buried treasure."

"I am," I exclaimed. "Always have been."

"Have you," he demanded searchingly, "any practical experience?"

I tried to appear at ease; but I knew then just how the man who applies to look after your furnace feels, when you ask him if he can also run a sixty horse-power dynamo.

"I have never actually *found* any buried treasure," I admitted; "but I know where lots of it *is*, and I know just how to go after it." I endeavored to dazzle him with expert knowledge.

"Of course," I went on airily, "I am familiar with all the expeditions that have tried for the one on Cocos Island, and I know all about the Peruvian treasure on Trinidad, and the lost treasures of Jalisco near Guadalajara, and the sunken galleon on the Grand Cayman, and when I was on the Isle of Pines I had several very tempting offers to search there. And the late Captain Boynton invited me——"

"But," interrupted Edgar in a tone that would tolerate no trifling, "you yourself have never financed or organized an expedition with the object in view of——"

MY BURIED TREASURE

"Oh, that part's easy!" I assured him. "The fitting-out part you can safely leave to me." I assumed a confidence that I hoped he might believe was real. "There's always a tramp steamer in the Erie Basin," I said, "that one can charter for any kind of adventure, and I have the addresses of enough soldiers of fortune, filibusters, and professional revolutionists to man a battle-ship, all fine fellows in a tight corner. And I'll promise you they'll follow us to hell, and back——"

"That!" exclaimed Edgar, "is exactly what I feared."

"I beg your pardon!" I exclaimed.

"That's exactly what I *don't* want," said Edgar sternly. "I don't *intend* to get into any tight corners. I don't *want* to go to hell!"

I saw that in my enthusiasm I had perhaps alarmed him. I continued more temperately.

"Any expedition after treasure," I pointed out, "is never without risk. You must have discipline, and you must have picked men. Suppose there's a mutiny? Suppose they try to rob us of the treasure on our way home? We must have men we can rely on, and men who know how to pump a Winchester. I can get you both. And Bannerman will furnish me with anything from a pair of leggins to a quick-firing gun, and on Clark Street they'll quote me a special rate on ship stores, hydraulic pumps, divers' helmets——"

Edgar's eye-glasses became frosted with cold, condemnatory scorn. He shook his head disgustedly.

"I was afraid of this!" he murmured.

I endeavored to reassure him.

"A little danger," I laughed, "only adds to the fun."

"I want you to understand," exclaimed Edgar indignantly, "there isn't going to be any danger. There isn't going to be any fun. This is a plain business proposition. I asked you those questions just to test you. And you approached the matter exactly as I feared you would. I was prepared for it. In fact," he explained shamefacedly, "I've read several of your little stories, and I find they run to adventure and blood and thunder; they are not of the analytical school of fiction. Judging from them," he added accusingly, "you have a tendency to the romantic." He spoke reluctantly as though saying I had a tendency to epileptic fits or the morphine habit.

"I am afraid," I was forced to admit, "that to me pirates and buried treasure always suggest adventure. And your criticism of my writings is well observed. Others have discovered the

MY BURIED TREASURE

same fatal weakness. We cannot all," I pointed out, "manufacture unshrinkable flannels."

At this compliment to his more fortunate condition, Edgar seemed to soften.

"I grant you," he said, "that the subject has almost invariably been approached from the point of view you take. And what," he demanded triumphantly, "has been the result? Failure, or at least, before success was attained, a most unnecessary and regrettable loss of blood and life. Now, on my expedition, I do not intend that any blood shall be shed, or that anybody shall lose his life. I have not entered into this matter hastily. I have taken out information, and mean to benefit by other people's mistakes. When I decided to go on with this," he explained, "I read all the books that bear on searches for buried treasure, and I found that in each case the same mistakes were made, and that then, in order to remedy the mistakes, it was invariably necessary to kill somebody. Now, by not making those mistakes, it will not be necessary for me to kill any one, and nobody is going to have a chance to kill me.

"You propose that we fit out a schooner and sign on a crew. What will happen? A man with a sabre cut across his forehead, or with a black patch over one eye, will inevitably be one of that crew. And, as soon as we sail, he will at once begin to plot against us. A cabin boy, who the conspirators think is asleep in his bunk, will overhear their plot and will run to the quarter-deck to give warning; but a pistol shot rings out, and the cabin boy falls at the foot of the companion ladder. The cabin boy is always the first one to go. After that the mutineers kill the first mate, and lock us in our cabin, and take over the ship. They will then broach a cask of rum, and all through the night we will listen to their drunken howlings, and from the cabin airport watch the body of the first mate rolling in the lee scuppers."

"But you forget," I protested eagerly, "there is always *one* faithful member of the crew, who——"

Edgar interrupted me impatiently.

"I have not overlooked him," he said. "He is a Jamaica negro of gigantic proportions, or the ship's cook; but he always gets his too, and he gets it good. They throw *him* to the sharks! Then we all camp out on a desert island inhabited only by goats, and we build a stockade, and the mutineers come to treat with us under a white flag, and we, trusting entirely to their honor, are fools enough to go out and talk with them. At which they shoot us up, and withdraw laughing scornfully." Edgar fixed his eyeglasses upon me accusingly.

MY BURIED TREASURE

"Am I right, or am I wrong?" he demanded. I was unable to answer.

"The only man," continued Edgar warmly, "who ever showed the slightest intelligence in the matter was the fellow in the 'Gold Bug.' *He* kept his mouth shut. He never let any one know that he was after buried treasure, until he found it. That's me! Now I know *exactly* where this treasure is, and——"

I suppose, involuntarily, I must have given a start of interest; for Edgar paused and shook his head, slyly and cunningly.

"And if you think I have the map on my person now," he declared in triumph, "you'll have to guess again!"

"Really," I protested, "I had no intention——"

"Not you, perhaps," said Edgar grudgingly; "but your Japanese valet conceals himself behind those curtains, follows me home, and at night——"

"I haven't got a valet," I objected.

Edgar merely smiled with the most aggravating self-sufficiency. "It makes no difference," he declared. "*No one* will ever find that map, or see that map, or know where that treasure is, until *I* point to the spot."

"Your caution is admirable," I said; "but what," I jeered, "makes you think you can point to the spot,—because your map says something

MY BURIED TREASURE

like, 'Through the Sunken Valley to Witch's Caldron, four points N. by N. E. to Gallows Hill where the shadow falls at sunrise, fifty fathoms west, fifty paces north as the crow flies, to the Seven Wells'? How the deuce," I demanded, "is any one going to point to *that* spot?"

"It isn't that kind of map," shouted Edgar triumphantly. "If it had been, I wouldn't have gone on with it. It's a map anybody can read except a half-caste Portuguese sailor. It's as plain as a laundry bill. It says," he paused apprehensively, and then continued with caution, "it says at such and such a place there is a something. So many somethings from that something are three what-you-may-call-'ems, and in the centre of these three what-you-may-call-'ems is buried the treasure. It's as plain as that!"

"Even with the few details you have let escape you," I said, "I could find *that* spot in my sleep."

"I don't think you could," said Edgar uncomfortably; but I could see that he had mentally warned himself to be less communicative. "And," he went on, "I am willing to lead you to it, if you subscribe to certain conditions."

Edgar's insulting caution had ruffled my spirit.

MY BURIED TREASURE

"Why do you think you can trust ME?" I asked haughtily. And then, remembering my share of the million dollars, I added in haste, "I accept the conditions."

"Of course, as you say, one has got to take *some* risk," Edgar continued; "but I feel sure," he said, regarding me doubtfully, "you would not stoop to open robbery." I thanked him.

"Well, until one is tempted," said Edgar, "one never knows *what* he might do. And I've simply *got* to have one other man, and I picked on you because I thought you could write about it——"

"I see," I said, "I am to act as the historian of the expedition."

"That will be arranged later," said Edgar. "What I chiefly want you for is to dig. *Can* you dig?" he asked eagerly. I told him I could; but that I would rather do almost anything else.

"I *must* have one other man," repeated Edgar, "a man who is strong enough to dig, and strong enough to resist the temptation to murder me." The retort was so easy that I let it pass. Besides, on Edgar, it would have been wasted.

"I *think* you will do," he said with reluctance. "And now the conditions!"

I smiled agreeably.

"You are already sworn to secrecy," said

MY BURIED TREASURE

Edgar. "And you now agree in every detail to obey me implicitly, and to accompany me to a certain place, where you will dig. If I find the treasure, you agree to help me guard it, and convey it to wherever I decide it is safe to leave it. Your responsibility is then at an end. One year after the treasure is discovered, you will be free to write the account of the expedition. For what you write, some magazine may pay you. What it pays you will be your share of the treasure."

Of my part of the million dollars, which I had hastily calculated could not be less than one-fifth, I had already spent over one hundred thousand dollars and was living far beyond my means. I had bought a farm with a water-front on the Sound, a motor-boat, and, as I was not sure which make I preferred, three automobiles. I had at my own expense produced a play of mine that no manager had appreciated, and its name in electric lights was already blinding Broadway. I had purchased a Hollander express rifle, a *real* amber cigar holder, a private secretary who could play both rag-time and tennis, and a fur coat. So Edgar's generous offer left me naked. When I had again accustomed myself to the narrow confines of my flat, and the jolt of the surface cars, I asked humbly:

MY BURIED TREASURE

"Is that ALL I get?"

"Why should you expect any more?" demanded Edgar. "It isn't *your* treasure. You wouldn't expect me to make you a present of an interest in my mills; why should you get a share of my treasure?" He gazed at me reproachfully. "I thought you'd be pleased," he said. "It must be hard to think of things to write about, and I'm giving you a subject for nothing. I thought," he remonstrated, "you'd jump at the chance. It isn't every day a man can dig for buried treasure."

"That's all right," I said. "Perhaps I appreciate that quite as well as you do. But my time has a certain small value, and I can't leave my work just for excitement. We may be weeks, months— How long do you think we——"

Behind his eye-glasses Edgar winked reprovingly.

"That is a leading question," he said. "I will pay all your legitimate expenses—transportation, food, lodging. It won't cost you a cent. And you write the story—with my name left out," he added hastily; "it would hurt my standing in the trade," he explained—"and get paid for it."

I saw a sea voyage at Edgar's expense. I saw palm leaves, coral reefs. I felt my muscles aching and the sweat run from my neck and

MY BURIED TREASURE

shoulders as I drove my pick into the chest of gold.

"I'll go you!" I said. We shook hands on it. "When do we start?" I asked.

"Now!" said Edgar. I thought he wished to test me; he had touched upon one of my pet vanities.

"You can't do that with me!" I said. "My bags are packed and ready for any place in the wide world, except the cold places. I can start this minute. Where is it, the Gold Coast, the Ivory Coast, the Spanish Main——"

Edgar frowned inscrutably. "Have you an empty suit-case?" he asked.

"Why EMPTY?" I demanded.

"To carry the treasure," said Edgar. "I left mine in the hall. We will need two."

"And your trunks?" I said.

"There aren't going to be any trunks," said Edgar. From his pocket he had taken a folder of the New Jersey Central Railroad. "If we hurry," he exclaimed, "we can catch the ten-thirty express, and return to New York in time for dinner."

"And what about the treasure?" I roared.

"We'll bring it with us," said Edgar.

I asked for information. I demanded confidences. Edgar refused both. I insisted that I might be allowed at least to carry my automatic

MY BURIED TREASURE

pistol. "Suppose some one tries to take the treasure from us?" I pointed out.

"No one," said Edgar severely, "would be such an ass as to imagine we are carrying buried treasure in a suit-case. He will think it contains pajamas."

"For local color, then," I begged, "I want to say in my story that I went heavily armed."

"Say it, then," snapped Edgar. "But you can't DO it! Not with me, you can't! How do I know you mightn't—" He shook his head warily.

It was a day in early October, the haze of Indian summer was in the air, and as we crossed the North River by the Twenty-third Street Ferry the sun flashed upon the white clouds overhead and the tumbling waters below. On each side of us great vessels with the Blue Peter at the fore lay at the wharfs ready to cast off, or were already nosing their way down the channel toward strange and beautiful ports. Lamport and Holt were rolling down to Rio; the Royal Mail's *Magdalena,* no longer "white and gold," was off to Kingston, where once seven pirates swung in chains; the *Clyde* was on her way to Hayti where the buccaneers came from; the *Morro Castle* was bound for Havana, which Morgan, king of all the pirates, had once made his own; and the *Red D* was steaming to

MY BURIED TREASURE

Porto Cabello where Sir Francis Drake, as big a buccaneer as any of them, lies entombed in her harbor. And *I* was setting forth on a buried-treasure expedition on a snub-nosed, flat-bellied, fresh-water ferry-boat, bound for Jersey City! No one will ever know my sense of humiliation. And, when the Italian boy insulted my immaculate tan shoes by pointing at them and saying, "Shine?" I could have slain him. Fancy digging for buried treasure in freshly varnished boots! But Edgar did not mind. To him there was nothing lacking; it was just as it should be. He was deeply engrossed in calculating how many offices were for rent in the Singer Building!

When we reached the other side, he refused to answer any of my eager questions. He would not let me know even for what place on the line he had purchased our tickets, and, as a hint that I should not disturb him, he stuffed into my hands the latest magazines. "At least tell me this," I demanded. "Have you ever been to this place before to-day?"

"Once," said Edgar shortly, "last week. That's when I found out I would need some one with me who could dig."

"How do you know it's the *right* place?" I whispered.

The summer season was over, and of the chair

MY BURIED TREASURE

car we were the only occupants; but, before he answered, Edgar looked cautiously round him and out of the window. We had just passed Red Bank.

"Because the map told me," he answered. "Suppose," he continued fretfully, "you had a map of New York City with the streets marked on it plainly? Suppose the map said that if you walked to where Broadway and Fifth Avenue meet, you would find the Flatiron Building. Do you think you could find it?"

"Was it as easy as *that*?" I gasped.

"It was as easy as *that*!" said Edgar.

I sank back into my chair and let the magazines slide to the floor. What fiction story was there in any one of them so enthralling as the actual possibilities that lay before me? In two hours I might be bending over a pot of gold, a sea chest stuffed with pearls and rubies!

I began to recall all the stories I had heard as a boy of treasure buried along the coast by Kidd on his return voyage from the Indies. Where along the Jersey sea-line were there safe harbors? The train on which we were racing south had its rail head at Barnegat Bay. And between Barnegat and Red Bank there now was but one other inlet, that of the Manasquan River. It might be Barnegat; it might be Manasquan. It could not be a great distance from either;

MY BURIED TREASURE

for sailors would not have carried their burden far from the ship. I glanced appealingly at Edgar. He was smiling happily over "Pickings from Puck." We passed Asbury Park and Ocean Grove, halted at Sea Girt, and again at Manasquan; but Edgar did not move. The next station was Point Pleasant, and as the train drew to a stop, Edgar rose calmly and grasped his suit-case.

"We get out here," he said.

Drawn up at the station were three open-work hacks with fringe around the top. From each a small boy waved at us with his whip.

"Curtis House? The Gladstone? The Cottage in the Pines?" they chanted invitingly.

"Take me to a hardware store," said Edgar, "where one can buy a spade." When we stopped I made a move to get down; but Edgar stopped me.

I protested indignantly, "I haven't *much* to say about this expedition," I exclaimed; "but, as *I* have to do the digging, I intend to choose my own spade."

Edgar's eye-glasses flashed defiance. "You have given your word to obey me," he said sternly. "If you do not intend to obey me, you can return in ten minutes by the next train."

I sank into my seat. In a moment the mutiny had been crushed. Not even a cabin boy had

MY BURIED TREASURE

fallen! Edgar returned with a spade, an axe, and a pick. He placed them in the seat beside the boy driver.

"What is your name, boy?" he asked.

"Rupert," said the boy.

"Rupert," continued Edgar, "drive us to the beach. When you get to the bathing pavilions keep on along the shore toward Manasquan Inlet." He touched the spade with his hand. "I have bought a building lot on the beach," he explained, "and am going to dig a hole, and plant a flagpole."

I was choked with indignation. As a writer of fiction my self-respect was insulted.

"If there are any more lies to be told," I whispered, "please let *me* tell them. Your invention is crude, ridiculous! Why," I demanded, "should anybody want to plant a flagpole on a wind-swept beach in October? It's not the season for flagpoles. Besides," I jeered, "where is your flagpole? Is it concealed in the suit-case?"

Edgar frowned uneasily, and touched the boy on the shoulder.

"The flagpole itself," he explained, "is coming down to-morrow by express."

The boy yawned, and slapped the flanks of his horse with the reins. "Gat up!" he said.

We crossed the railroad tracks and moved

MY BURIED TREASURE

toward the ocean down a broad, sandy road. The season had passed and the windows of the cottages and bungalows on either side of the road were barricaded with planks. On the verandas hammocks abandoned to the winds hung in tatters, on the back porches the doors of empty refrigerators swung open on one hinge, and on every side above the fields of gorgeous golden-rod rose signs reading "For Rent." When we had progressed in silence for a mile, the sandy avenue lost itself in the deeper sand of the beach, and the horse of his own will came to a halt. On one side we were surrounded by locked and deserted bathing houses, on the other by empty pavilions shuttered and barred against the winter, but still inviting one to "Try our salt water taffy" or to "*Keep cool* with an ice-cream soda." Rupert turned and looked inquiringly at Edgar. To the north the beach stretched in an unbroken line to Manasquan Inlet. To the south three miles away we could see floating on the horizon-like a mirage the hotels and summer cottages of Bay Head.

"Drive toward the inlet," directed Edgar. "This gentleman and I will walk."

Relieved of our weight, the horse stumbled bravely into the trackless sand, while below on the damper and firmer shingle we walked by the edge of the water.

MY BURIED TREASURE

The tide was coming in and the spent waves, spreading before them an advance guard of tiny shells and pebbles, threatened our boots, and at the same time in soothing, lazy whispers warned us of their attack. These lisping murmurs and the crash and roar of each incoming wave as it broke were the only sounds. And on the beach we were the only human figures. At last the scene began to bear some resemblance to one set for an adventure. The rolling ocean, a coast steamer dragging a great column of black smoke, and cast high upon the beach the wreck of a schooner, her masts tilting drunkenly, gave color to our purpose. It became filled with greater promise of drama, more picturesque. I began to thrill with excitement. I regarded Edgar appealingly, in eager supplication. At last he broke the silence that was torturing me.

"We will now walk higher up," he commanded. "If we get our feet wet, we may take cold."

My spirit was too far broken to make reply. But to my relief I saw that in leaving the beach Edgar had some second purpose. With each heavy step he was drawing toward two high banks of sand in a hollow behind which, protected by the banks, were three stunted, wind-driven pines. His words came back to me. "So many what-you-may-call-'ems." Were

MY BURIED TREASURE

these pines the three somethings from something, the what-you-may-call-'ems? The thought chilled me to the spine. I gazed at them fascinated. I felt like falling on my knees in the sand and tearing their secret from them with my bare hands. I was strong enough to dig them up by the roots, strong enough to dig the Panama Canal! I glanced tremulously at Edgar. His eyes were wide open and, eloquent with dismay, his lower jaw had fallen. He turned and looked at me for the first time with consideration. Apology and remorse were written in every line of his countenance.

"I'm sorry," he stammered. I had a cruel premonition. I exclaimed with distress.

"You have lost the map!" I hissed.

"No, no," protested Edgar; "but I entirely forgot to bring any lunch!"

With violent mutterings I tore off my upper and outer garments and tossed them into the hack.

"Where do I begin?" I asked.

Edgar pointed to a spot inside the triangle formed by the three trees and equally distant from each.

"Put that horse behind the bank," I commanded, "where no one can see him! And both you and Rupert keep off the sky-line!"

From the north and south we were now all

MY BURIED TREASURE

three hidden by the two high banks of sand; to the east lay the beach and the Atlantic Ocean, and to the west stretches of marshes that a mile away met a wood of pine trees and the railroad round-house.

I began to dig. I knew that weary hours lay before me, and I attacked the sand leisurely and with deliberation. It was at first no great effort; but as the hole grew in depth, and the roots of the trees were exposed, the work was sufficient for several men. Still, as Edgar had said, it is not every day that one can dig for treasure, and in thinking of what was to come I forgot my hands that quickly blistered, and my breaking back. After an hour I insisted that Edgar should take a turn; but he made such poor headway that my patience could not contain me, and I told him I was sufficiently rested and would continue. With alacrity he scrambled out of the hole, and, taking a cigar from my case, seated himself comfortably in the hack. I took MY comfort in anticipating the thrill that would be mine when the spade would ring on the ironbound chest; when, with a blow of the axe, I would expose to view the hidden jewels, the pieces of eight, coated with verdigris, the string of pearls, the chains of yellow gold. Edgar had said a million dollars. That must mean there would be diamonds, many dia-

MY BURIED TREASURE

monds. I would hold them in my hands, watch them, at the sudden sunshine, blink their eyes and burst into tiny, burning fires. In imagination I would replace them in the setting, from which, years before, they had been stolen. I would try to guess whence they came—from a jewelled chalice in some dim cathedral, from the breast of a great lady, from the hilt of an admiral's sword.

After another hour I lifted my aching shoulders and, wiping the sweat from my eyes, looked over the edge of the hole. Rupert, with his back to the sand-hill, was asleep. Edgar with one hand was waving away the mosquitoes and in the other was holding one of the magazines he had bought on the way down. I could even see the page upon which his eyes were riveted. It was an advertisement for breakfast food. In my indignation the spade slipped through my cramped and perspiring fingers, and as it struck the bottom of the pit, something —a band of iron, a steel lock, an iron ring— gave forth a muffled sound. My heart stopped beating as suddenly as though Mr. Corbett had hit it with his closed fist. My blood turned to melted ice. I drove the spade down as fiercely as though it was a dagger. It sank into rotten wood. I had made no sound; for I could hardly breathe. But the slight noise of the

MY BURIED TREASURE

blow had reached Edgar. I heard the springs of the hack creak as he vaulted from it, and the next moment he was towering above me, peering down into the pit. His eyes were wide with excitement, greed, and fear. In his hands he clutched the two suit-cases. Like a lion defending his cubs he glared at me.

"Get out!" he shouted.

"Like hell!" I said.

"Get out!" he roared. "I'll do the rest. That's mine, not yours! *Get out!*"

With a swift kick I brushed away the sand. I found I was standing on a squat wooden box, bound with bands of rusty iron. I had only to stoop to touch it. It was so rotten that I could have torn it apart with my bare hands. Edgar was dancing on the edge of the pit, incidentally kicking sand into my mouth and nostrils.

"You *promised* me!" he roared. "You *promised* to obey me!"

"You ass!" I shouted. "Haven't I done all the work? Don't I get——"

"You get out!" roared Edgar.

Slowly, disgustedly, with what dignity one can display in crawling out of a sand-pit, I scrambled to the top.

"Go over there," commanded Edgar pointing, "and sit down."

In furious silence I seated myself beside

MY BURIED TREASURE

Rupert. He was still slumbering and snoring happily. From where I sat I could see nothing of what was going forward in the pit, save once, when the head of Edgar, his eyes aflame and his hair and eye-glasses sprinkled with sand, appeared above it. Apparently he was fearful lest I had moved from the spot where he had placed me. I had not; but had he known my inmost feelings he would have taken the axe into the pit with him.

I must have sat so for half an hour. In the sky above me a fish-hawk drifted lazily. From the beach sounded the steady beat of the waves, and from the town across the marshes came the puffing of a locomotive and the clanging bells of the freight trains. The breeze from the sea cooled the sweat on my aching body; but it could not cool the rage in my heart. If I had had the courage of my feelings, I would have cracked Edgar over the head with the spade, buried him in the pit, bribed Rupert, and forever after lived happily on my ill-gotten gains. That was how Kidd, or Morgan, or Blackbeard would have acted. I cursed the effete civilization which had taught me to want many pleasures but had left me with a conscience that would not let me take human life to obtain them, not even Edgar's life.

In half an hour a suit-case was lifted into view

In his hands he clutched the two suit-cases.... "Get out!" he shouted.

and dropped on the edge of the pit. It was followed by the other, and then by Edgar. Without asking me to help him, because he probably knew I would not, he shovelled the sand into the hole, and then placed the suit-cases in the carriage. With increasing anger I observed that the contents of each were so heavy that to lift it he used both hands.

"There is no use your asking any questions," he announced, "because I won't answer them."

I gave him minute directions as to where he could go; but instead we drove in black silence to the station. There Edgar rewarded Rupert with a dime, and while we waited for the train to New York placed the two suit-cases against the wall of the ticket office and sat upon them. When the train arrived he warned me in a hoarse whisper that I had promised to help him guard the treasure, and gave me one of the suit-cases. It weighed a ton. Just to spite Edgar, I had a plan to kick it open, so that every one on the platform might scramble for the contents. But again my infernal New England conscience restrained me.

Edgar had secured the drawing-room in the parlor-car, and when we were safely inside and the door bolted my curiosity became stronger than my pride.

"Edgar," I said, "your ingratitude is contemptible. Your suspicions are ridiculous; but, under these most unusual conditions, I don't blame you. But we are quite safe now. The door is fastened," I pointed out ingratiatingly, "and this train doesn't stop for another forty minutes. I think this would be an excellent time to look at the treasure."

"I don't!" said Edgar.

I sank back into my chair. With intense enjoyment I imagined the train in which we were seated hurling itself into another train; and everybody, including Edgar, or, rather, especially Edgar, being instantly but painlessly killed. By such an act of an all-wise Providence I would at once become heir to one million dollars. It was a beautiful, satisfying dream. Even *my* conscience accepted it with a smug smile. It was so vivid a dream that I sat guiltily expectant, waiting for the crash to come, for the shrieks and screams, for the rush of escaping steam and breaking window-panes.

But it was far too good to be true. Without a jar the train carried us and its precious burden in safety to the Jersey City terminal. And each, with half a million dollars in his hand, hurried to the ferry, assailed by porters, newsboys, hackmen. To them we were a couple of commuters saving a dime by carrying our own hand-bags.

MY BURIED TREASURE

It was now six o'clock, and I pointed out to Edgar that at that hour the only vaults open were those of the Night and Day Bank. And to that institution in a taxicab we at once made our way. I paid the chauffeur, and two minutes later, with a gasp of relief and rejoicing, I dropped the suit-case I had carried on a table in the steel-walled fastnesses of the vaults. Gathered excitedly around us were the officials of the bank, summoned hastily from above, and watchmen in plain clothes, and watchmen in uniforms of gray. Great bars as thick as my leg protected us. Walls of chilled steel rising from solid rock stood between our treasure and the outer world. Until then I had not known how tremendous the nervous strain had been; but now it came home to me. I mopped the perspiration from my forehead, I drew a deep breath.

"Edgar," I exclaimed happily, "I congratulate you!"

I found Edgar extending toward me a two-dollar bill. "You gave the chauffeur two dollars," he said. "The fare was really one dollar eighty; so you owe me twenty cents."

Mechanically I laid two dimes upon the table.

"All the other expenses," continued Edgar, "which I agreed to pay, I have paid." He made

MY BURIED TREASURE

a peremptory gesture. "I won't detain you any longer," he said. "Good-night!"

"Good-night!" I cried. "Don't I see the treasure?" Against the walls of chilled steel my voice rose like that of a tortured soul. "Don't I touch it!" I yelled. "Don't I even get a squint?"

Even the watchmen looked sorry for me.

"You do not!" said Edgar calmly. "You have fulfilled your part of the agreement. I have fulfilled mine. A year from now you can write the story." As I moved in a dazed state toward the steel door, his voice halted me.

"And you can say in your story," called Edgar, "that there is only one way to get a buried treasure. That is to go, and get it!"

THE CONSUL

FOR over forty years, in one part of the world or another, old man Marshall had served his country as a United States consul. He had been appointed by Lincoln. For a quarter of a century that fact was his distinction. It was now his epitaph. But in former years, as each new administration succeeded the old, it had again and again saved his official head. When victorious and voracious place-hunters, searching the map of the world for spoils, dug out his hiding-place and demanded his consular sign as a reward for a younger and more aggressive party worker, the ghost of the dead President protected him. In the State Department, Marshall had become a tradition. "You can't touch HIM!" the State Department would say; "why, HE was appointed by Lincoln!" Secretly, for this weapon against the hungry head-hunters, the department was infinitely grateful. Old man Marshall was a consul after its own heart. Like a soldier, he was obedient, disciplined; wherever he was sent, there, without question, he would go. Never against exile, against ill-health, against climate did he make complaint. Nor when he was moved on and down to make way for some ne'er-do-well with influence, with a brother-in-law in the Senate, with a cousin owning a newspaper, with rich relatives who desired him to drink himself to death at the expense of the government rather than at their own, did old man Marshall point to his record as a claim for more just treatment.

And it had been an excellent record. His official reports, in a quaint, stately hand, were models of English; full of information, intelligent, valuable, well observed. And those few of his countrymen, who stumbled upon him in the out-of-the-world places to which of late he had been banished, wrote of him to the department in terms of admiration and awe. Never had he or his friends petitioned for promotion, until it was at last apparent that, save for his record and the memory of his dead patron, he had no friends. But, still in the department the tradition held and, though he was not advanced, he was not dismissed.

"If that old man's been feeding from the public trough ever since the Civil War," protested a "practical" politician, "it seems to me, Mr. Secretary, that he's about had his share. Ain't it time he give some one else a bite? Some of us that has done the work, that has borne the brunt——"

THE CONSUL

"This place he now holds," interrupted the Secretary of State suavely, "is one hardly commensurate with services like yours. I can't pronounce the name of it, and I'm not sure just where it is, but I see that, of the last six consuls we sent there, three resigned within a month and the other three died of yellow-fever. Still, if you insist——"

The practical politician reconsidered hastily. "I'm not the sort," he protested, "to turn out a man appointed by our martyred President. Besides, he's so old now, if the fever don't catch him, he'll die of old age, anyway."

The Secretary coughed uncomfortably. "And they say," he murmured, "republics are ungrateful."

"I don't quite get that," said the practical politician.

Of Porto Banos, of the Republic of Colombia, where as consul Mr. Marshall was upholding the dignity of the United States, little could be said except that it possessed a sure harbor. When driven from the Caribbean Sea by stress of weather, the largest of ocean tramps, and even battle-ships, could find in its protecting arms of coral a safe shelter. But, as young Mr. Aiken, the wireless operator, pointed out, unless driven by a hurricane and the fear of death, no one ever visited it. Back of the ancient

THE CONSUL

wharfs, that dated from the days when Porto Banos was a receiver of stolen goods for buccaneers and pirates, were rows of thatched huts, streets, according to the season, of dust or mud, a few iron-barred, jail-like barracks, custom-houses, municipal buildings, and the white-washed adobe houses of the consuls. The back yard of the town was a swamp. Through this at five each morning a rusty engine pulled a train of flat cars to the base of the mountains, and, if meanwhile the rails had not disappeared into the swamp, at five in the evening brought back the flat cars laden with odorous coffee-sacks.

In the daily life of Porto Banos, waiting for the return of the train, and betting if it would return, was the chief interest. Each night the consuls, the foreign residents, the wireless operator, the manager of the rusty railroad met for dinner. There at the head of the long table, by virtue of his years, of his courtesy and distinguished manner, of his office, Mr. Marshall presided. Of the little band of exiles he was the chosen ruler. His rule was gentle. By force of example he had made existence in Porto Banos more possible. For women and children Porto Banos was a death-trap, and before "old man Marshall" came there had been no influence to remind the enforced bachelors of other days.

THE CONSUL

They had lost interest, had grown lax, irritable, morose. Their white duck was seldom white. Their cheeks were unshaven. When the sun sank into the swamp and the heat still turned Porto Banos into a Turkish bath, they threw dice on the greasy tables of the Café Bolivar for drinks. The petty gambling led to petty quarrels; the drinks to fever. The coming of Mr. Marshall changed that. His standard of life, his tact, his worldly wisdom, his cheerful courtesy, his fastidious personal neatness shamed the younger men; the desire to please him, to stand well in his good opinion, brought back pride and self-esteem.

The lieutenant of her Majesty's gun-boat *Plover* noted the change.

"Used to be," he exclaimed, "you couldn't get out of the Café Bolivar without some one sticking a knife in you; now it's a debating club. They all sit round a table and listen to an old gentleman talk world politics."

If Henry Marshall brought content to the exiles of Porto Banos, there was little in return that Porto Banos could give to him. Magazines and correspondents in six languages kept him in touch with those foreign lands in which he had represented his country, but of the country he had represented, newspapers and periodicals showed him only too clearly that in

THE CONSUL

forty years it had grown away from him, had changed beyond recognition.

When last he had called at the State Department, he had been made to feel he was a man without a country, and when he visited his home town in Vermont, he was looked upon as a Rip Van Winkle. Those of his boyhood friends who were not dead had long thought of him as dead. And the sleepy, pretty village had become a bustling commercial centre. In the lanes where, as a young man, he had walked among wheat-fields, trolley-cars whirled between rows of mills and factories. The children had grown to manhood, with children of their own.

Like a ghost, he searched for house after house, where once he had been made welcome, only to find in its place a towering office building. "All had gone, the old familiar faces." In vain he scanned even the shop fronts for a friendly, homelike name. Whether the fault was his, whether he would better have served his own interests than those of his government, it now was too late to determine. In his own home, he was a stranger among strangers. In the service he had so faithfully followed, rank by rank, he had been dropped, until now he, who twice had been a consul-general, was an exile, banished to a fever swamp. The great Ship of State had dropped him overside, had "marooned" him, and sailed away.

THE CONSUL

Twice a day he walked along the shell road to the Café Bolivar, and back again to the consulate. There, as he entered the outer office, José, the Colombian clerk, would rise and bow profoundly.

"Any papers for me to sign, José?" the consul would ask.

"Not to-day, Excellency," the clerk would reply. Then José would return to writing a letter to his lady-love; not that there was anything to tell her, but because writing on the official paper of the consulate gave him importance in his eyes, and in hers. And in the inner office the consul would continue to gaze at the empty harbor, the empty coral reefs, the empty, burning sky.

The little band of exiles were at second breakfast when the wireless man came in late to announce that a Red D. boat and the island of Curaçoa had both reported a hurricane coming north. Also, that much concern was felt for the safety of the yacht *Serapis*. Three days before, in advance of her coming, she had sent a wireless to Wilhelmstad, asking the captain of the port to reserve a berth for her. She expected to arrive the following morning.

But for forty-eight hours nothing had been heard from her, and it was believed she had been overhauled by the hurricane. Owing to the presence on board of Senator Hanley, the closest friend of the new President, the man who had made him president, much concern was felt at Washington. To try to pick her up by wireless, the gun-boat *Newark* had been ordered from Culebra, the cruiser *Raleigh*, with Admiral Hardy on board, from Colon. It was possible she would seek shelter at Porto Banos. The consul was ordered to report.

As Marshall wrote out his answer, the French consul exclaimed with interest:

"He is of importance, then, this senator?" he asked. "Is it that in your country ships of war are at the service of a senator?"

Aiken, the wireless operator, grinned derisively.

"At the service of *this* senator, they are!" he answered. "They call him the 'king-maker,' the man behind the throne."

"But in your country," protested the Frenchman, "there is no throne. I thought your president was elected by the people?"

"That's what the people think," answered Aiken. "In God's country," he explained, "the trusts want a rich man in the Senate, with the same interests as their own, to represent them. They chose Hanley. He picked out of the candidates for the presidency the man he thought would help the interests. He nominated him,

THE CONSUL

and the people voted for him. Hanley is what we call a 'boss.'"

The Frenchman looked inquiringly at Marshall.

"The position of the boss is the more dangerous," said Marshall gravely, "because it is unofficial, because there are no laws to curtail his powers. Men like Senator Hanley are a menace to good government. They see in public office only a reward for party workers."

"That's right," assented Aiken. "Your forty years' service, Mr. Consul, wouldn't count with Hanley. If he wanted your job, he'd throw you out as quick as he would a drunken cook."

Mr. Marshall flushed painfully, and the French consul hastened to interrupt.

"Then, let us pray," he exclaimed, with fervor, "that the hurricane has sunk the *Serapis*, and all on board."

Two hours later, the *Serapis*, showing she had met the hurricane and had come out second best, steamed into the harbor.

Her owner was young Herbert Livingstone, of Washington. He once had been in the diplomatic service, and, as minister to The Hague, wished to return to it. In order to bring this about he had subscribed liberally to the party campaign fund.

With him, among other distinguished persons,

was the all-powerful Hanley. The kidnapping of Hanley for the cruise, in itself, demonstrated the ability of Livingstone as a diplomat. It was the opinion of many that it would surely lead to his appointment as a minister plenipotentiary. Livingstone was of the same opinion. He had not lived long in the nation's capital without observing the value of propinquity. How many men he knew were now paymasters, and secretaries of legation, solely because those high in the government met them daily at the Metropolitan Club, and preferred them in almost any other place. And if, after three weeks as his guest on board what the newspapers called his floating palace, the senator could refuse him even the prize legation of Europe, there was no value in modest merit. As yet, Livingstone had not hinted at his ambition. There was no need. To a statesman of Hanley's astuteness, the largeness of Livingstone's contribution to the campaign fund was self-explanatory.

After her wrestling-match with the hurricane, all those on board the *Serapis* seemed to find in land, even in the swamp land of Porto Banos, a compelling attraction. Before the anchors hit the water, they were in the launch. On reaching shore, they made at once for the consulate. There were many cables they wished

THE CONSUL

to start on their way by wireless; cables to friends, to newspapers, to the government.

José, the Colombian clerk, appalled by the unprecedented invasion of visitors, of visitors so distinguished, and Marshall, grateful for a chance to serve his fellow-countrymen, and especially his countrywomen, were ubiquitous, eager, indispensable. At José's desk the great senator, rolling his cigar between his teeth, was using, to José's ecstasy, José's own pen to write a reassuring message to the White House. At the consul's desk a beautiful creature, all in lace and pearls, was struggling to compress the very low opinion she held of a hurricane into ten words. On his knee, Henry Cairns, the banker, was inditing instructions to his Wall Street office, and upon himself Livingstone had taken the responsibility of replying to the inquiries heaped upon Marshall's desk, from many newspapers.

It was just before sunset, and Marshall produced his tea things, and the young person in pearls and lace, who was Miss Cairns, made tea for the women, and the men mixed gin and limes with tepid water. The consul apologized for proposing a toast in which they could not join. He begged to drink to those who had escaped the perils of the sea. Had they been his oldest and nearest friends, his little speech could not have been more heart-felt and sincere. To his distress, it moved one of the ladies to tears, and in embarrassment he turned to the men.

"I regret there is no ice," he said, "but you know the rule of the tropics; as soon as a ship enters port, the ice-machine bursts."

"I'll tell the steward to send you some, sir," said Livingstone, "and as long as we're here——"

The senator showed his concern.

"As long as we're here?" he gasped.

"Not over two days," answered the owner nervously. "The chief says it will take all of that to get her in shape. As you ought to know, Senator, she was pretty badly mauled."

The senator gazed blankly out of the window. Beyond it lay the naked coral reefs, the empty sky, and the ragged palms of Porto Banos.

Livingstone felt that his legation was slipping from him.

"That wireless operator," he continued hastily, "tells me there is a most amusing place a a few miles down the coast, Las Bocas, a sort of Coney Island, where the government people go for the summer. There's surf bathing and roulette and cafés chantants. He says there's some Spanish dancers——"

The guests of the *Serapis* exclaimed with

THE CONSUL

interest; the senator smiled. To Marshall the general enthusiasm over the thought of a ride on a merry-go-round suggested that the friends of Mr. Livingstone had found their own society far from satisfying.

Greatly encouraged, Livingstone continued, with enthusiasm:

"And that wireless man said," he added, "that with the launch we can get there in half an hour. We might run down after dinner."

He turned to Marshall.

"Will you join us, Mr. Consul?" he asked, "and dine with us, first?"

Marshall accepted with genuine pleasure. It had been many months since he had sat at table with his own people. But he shook his head doubtfully.

"I was wondering about Las Bocas," he explained, "if your going there might not get you in trouble at the next port. With a yacht, I think it is different, but Las Bocas is under quarantine——"

There was a chorus of exclamations.

"It's not serious," Marshall explained. "There was bubonic plague there, or something like it. You would be in no danger from that. It is only that you might be held up by the regulations. Passenger steamers can't land any one who has been there at any other port of the

THE CONSUL

West Indies. The English are especially strict. The Royal Mail won't even receive any one on board here without a certificate from the English consul saying he has not visited Las Bocas. For an American they would require the same guarantee from me. But I don't think the regulations extend to yachts. I will inquire. I don't wish to deprive you of any of the many pleasures of Porto Banos," he added, smiling, "but if you were refused a landing at your next port I would blame myself."

"It's all right," declared Livingstone decidedly. "It's just as you say; yachts and warships are exempt. Besides, I carry my own doctor, and if he won't give us a clean bill of health, I'll make him walk the plank. At eight, then, at dinner. I'll send the cutter for you. I can't give you a salute, Mr. Consul, but you shall have all the side boys I can muster."

Those from the yacht parted from their consul in the most friendly spirit.

"I think he's charming!" exclaimed Miss Cairns. "And did you notice his novels? They were in every language. It must be terribly lonely down here, for a man like that."

"He's the first of our consuls we've met on this trip," growled her father, "that we've caught sober."

"Sober!" exclaimed his wife indignantly.

THE CONSUL

"He's one of the Marshalls of Vermont. I asked him."

"I wonder," mused Hanley, "how much the place is worth? Hamilton, one of the new senators, has been deviling the life out of me to send his son somewhere. Says if he stays in Washington he'll disgrace the family. I should think this place would drive any man to drink himself to death in three months, and young Hamilton, from what I've seen of him, ought to be able to do it in a week. That would leave the place open for the next man."

"There's a postmaster in my State thinks he carried it." The senator smiled grimly. "He has consumption, and wants us to give him a consulship in the tropics. I'll tell him I've seen Porto Banos, and that it's just the place for him."

The senator's pleasantry was not well received. But Miss Cairns alone had the temerity to speak of what the others were thinking.

"What would become of Mr. Marshall?" she asked.

The senator smiled tolerantly.

"I don't know that I was thinking of Mr. Marshall," he said. "I can't recall anything he has done for this administration. You see, Miss Cairns," he explained, in the tone of one addressing a small child, "Marshall has been abroad now for forty years, at the expense of

THE CONSUL

the taxpayers. Some of us think men who have lived that long on their fellow-countrymen had better come home and get to work."

Livingstone nodded solemnly in assent. He did not wish a post abroad at the expense of the taxpayers. He was willing to pay for it. And then, with "ex-Minister" on his visiting cards, and a sense of duty well performed, for the rest of his life he could join the other expatriates in Paris.

Just before dinner, the cruiser *Raleigh* having discovered the whereabouts of the *Serapis* by wireless, entered the harbor, and Admiral Hardy came to the yacht to call upon the senator, in whose behalf he had been scouring the Caribbean Seas. Having paid his respects to that personage, the admiral fell boisterously upon Marshall.

The two old gentlemen were friends of many years. They had met, officially and unofficially, in many strange parts of the world. To each the chance reunion was a piece of tremendous good fortune. And throughout dinner the guests of Livingstone, already bored with each other, found in them and their talk of former days new and delightful entertainment. So much so that when, Marshall having assured them that the local quarantine regulations did not extend to a yacht, the men departed for

THE CONSUL

Las Bocas, the women insisted that he and the admiral remain behind.

It was for Marshall a wondrous evening. To foregather with his old friend, whom he had known since Hardy was a mad midshipman, to sit at the feet of his own charming countrywomen, to listen to their soft, modulated laughter, to note how quickly they saw that to him the evening was a great event, and with what tact each contributed to make it the more memorable; all served to wipe out the months of bitter loneliness, the stigma of failure, the sense of undeserved neglect. In the moonlight, on the cool quarter-deck, they sat, in a half-circle, each of the two friends telling tales out of school, tales of which the other was the hero or the victim, "inside" stories of great occasions, ceremonies, bombardments, unrecorded "shirt-sleeve" diplomacy.

Hardy had helped to open the Suez Canal. Marshall had assisted the Queen of Madagascar to escape from the French invaders. On the Barbary Coast Hardy had chased pirates. In Edinburgh Marshall had played chess with Carlyle. He had seen Paris in mourning in the days of the siege, Paris in terror in the days of the Commune; he had known Garibaldi, Gambetta, the younger Dumas, the creator of Pickwick.

THE CONSUL

"Do you remember that time in Tangier," the admiral urged, "when I was a midshipman, and got into the bashaw's harem?"

"Do you remember how I got you out?" Marshall replied grimly.

"And," demanded Hardy, "do you remember when Adelina Patti paid a visit to the *Kearsarge* at Marseilles in '65—George Dewey was our second officer—and you were bowing and backing away from her, and you backed into an open hatch, and she said—my French isn't up to it—what was it she said?"

"I didn't hear it," said Marshall; "I was too far down the hatch."

"Do you mean the old *Kearsarge?*" asked Mrs. Cairns. "Were you in the service then, Mr. Marshall?"

With loyal pride in his friend, the admiral answered for him:

"He was our consul-general at Marseilles!"

There was an uncomfortable moment. Even those denied imagination could not escape the contrast, could see in their mind's eye the great harbor of Marseilles, crowded with the shipping of the world, surrounding it the beautiful city, the rival of Paris to the north, and on the battleship the young consul-general making his bow to the young Empress of Song. And now, before their actual eyes, they saw the village

THE CONSUL

of Porto Banos, a black streak in the night, a row of mud shacks, at the end of the wharf a single lantern yellow in the clear moonlight.

Later in the evening Miss Cairns led the admiral to one side.

"Admiral," she began eagerly, "tell me about your friend. Why is he here? Why don't they give him a place worthy of him? I've seen many of our representatives abroad, and I know we cannot afford to waste men like that." The girl exclaimed indignantly: "He's one of the most interesting men I've ever met! He's lived everywhere, known every one. He's a distinguished man, a cultivated man; even I can see he knows his work, that he's a diplomat, born, trained, that he's——"

The admiral interrupted with a growl.

"You don't have to tell ME about Henry," he protested. "I've known Henry twenty-five years. If Henry got his deserts," he exclaimed hotly, "he wouldn't be a consul on this coral reef; he'd be a minister in Europe. Look at me! We're the same age. We started together. When Lincoln sent him to Morocco as consul, he signed my commission as a midshipman. Now I'm an admiral. Henry has twice my brains and he's been a consul-general, and he's *here*, back at the foot of the ladder!"

"Why?" demanded the girl.

THE CONSUL

"Because the navy is a service and the consular service isn't a service. Men like Senator Hanley use it to pay their debts. While Henry's been serving his country abroad, he's lost his friends, lost his 'pull.' Those politicians up at Washington have no use for him. They don't consider that a consul like Henry can make a million dollars for his countrymen. He can keep them from shipping goods where there's no market, show them where there is a market." The admiral snorted contemptuously. "You don't have to tell ME the value of a good consul. But those politicians don't consider that. They only see that he has a job worth a few hundred dollars, and they want it, and if he hasn't other politicians to protect him, they'll take it."

The girl raised her head.

"Why don't you speak to the senator?" she asked. "Tell him you've known him for years, that——"

"Glad to do it!" exclaimed the admiral heartily. "It won't be the first time. But Henry mustn't know. He's too confoundedly touchy. He hates the *idea* of influence, hates men like Hanley, who abuse it. If he thought anything was given to him except on his merits, he wouldn't take it."

"Then we won't tell him," said the girl. For a moment she hesitated.

THE CONSUL

"If I spoke to Mr. Hanley," she asked, "told him what I learned to-night of Mr. Marshall, would it have any effect?"

"Don't know how it will affect Hanley," said the sailor, "but if you asked *me* to make anybody a consul-general, I'd make him an ambassador."

Later in the evening Hanley and Livingstone were seated alone on deck. The visit to Las Bocas had not proved amusing, but, much to Livingstone's relief, his honored guest was now in good-humor. He took his cigar from his lips, only to sip at a long cool drink. He was in a mood flatteringly confidential and communicative.

"People have the strangest idea of what I can do for them," he laughed. It was his pose to pretend he was without authority. "They believe I've only to wave a wand, and get them anything they want. I thought I'd be safe from them on board a yacht."

Livingstone, in ignorance of what was coming, squirmed apprehensively.

"But it seems," the senator went on, "I'm at the mercy of a conspiracy. The women folk want me to do something for this fellow Marshall. If they had their way, they'd send him to the Court of St. James. And old Hardy, too, tackled me about him. So did Miss Cairns.

THE CONSUL

And then Marshall himself got me behind the wheel-house, and I thought he was going to tell me how good he was, too! But he didn't."

As though the joke were on himself, the senator laughed appreciatively.

"Told me, instead, that Hardy ought to be a vice-admiral."

Livingstone, also, laughed, with the satisfied air of one who cannot be tricked.

"They fixed it up between them," he explained, "each was to put in a good word for the other." He nodded eagerly. "That's what *I* think."

There were moments during the cruise when Senator Hanley would have found relief in dropping his host overboard. With mock deference, the older man inclined his head.

"That's what *you* think, is it?" he asked. "Livingstone," he added, "you certainly are a great judge of men!"

The next morning, old man Marshall woke with a lightness at his heart that had been long absent. For a moment, conscious only that he was happy, he lay between sleep and waking, frowning up at his canopy of mosquito net, trying to realize what change had come to him. Then he remembered. His old friend had returned. New friends had come into his life and welcomed him kindly. He was no longer

THE CONSUL

lonely. As eager as a boy, he ran to the window. He had not been dreaming. In the harbor lay the pretty yacht, the stately, white-hulled warship. The flag that drooped from the stern of each caused his throat to tighten, brought warm tears to his eyes, fresh resolve to his discouraged, troubled spirit. When he knelt beside his bed, his heart poured out his thanks in gratitude and gladness.

While he was dressing, a blue-jacket brought a note from the admiral. It invited him to tea on board the war-ship, with the guests of the *Serapis*. His old friend added that he was coming to lunch with his consul, and wanted time reserved for a long talk. The consul agreed gladly. He was in holiday humor. The day promised to repeat the good moments of the night previous.

At nine o'clock, through the open door of the consulate, Marshall saw Aiken, the wireless operator, signalling from the wharf excitedly to the yacht, and a boat leave the ship and return. Almost immediately the launch, carrying several passengers, again made the trip shoreward.

Half an hour later, Senator Hanley, Miss Cairns, and Livingstone came up the waterfront, and entering the consulate, seated themselves around Marshall's desk. Livingstone was sunk in melancholy. The senator, on the con-

THE CONSUL

trary, was smiling broadly. His manner was one of distinct relief. He greeted the consul with hearty good-humor.

"I'm ordered home!" he announced gleefully. Then, remembering the presence of Livingstone, he hastened to add: "I needn't say how sorry I am to give up my yachting trip, but orders are orders. The President," he explained to Marshall, "cables me this morning to come back and take my coat off."

The prospect, as a change from playing bridge on a pleasure boat, seemed far from depressing him.

"Those filibusters in the Senate," he continued genially, "are making trouble again. They think they've got me out of the way for another month, but they'll find they're wrong. When that bill comes up, they'll find me at the old stand and ready for business!" Marshall did not attempt to conceal his personal disappointment.

"I am so sorry you are leaving," he said; "selfishly sorry, I mean. I'd hoped you all would be here for several days."

He looked inquiringly toward Livingstone.

"I understood the *Serapis* was disabled," he explained.

"She is," answered Hanley. "So's the *Raleigh*. At a pinch, the admiral might have

THE CONSUL

stretched the regulations and carried me to Jamaica, but the *Raleigh's* engines are knocked about too. I've *got* to reach Kingston Thursday. The German boat leaves there Thursday for New York. At first it looked as though I couldn't do it, but we find that the Royal Mail is due to-day, and she can get to Kingston Wednesday night. It's a great piece of luck. I wouldn't bother you with my troubles," the senator explained pleasantly, "but the agent of the Royal Mail here won't sell me a ticket until you've put your seal to this."

He extended a piece of printed paper.

As Hanley had been talking, the face of the consul had grown grave. He accepted the paper, but did not look at it. Instead, he regarded the senator with troubled eyes. When he spoke, his tone was one of genuine concern.

"It is most unfortunate," he said. "But I am afraid the *Royal Mail* will not take you on board. Because of Las Bocas," he explained. "If we had only known!" he added remorsefully. "It is *most* unfortunate."

"Because of Las Bocas?" echoed Hanley. "You don't mean they'll refuse to take me to Jamaica because I spent half an hour at the end of a wharf listening to a squeaky gramophone?"

"The trouble," explained Marshall, "is this:

if they carried you, all the other passengers would be held in quarantine for ten days, and there are fines to pay, and there would be difficulties over the mails. But," he added hopefully, "maybe the regulations have been altered. I will see her captain, and tell him——"

"See her captain!" objected Hanley. "Why see the captain? He doesn't know I've been to that place. Why tell *him?* All I need is a clean bill of health from you. That's all HE wants. You have only to sign that paper."

Marshall regarded the senator with surprise.

"But I can't," he said.

"You can't? Why not?"

"Because it certifies to the fact that you have not visited Las Bocas. Unfortunately, you have visited Las Bocas."

The senator had been walking up and down the room. Now he seated himself, and stared at Marshall curiously.

"It's like this, Mr. Marshall," he began quietly. "The President desires my presence in Washington, thinks I can be of some use to him there in helping carry out certain party measures—measures to which he pledged himself before his election. Down here, a British steamship line has laid down local rules which, in my case anyway, are ridiculous. The question is, are you going to be bound by the red

THE CONSUL

tape of a ha'penny British colony, or by your oath to the President of the United States?"

The sophistry amused Marshall. He smiled good-naturedly and shook his head.

"I'm afraid, Senator," he said, "that way of putting it is hardly fair. Unfortunately, the question is one of fact. I will explain to the captain——"

"You will explain nothing to the captain!" interrupted Hanley. "This is a matter which concerns no one but our two selves. I am not asking favors of steamboat captains. I am asking an American consul to assist an American citizen in trouble, and," he added, with heavy sarcasm, "incidentally, to carry out the wishes of his President."

Marshall regarded the senator with an expression of both surprise and disbelief.

"Are you asking me to put my name to what is not so?" he said. "Are you serious?"

"That paper, Mr. Marshall," returned Hanley steadily, "is a mere form, a piece of red tape. There's no more danger of my carrying the plague to Jamaica than of my carrying a dynamite bomb. You *know* that."

"I *do* know that," assented Marshall heartily. "I appreciate your position, and I regret it exceedingly. You are the innocent victim of a regulation which is a wise regulation, but which

THE CONSUL

is most unfair to you. My own position," he added, "is not important, but you can believe me, it is not easy. It is certainly no pleasure for me to be unable to help you."

Hanley was leaning forward, his hands on his knees, his eyes watching Marshall closely.

"Then you refuse?" he said. "Why?"

Marshall regarded the senator steadily. His manner was untroubled. The look he turned upon Hanley was one of grave disapproval.

"You know why," he answered quietly. "It is impossible."

In sudden anger Hanley rose. Marshall, who had been seated behind his desk, also rose. For a moment, in silence, the two men confronted each other. Then Hanley spoke; his tone was harsh and threatening.

"Then I am to understand," he exclaimed, "that you refuse to carry out the wishes of a United States Senator and of the President of the United States?"

In front of Marshall, on his desk, was the little iron stamp of the consulate. Protectingly, almost caressingly, he laid his hand upon it.

"I refuse," he corrected, "to place the seal of this consulate on a lie."

There was a moment's pause. Miss Cairns, unwilling to remain, and unable to withdraw,

"Then I am to understand," he exclaimed, "that you refuse to carry out the wishes of a United States Senator and of the President of the United States?"

THE CONSUL

clasped her hands unhappily and stared at the floor. Livingstone exclaimed in indignant protest. Hanley moved a step nearer and, to emphasize what he said, tapped his knuckles on the desk. With the air of one confident of his advantage, he spoke slowly and softly.

"Do you appreciate," he asked, "that, while you may be of some importance down here in this fever swamp, in Washington I am supposed to carry some weight? Do you appreciate that I am a senator from a State that numbers four millions of people, and that you are preventing me from serving those people?"

Marshall inclined his head gravely and politely.

"And I want you to appreciate," he said, "that while I have no weight at Washington, in this fever swamp I have the honor to represent eighty millions of people, and as long as that consular sign is over my door I don't intend to prostitute it for *you*, or the President of the United States, or any one of those eighty millions."

Of the two men, the first to lower his eyes was Hanley. He laughed shortly, and walked to the door. There he turned, and indifferently, as though the incident no longer interested him, drew out his watch.

"Mr. Marshall," he said, "if the cable is

THE CONSUL

working, I'll take your tin sign away from you by sunset."

For one of Marshall's traditions, to such a speech there was no answer save silence. He bowed, and, apparently serene and undismayed, resumed his seat. From the contest, judging from the manner of each, it was Marshall, not Hanley, who had emerged victorious.

But Miss Cairns was not deceived. Under the unexpected blow, Marshall had turned older. His clear blue eyes had grown less alert, his broad shoulders seemed to stoop. In sympathy, her own eyes filled with sudden tears.

"What will you do?" she whispered.

"I don't know what I shall do," said Marshall simply. "I should have liked to have resigned. It's a prettier finish. After forty years—to be dismissed by cable is—it's a poor way of ending it."

Miss Cairns rose and walked to the door. There she turned and looked back.

"I am sorry," she said. And both understood that in saying no more than that she had best shown her sympathy.

An hour later the sympathy of Admiral Hardy was expressed more directly.

"If he comes on board my ship," roared that gentleman, "I'll push him down an ammunition hoist and break his damned neck!"

THE CONSUL

Marshall laughed delightedly. The loyalty of his old friend was never so welcome.

"You'll treat him with every courtesy," he said. "The only satisfaction he gets out of this is to see that he has hurt me. We will not give him that satisfaction."

But Marshall found that to conceal his wound was more difficult than he had anticipated. When, at tea time, on the deck of the war-ship, he again met Senator Hanley and the guests of the *Serapis*, he could not forget that his career had come to an end. There was much to remind him that this was so. He was made aware of it by the sad, sympathetic glances of the women; by their tactful courtesies; by the fact that Livingstone, anxious to propitiate Hanley, treated him rudely; by the sight of the young officers, each just starting upon a career of honor, and possible glory, as his career ended in humiliation; and by the big war-ship herself, that recalled certain crises when he had only to press a button and war-ships had come at his bidding.

At five o'clock there was an awkward moment. The Royal Mail boat, having taken on her cargo, passed out of the harbor on her way to Jamaica, and dipped her colors. Senator Hanley, abandoned to his fate, observed her departure in silence.

THE CONSUL

Livingstone, hovering at his side, asked sympathetically:

"Have they answered your cable, sir?"

"They have," said Hanley gruffly.

"Was it—was it satisfactory?" pursued the diplomat.

"It *was*," said the senator, with emphasis.

Far from discouraged, Livingstone continued his inquiries.

"And when," he asked eagerly, "are you going to tell him?"

"Now!" said the senator.

The guests were leaving the ship. When all were seated in the admiral's steam launch, the admiral descended the accommodation ladder and himself picked up the tiller ropes.

"Mr. Marshall," he called, "when I bring the launch broadside to the ship and stop her, you will stand ready to receive the consul's salute."

Involuntarily, Marshall uttered an exclamation of protest. He had forgotten that on leaving the war-ship, as consul, he was entitled to seven guns. Had he remembered, he would have insisted that the ceremony be omitted. He knew that the admiral wished to show his loyalty, knew that his old friend was now paying him this honor only as a rebuke to Hanley. But the ceremony was no longer an honor.

THE CONSUL

Hanley had made of it a mockery. It served only to emphasize what had been taken from him. But, without a scene, it now was too late to avoid it. The first of the seven guns had roared from the bow, and, as often he had stood before, as never he would so stand again, Marshall took his place at the gangway of the launch. His eyes were fixed on the flag, his gray head was uncovered, his hat was pressed above his heart.

For the first time since Hanley had left the consulate, he fell into sudden terror lest he might give way to his emotions. Indignant at the thought, he held himself erect. His face was set like a mask, his eyes were untroubled. He was determined they should not see that he was suffering.

Another gun spat out a burst of white smoke, a stab of flame. There was an echoing roar. Another and another followed. Marshall counted seven, and then, with a bow to the admiral, backed from the gangway.

And then another gun shattered the hot, heavy silence. Marshall, confused, embarrassed, assuming he had counted wrong, hastily returned to his place. But again before he could leave it, in savage haste a ninth gun roared out its greeting. He could not still be mistaken. He turned appealingly to his friend.

THE CONSUL

The eyes of the admiral were fixed upon the war-ship. Again a gun shattered the silence. Was it a jest? Were they laughing at him? Marshall flushed miserably. He gave a swift glance toward the others. They were smiling. Then it *was* a jest. Behind his back, something of which they all were cognizant was going forward. The face of Livingstone alone betrayed a like bewilderment to his own. But the others, who knew, were mocking him.

For the thirteenth time a gun shook the brooding swamp land of Porto Banos. And then, and not until then, did the flag crawl slowly from the mast-head. Mary Cairns broke the tenseness by bursting into tears. But Marshall saw that every one else, save she and Livingstone, were still smiling. Even the bluejackets in charge of the launch were grinning at him. He was beset by smiling faces. And then from the war-ship, unchecked, came, against all regulations, three long, splendid cheers.

Marshall felt his lips quivering, the warm tears forcing their way to his eyes. He turned beseechingly to his friend. His voice trembled.

"Charles," he begged, "are they laughing at me?"

Eagerly, before the other would answer, Senator Hanley tossed his cigar into the water

THE CONSUL

and, scrambling forward, seized Marshall by the hand.

"Mr. Marshall," he cried, "our President has great faith in Abraham Lincoln's judgment of men. And this salute means that this morning he appointed you our new minister to The Hague. I'm one of those politicians who keeps his word. I *told* you I'd take your tin sign away from you by sunset. I've done it!"

THE NATURE FAKER

Richard Herrick was a young man with a gentle disposition, much money, and no sense of humor. His object in life was to marry Miss Catherweight. For three years she had tried to persuade him this could not be, and finally, in order to convince him, married some one else. When the woman he loves marries another man, the rejected one is popularly supposed to take to drink or to foreign travel. Statistics show that, instead, he instantly falls in love with the best friend of the girl who refused him. But, as Herrick truly loved Miss Catherweight, he could not worship any other woman, and so he became a lover of nature. Nature, he assured his men friends, does not disappoint you. The more thought, care, affection you give to nature, the more she gives you in return, and while, so he admitted, in wooing nature there are no great moments, there are no heartaches. Jackson, one of the men friends, and of a frivolous disposition, said that he also could admire a landscape, but he would rather look at the beautiful eyes of a girl he knew than at

THE NATURE FAKER

the Lakes of Killarney, with a full moon, a setting sun, and the aurora borealis for a background. Herrick suggested that, while the beautiful eyes might seek those of another man, the Lakes of Killarney would always remain where you could find them.

Herrick pursued his new love in Connecticut on an abandoned farm which he converted into a "model" one. On it he established model dairies and model incubators. He laid out old-fashioned gardens, sunken gardens, Italian gardens, landscape gardens, and a game preserve. The game preserve was his own especial care and pleasure. It consisted of two hundred acres of dense forest and hills and ridges of rock. It was filled with mysterious caves, deep chasms, tiny gurgling streams, nestling springs, and wild laurel. It was barricaded with fallen tree-trunks and moss-covered rocks that had never felt the foot of man since that foot had worn a moccasin. Around the preserve was a high fence stout enough to keep poachers on the outside and to persuade the wild animals that inhabited it to linger on the inside. These wild animals were squirrels, rabbits, and raccoons. Every day, in sunshine or in rain, entering through a private gate, Herrick would explore this holy of holies. For such vermin as would destroy the gentler animals he carried a

THE NATURE FAKER

gun. But it was turned only on those that preyed upon his favorites. For hours he would climb through this wilderness, or, seated on a rock, watch a bluebird building her nest or a squirrel laying in rations against the coming of the snow. In time he grew to think he knew and understood the inhabitants of this wild place of which he was the overlord. He looked upon them not as his tenants but as his guests. And when they fled from him in terror to caves and hollow tree-trunks, he wished he might call them back and explain he was their friend, that it was due to him they lived in peace. He was glad they were happy. He was glad it was through him that, undisturbed, they could live the simple life.

His fall came through ambition. Herrick himself attributed it to his too great devotion to nature and nature's children. Jackson, he of the frivolous mind, attributed it to the fact that any man is sure to come to grief who turns from the worship of God's noblest handiwork, by which Jackson meant woman, to worship chipmunks and Plymouth Rock hens.

One night Jackson lured Herrick into New York to a dinner and a music hall. He invited also one Kelly, a mutual friend of a cynical and combative disposition. Jackson liked to hear him and Herrick abuse each other, and always

THE NATURE FAKER

introduced subjects he knew would cause each to lose his temper.

But, on this night, Herrick needed no goading. He was in an ungrateful mood. Accustomed to food fresh from the soil and the farmyard, he sneered at hothouse asparagus, hothouse grapes, and cold-storage quail. At the music hall he was even more difficult. In front of him sat a stout lady who when she shook with laughter shed patchouli and a man who smoked American cigarettes. At these and the steam heat, the nostrils of Herrick, trained to the odor of balsam and the smoke of open wood fires, took offense. He refused to be amused. The monologue artist, in whom Jackson found delight, caused Herrick only to groan; the knockabout comedians he hoped would break their collarbones; the lady who danced Salome, and who fascinated Kelly, Herrick prayed would catch pneumonia and die of it. And when the drop rose upon the Countess Zichy's bears, his dissatisfaction reached a climax.

There were three bears—a large papa bear, a mamma bear, and the baby bear. On the programme they were described as Bruno, Clara, and Ikey. They were of a dusty brown, with long, curling noses tipped with white, and fat, tan-colored bellies. When father Bruno, on his hind legs and bare feet, waddled down the

THE NATURE FAKER

stage, he resembled a Hebrew gentleman in a brown bathing suit who had lost his waist-line. As he tripped doubtfully forward, with mincing steps, he continually and mournfully wagged his head. He seemed to be saying: "This water is much too cold for *me*." The mamma bear was dressed in a poke bonnet and white apron, and resembled the wolf who frightened Little Red Riding-Hood, and Ikey, the baby bear, wore rakishly over one eye the pointed cap of a clown. To those who knew their vaudeville, this was indisputable evidence that Ikey would furnish the comic relief. Nor did Ikey disappoint them. He was a wayward son. When his parents were laboriously engaged in a boxing-match, or dancing to the "Merry Widow Waltz," or balancing on step-ladders, Ikey, on all fours, would scamper to the foot-lights and, leaning over, make a swift grab at the head of the first trombone. And when the Countess Zichy, apprised by the shouts of the audience of Ikey's misconduct, waved a toy whip, Ikey would gallop back to his pedestal and howl at her. To every one, except Herrick and the first trombone, this playfulness on the part of Ikey furnished great delight.

The performances of the bears ended with Bruno and Clara dancing heavily to the refrain of the "Merry Widow Waltz," while Ikey pre-

THE NATURE FAKER

tended to conduct the music of the orchestra. On the final call, Madame Zichy threw to each of the animals a beer bottle filled with milk; and the gusto with which the savage-looking beasts uncorked the bottles and drank from them greatly amused the audience. Ikey, standing on his hind legs, his head thrown back, with both paws clasping the base of the bottle, shoved the neck far down his throat, and then, hurling it from him, and cocking his clown's hat over his eyes, gave a masterful imitation of a very intoxicated bear.

"That," exclaimed Herrick hotly, "is a degrading spectacle. It degrades the bear and degrades me and you."

"No, it bores me," said Kelly.

"If you understood nature," retorted Herrick, "and nature's children, it would infuriate you."

"I don't go to a music hall to get infuriated," said Kelly.

"Trained dogs I don't mind," exclaimed Herrick. "Dogs are not wild animals. The things they're trained to do are of USE. They can guard the house, or herd sheep. But a bear is a wild beast. Always will be a wild beast. You can't train him to be of use. It's degrading to make him ride a bicycle. I hate it! If I'd known there were to be performing bears tonight, I wouldn't have come!"

THE NATURE FAKER

"And if I'd known *you* were to be here to-night, *I* wouldn't have come!" said Kelly. "Where do we go to next?"

They went next to a restaurant in a gayly decorated cellar. Into this young men like themselves and beautiful ladies were so anxious to hurl themselves that to restrain them a rope was swung across the entrance and page boys stood on guard. When a young man became too anxious to spend his money, the page boys pushed in his shirt front. After they had fought their way to a table, Herrick ungraciously remarked he would prefer to sup in a subway station. The people, he pointed out, would be more human, the decorations were much of the same Turkish-bath school of art, and the air was no worse.

"Cheer up, Clarence!" begged Jackson, "you'll soon be dead. To-morrow you'll be back among your tree-toads and sunsets. And, let us hope," he sighed, "no one will try to stop you!"

"What worries me is this," explained Herrick. "I can't help thinking that, if one night of this artificial life is so hard upon me, what must it be to those bears!"

Kelly exclaimed, with exasperation: "Confound the bears!" he cried. "If you must spoil my supper weeping over animals, weep over cart-horses. *They* work. Those bears are loaf-

THE NATURE FAKER

ers. They're as well fed as pet canaries. They're aristocrats."

"But it's not a free life!" protested Herrick. "It's not the life they love."

"It's a darned sight better," declared Kelly, "than sleeping in a damp wood, eating raw blackberries——"

"The more you say," retorted Herrick, "the more you show you know nothing whatsoever of nature's children and their habits."

"And all you know of them," returned Kelly, "is that a cat has nine lives, and a barking dog won't bite. You're a nature faker."

Herrick refused to be diverted.

"It hurt me," he said. "They were so big, and good-natured, and helpless. I'll bet that woman beats them! I kept thinking of them as they were in the woods, tramping over the clean pine needles, eating nuts, and—and honey, and——"

"Buns!" suggested Jackson.

"I can't forget them," said Herrick. "It's going to haunt me, to-morrow, when I'm back in the woods; I'll think of those poor beasts capering in a hot theatre, when they ought to be out in the open as God meant they——"

"Well, then," protested Kelly, "take 'em to the open. And turn 'em loose! And I hope they bite you!"

At this Herrick frowned so deeply that Kelly

THE NATURE FAKER

feared he had gone too far. Inwardly, he reproved himself for not remembering that his friend lacked a sense of humor. But Herrick undeceived him.

"You are right!" he exclaimed. "To-morrow I will buy those bears, take them to the farm, and turn them loose!"

No objections his friend could offer could divert him from his purpose. When they urged that to spend so much money in such a manner was criminally wasteful, he pointed out that he was sufficiently rich to indulge any extravagant fancy, whether in polo ponies or bears; when they warned him that if he did not look out the bears would catch him alone in the woods, and eat him, he retorted that the bears were now educated to a different diet; when they said he should consider the peace of mind of his neighbors, he assured them the fence around his game preserve would restrain an elephant.

"Besides," protested Kelly, "what you propose to do is not only impracticable, but it's cruelty to animals. A domesticated animal can't return to a state of nature, and live."

"Can't it?" jeered Herrick. "Did you ever read 'The Call of the Wild'?"

"Did you ever read," retorted Kelly, "what happened at the siege of Ladysmith when the oats ran low and they drove the artillery horses

THE NATURE FAKER

out to grass? They starved, that's all. And if you don't feed your bears on milk out of a bottle they'll starve too."

"That's what will happen," cried Jackson; "those bears have forgotten what a pine forest smells like. Maybe it's a pity, but it's the fact. I'll bet if you could ask 'em whether they'd rather sleep in a cave on your farm or be headliners in vaudeville, they'd tell you they were 'devoted to their art.'"

"Why!" exclaimed Kelly, "they're so far from nature that if they didn't have that colored boy to comb and brush them twice a day they'd be ashamed to look each other in the eyes."

"And another thing," continued Jackson, "trained animals love to 'show off.' They're like children. Those bears *enjoy* doing those tricks. They *enjoy* the applause. They enjoy dancing to the 'Merry Widow Waltz.' And if you lock them up in your jungle, they'll get so homesick that they'll give a performance twice a day to the squirrels and woodpeckers."

"It's just as hard to unlearn a thing as to learn it," said Kelly sententiously. "You can't make a man who has learned to wear shoes enjoy going around in his bare feet."

"Rot!" cried Herrick. "Look at me. Didn't I love New York? I loved it so I never went to bed for fear I'd miss something. But

THE NATURE FAKER

when I went 'Back to the Land,' did it take me long to fall in love with the forests and the green fields? It took me a week. I go to bed now the same day I get up, and I've passed on my high hat and frock coat to a scarecrow. And I'll bet you when those bears once scent the wild woods they'll stampede for them like Croker going to a third alarm."

"And I repeat," cried Kelly, "you are a nature faker. And I'll leave it to the bears to prove it."

"We have done our best," sighed Jackson. "We have tried to save him money and trouble. And now all he can do for us in return is to give us seats for the opening performance."

What the bears cost Herrick he never told. But it was a very large sum. As the Countess Zichy pointed out, bears as bears, in a state of nature, are cheap. If it were just a bear he wanted, he himself could go to Pike County, Pennsylvania, and trap one. What he was paying for, she explained, was the time she had spent in educating the Bruno family, and added to that the time during which she must now remain idle while she educated another family.

Herrick knew for what he was paying. It was the pleasure of rescuing unwilling slaves from bondage. As to their expensive education, if they returned to a state of ignorance as

THE NATURE FAKER

rapidly as did most college graduates he knew, he would be satisfied. Two days later, when her engagement at the music hall closed, Madame Zichy reluctantly turned over her pets to their new manager. With Ikey she was especially loath to part.

"I'll never get one like him," she wailed. "Ikey is the funniest four-legged clown in America. He's a natural-born comedian. Folks think I learn him those tricks, but it's all his own stuff. Only last week we was playing Paoli's in Bridgeport, and when I was putting Bruno through the hoops, Ikey runs to the stage-box and grabs a pound of caramels out of a girl's lap—and swallows the box. And in St. Paul, if the trombone hadn't worn a wig, Ikey would have scalped him. Say, it was a scream! When the audience see the trombone snatched bald-headed, and him trying to get back his wig, and Ikey chewing it, they went crazy. You can't learn a bear tricks like that. It's just genius. Some folks think I taught him to act like he was intoxicated, but he picked that up, too, all by himself, through watching my husband. And Ikey's very fond of beer on his own account. If I don't stop 'em the stage hands would be always slipping him drinks. I hope you won't give him none."

"I will not!" said Herrick.

THE NATURE FAKER

The bears, Ikey in one cage and Bruno and Clara in another, travelled by express to the station nearest the Herrick estate. There they were transferred to a farm wagon, and grumbling and growling, and with Ikey howling like an unspanked child, they were conveyed to the game preserve. At the only gate that entered it, Kelly and Jackson and a specially invited house party of youths and maidens were gathered to receive them. At a greater distance stood all of the servants and farm hands, and as the wagon backed against the gate, with the door of Ikey's cage opening against it, the entire audience, with one accord, moved solidly to the rear. Herrick, with a pleased but somewhat nervous smile, mounted the wagon. But before he could unlock the cage Kelly demanded to be heard. He insisted that, following the custom of all great artists, the bears should give a "positively farewell performance."

He begged that Bruno and Clara might be permitted to dance together. He pointed out that this would be the last time they could listen to the strains of the "Merry Widow Waltz." He called upon everybody present to whistle it.

The suggestion of an open-air performance was received coldly. At the moment no one seemed able to pucker his lips into a whistle, and some even explained that with that famous waltz they were unfamiliar.

One girl attained an instant popularity by pointing out that the bears could waltz just as well on one side of the fence as the other. Kelly, cheated of his free performance, then begged that before Herrick condemned the bears to starve on acorns, he should give them a farewell drink, and Herrick, who was slightly rattled, replied excitedly that he had not ransomed the animals only to degrade them. The argument was interrupted by the French chef falling out of a tree. He had climbed it, he explained, in order to obtain a better view.

When, in turn, it was explained to him that a bear also could climb a tree, he remembered he had left his oven door open. His departure reminded other servants of duties they had neglected, and one of the guests, also, on remembering he had put in a long-distance call, hastened to the house. Jackson suggested that perhaps they had better all return with him, as the presence of so many people might frighten the bears. At the moment he spoke, Ikey emitted a hideous howl, whether of joy or rage no one knew, and few remained to find out. It was not until Herrick had investigated and reported that Ikey was still behind the bars that the house party cautiously returned. The house party then filed a vigorous protest. Its members, with Jackson as spokesman, complained that Herrick was relying entirely too much on his supposition that the bears would be anxious to enter the forest. Jackson pointed out that, should they not care to do so, there was nothing to prevent them from doubling back under the wagon; in which case the house party and all of the United States lay before them. It was not until a lawn-tennis net and much chicken wire was stretched in intricate thicknesses across the lower half of the gate that Herrick was allowed to proceed. Unassisted, he slid back the cage door, and without a moment's hesitation Ikey leaped from the wagon through the gate and into the preserve. For an instant, dazed by the sudden sunlight, he remained motionless, and then, after sniffing delightedly at the air, stuck his nose deep into the autumn leaves. Turning on his back, he luxuriously and joyfully kicked his legs, and rolled from side to side.

Herrick gave a shout of joy and triumph. "What did I tell you!" he called. "See how he loves it! See how happy he is."

"Not at all," protested Kelly. "He thought you gave him the sign to 'roll over.' Tell him to 'play dead,' and he'll do that."

THE NATURE FAKER

"Tell ALL the bears to 'play dead,'" begged Jackson, "until I'm back in the billiard-room."

Flushed with happiness, Herrick tossed Ikey's cage out of the wagon, and opened the door of the one that held Bruno and Clara. On their part, there was a moment of doubt. As though suspecting a trap, they moved to the edge of the cage, and gazed critically at the screen of trees and tangled vines that rose before them.

"They think it's a new backdrop," explained Kelly.

But the delight with which Ikey was enjoying his bath in the autumn leaves was not lost upon his parents. Slowly and clumsily they dropped to the ground. As though they expected to be recalled, each turned to look at the group of people who had now run to peer through the wire meshes of the fence. But, as no one spoke and no one signalled, the three bears, in single file, started toward the edge of the forest. They had of cleared space to cover only a little distance, and at each step, as though fearful they would be stopped and punished, one or the other turned his head. But no one halted them. With quickening footsteps the bears, now almost at a gallop, plunged forward. The next instant they were lost to sight, and only the crackling of the underbrush told that they had come into their own.

THE NATURE FAKER

Herrick dropped to the ground and locked himself inside the preserve.

"I'm going after them," he called, "to see what they'll do."

There was a frantic chorus of cries and entreaties.

"Don't be an ass!" begged Jackson. "They'll eat you."

Herrick waved his hand reassuringly.

"They won't even see me," he explained. "I can find my way about this place better than they can. And I'll keep to windward of them, and watch them. Go to the house," he commanded. "I'll be with you in an hour, and report."

It was with real relief that, on assembling for dinner, the house party found Herrick, in high spirits, with the usual number of limbs, and awaiting them. The experiment had proved a great success. He told how, unheeded by the bears, he had, without difficulty, followed in their tracks. For an hour he had watched them. No happy school-children, let loose at recess, could have embraced their freedom with more obvious delight. They drank from the running streams, for honey they explored the hollow tree-trunks, they sharpened their claws on moss-grown rocks, and among the fallen oak leaves scratched violently for acorns.

THE NATURE FAKER

So satisfied was Herrick with what he had seen, with the success of his experiment, and so genuine and unselfish was he in the thought of the happiness he had brought to the beasts of the forests, that for him no dinner ever passed more pleasantly. Miss Waring, who sat next to her host, thought she had seldom met a man with so kind and simple a nature. She rather resented the fact, and she was inwardly indignant that so much right feeling and affection could be wasted on farmyard fowls, and four-footed animals. She felt sure that some nice girl, seated at the other end of the table, smiling through the light of the wax candles upon Herrick, would soon make him forget his love of "Nature and Nature's children." She even saw herself there, and this may have made her exhibit more interest in Herrick's experiment than she really felt. In any event, Herrick found her most sympathetic, and when dinner was over carried her off to a corner of the terrace. It was a warm night in early October, and the great woods of the game preserve that stretched below them were lit with a full moon. On his way to the lake for a moonlight row with one of the house party who belonged to that sex that does not row, but looks well in the moonlight, Kelly halted, and jeered mockingly.

"How can you sit there," he demanded,

"while those poor beasts are freezing in a cave, with not even a silk coverlet or a pillow-sham. You and your valet ought to be down there now carrying them pajamas."

"Kelly," declared Herrick, unruffled in his moment of triumph, "I hate to say, 'I told you so,' but you force me. Go away," he commanded. "You have neither imagination nor soul."

"And that's true," he assured Miss Waring, as Kelly and his companion left them. "Now, I see nothing in what I accomplished that is ridiculous. Had you watched those bears as I did, you would have felt that sympathy that exists between all who love the out-of-door life. A dog loves to see his master pick up his stick and his hat to take him for a walk, and the man enjoys seeing the dog leaping and quartering the fields before him. They are both the happier. At least I am happier to-night, knowing those bears are at peace and at home, than I would be if I thought of them being whipped through their tricks in a dirty theatre." Herrick pointed to the great forest trees of the preserve, their tops showing dimly in the mist of moonlight. "Somewhere, down in that valley," he murmured, "are three happy animals. They are no longer slaves and puppets—they are their own masters. For the rest of their lives

THE NATURE FAKER

they can sleep on pine needles and dine on nuts and honey. No one shall molest them, no one shall force them through degrading tricks. Hereafter they can choose their life, and their own home among the rocks, and the——"

Herrick's words were frozen on his tongue.

From the other end of the terrace came a scream so fierce, so long, so full of human suffering, that at the sound the blood of all that heard it turned to water. It was so appalling that for an instant no one moved, and then from every part of the house, along the garden walks, from the servants' quarters, came the sound of pounding feet. Herrick, with Miss Waring clutching at his sleeve, raced toward the other end of the terrace. They had not far to go. Directly in front of them they saw what had dragged from the very soul of the woman the scream of terror.

The drawing-room opened upon the terrace, and, seated at the piano, Jackson had been playing for those in the room to dance. The windows to the terrace were open. The terrace itself was flooded with moonlight. Seeking the fresh air, one of the dancers stepped from the drawing-room to the flags outside. She had then raised the cry of terror and fallen in a faint. What she had seen, Herrick a moment later also saw. On the terrace in the moon-

THE NATURE FAKER

light, Bruno and Clara, on their hind legs, were solemnly waltzing. Neither the scream nor the cessation of the music disturbed them. Contentedly, proudly, they continued to revolve in hops and leaps. From their happy expression, it was evident they not only were enjoying themselves, but that they felt they were greatly affording immeasurable delight to others.

Sick at heart, furious, bitterly hurt, with roars of mocking laughter in his ears, Herrick ran toward the stables for help. At the farther end of the terrace the butler had placed a tray of liqueurs, whiskeys, and soda bottles. His back had been turned for only a few moments, but the time had sufficed.

Lolling with his legs out, stretched in a wicker chair, Herrick beheld the form of Ikey. Between his uplifted paws he held aloof the base of a decanter; between his teeth, and well jammed down his throat, was the long neck of the bottle. From it issued the sound of gentle gurgling. Herrick seized the decanter and hurled it crashing upon the terrace. With difficulty Ikey rose. Swaying and shaking his head reproachfully, he gave Herrick a perfectly accurate imitation of an intoxicated bear.

BILLY AND THE BIG STICK

Had the Wilmot Electric Light people remained content only to make light, had they not, as a by-product, attempted to make money, they need not have left Hayti.

When they flooded with radiance the unpaved streets of Port-au-Prince no one, except the police, who complained that the lights kept them awake, made objection; but when for this illumination the Wilmot Company demanded payment, every one up to President Hamilcar Poussevain was surprised and grieved. So grieved was President Ham, as he was lovingly designated, that he withdrew the Wilmot concession, surrounded the power-house with his barefooted army, and in a proclamation announced that for the future the furnishing of electric light would be a monopoly of the government.

In Hayti, as soon as it begins to make money, any industry, native or foreign, becomes a monopoly of the government. The thing works automatically. It is what in Hayti is understood as *haute finance*. The Wilmot people should have known that. Because they did not

BILLY AND THE BIG STICK

know that, they stood to lose what they had sunk in the electric-light plant, and after their departure to New York, which departure was accelerated as far as the wharf by seven generals and twelve privates, they proceeded to lose more money on lobbyists and lawyers who claimed to understand international law; even the law of Hayti. And lawyers who understand that are high-priced.

The only employee of the Wilmot force who was not escorted to the wharf under guard was Billy Barlow. He escaped the honor because he was superintendent of the power-house, and President Ham believed that without him the lightning would not strike. Accordingly by an executive order Billy became an employee of the government. With this arrangement the Wilmot people were much pleased. For they trusted Billy, and they knew while in the courts they were fighting to regain their property, he would see no harm came to it.

Billy's title was Directeur Général et Inspecteur Municipal de Luminaire Electrique, which is some title, and his salary was fifty dollars a week. In spite of Billy's color President Ham always treated his only white official with courtesy and gave him his full title. About giving him his full salary he was less particular. This neglect greatly annoyed Billy. He came

BILLY AND THE BIG STICK

of sturdy New England stock and possessed that New England conscience which makes the owner a torment to himself, and to every one else a nuisance. Like all the other Barlows of Barnstable on Cape Cod, Billy had worked for his every penny. He was no shirker. From the first day that he carried a pair of pliers in the leg pocket of his overalls, and in a sixty-knot gale stretched wires between ice-capped telegraph poles, he had more than earned his wages. Never, whether on time or at piece-work, had he by a slovenly job, or by beating the whistle, robbed his employer. And for his honest toil he was determined to be as honestly paid—even by President Hamilcar Poussevain. And President Ham never paid anybody; neither the Armenian street peddlers, in whose sweets he delighted, nor the Bethlehem Steel Company, nor the house of Rothschild.

Why he paid Billy even the small sums that from time to time Billy wrung from the president's strong box the foreign colony were at a loss to explain. Wagner, the new American consul, asked Billy how he managed it. As an American minister had not yet been appointed to the duties of the consul, as Wagner assured everybody, were added those of diplomacy. But Haytian diplomacy he had yet to master. At the seaport in Scotland where he had served

BILLY AND THE BIG STICK

as vice-consul, law and order were as solidly established as the stone jetties, and by contrast the eccentricities of the Black Republic baffled and distressed him.

"It can't be that you blackmail the president," said the consul, "because I understand he boasts he has committed all the known crimes."

"And several he invented," agreed Billy.

"And you can't do it with a gun, because they tell me the president isn't afraid of anything except a voodoo priestess. What is your secret?" coaxed the consul. "If you'll only sell it, I know several Powers that would give you your price."

Billy smiled modestly.

"It's very simple," he said. "The first time my wages were shy I went to the palace and told him if he didn't come across I'd shut off the juice. I think he was so stunned at anybody asking him for real money that while he was still stunned he opened his safe and handed me two thousand francs. I think he did it more in admiration for my nerve than because he owed it. The next time pay-day arrived, and the pay did not, I didn't go to the palace. I just went to bed, and the lights went to bed, too. You may remember?"

The consul snorted indignantly.

BILLY AND THE BIG STICK

"I was holding three queens at the time," he protested. "Was it *you* did that?"

"It was," said Billy. "The police came for me to start the current going again, but I said I was too ill. Then the president's own doctor came, old Gautier, and Gautier examined me with a lantern and said that in Hayti my disease frequently proved fatal, but he thought if I turned on the lights I might recover. I told him I was tired of life, anyway, but that if I could see three thousand francs it might give me an incentive. He reported back to the president and the three thousand francs arrived almost instantly, and a chicken broth from Ham's own chef, with His Excellency's best wishes for the recovery of the invalid. My recovery was instantaneous, and I switched on the lights.

"I had just moved into the Widow Ducrot's hotel that week, and her daughter Claire wouldn't let me eat the broth. I thought it was because, as she's a dandy cook herself, she was professionally jealous. She put the broth on the top shelf of the pantry and wrote on a piece of paper, 'Gare!' But the next morning a perfectly good cat, who apparently couldn't read, was lying beside it dead."

The consul frowned reprovingly.

"You should not make such reckless charges,"

BILLY AND THE BIG STICK

he protested. "I would call it only a coincidence."

"You can call it what you please," said Billy, "but it won't bring the cat back. Anyway, the next time I went to the palace to collect, the president was ready for me. He said he'd been taking out information, and he found if I shut off the lights again he could hire another man in the States to turn them on. I told him he'd been deceived. I told him the Wilmot Electric Lights were produced by a secret process, and that only a trained Wilmot man could work them. And I pointed out to him if he dismissed me it wasn't likely the Wilmot people would loan him another expert; not while they were fighting him through the courts and the State Department. That impressed the old man; so I issued my ultimatum. I said if he must have electric lights he must have me, too. Whether he liked it or not, mine was a life job."

"What did he say to that?" gasped the new consul.

"Said it *wasn't* a life job, because he was going to have me shot at sunset."

"Then you said?"

"I said if he did that there wouldn't be any electric lights, and *you* would bring a warship and shoot Hayti off the map."

The new consul was most indignant.

BILLY AND THE BIG STICK

"You had no right to say that!" he protested. "You did very ill. My instructions are to avoid all serious complications."

"That was what I was trying to avoid," said Billy. "Don't you call being shot at sunset a serious complication? Or would that be just a coincidence, too? You're a hellofa consul!"

Since his talk with the representative of his country four months had passed and Billy still held his job. But each month the number of francs he was able to wrest from President Hamilcar dwindled, and were won only after verbal conflicts that each month increased in violence.

To the foreign colony it became evident that, in the side of President Ham, Billy was a thorn, sharp, irritating, virulent, and that at any moment Ham might pluck that thorn and Billy would leave Hayti in haste, and probably in hand-cuffs. This was evident to Billy, also, and the prospect was most disquieting. Not because he loved Hayti, but because since he went to lodge at the café of the Widow Ducrot, he had learned to love her daughter Claire, and Claire loved him.

On the two thousand dollars due him from Ham they plotted to marry. This was not as great an adventure as it might appear. Billy knew that from the Wilmot people he always

BILLY AND THE BIG STICK

was sure of a salary, and one which, with such an excellent housekeeper as was Claire, would support them both. But with his two thousand dollars as capital they could afford to plunge; they could go upon a honeymoon; they need not dread a rainy day, and, what was of greatest importance, they need not delay. There was good reason against delay, for the hand of the beautiful Claire was already promised. The Widow Ducrot had promised it to Paillard, he of the prosperous commission business, the prominent *embonpoint*, and four children. Monsieur Paillard possessed an establishment of his own, but it was a villa in the suburbs; and so, each day at noon, for his *déjeuné* he left his office and crossed the street to the Café Ducrot. For five years this had been his habit. At first it was the widow's cooking that attracted him, then for a time the widow herself; but when from the convent Claire came to assist her mother in the café, and when from a lanky, big-eyed, long-legged child she grew into a slim, joyous, and charming young woman, she alone was the attraction, and the Widower Paillard decided to make her his wife. Other men had made the same decision; and when it was announced that between Claire and the widower a marriage had been "arranged," the clerks in the foreign commission houses and the agents of the steamship lines drowned their sorrow in rum and ran the house flags to half-staff. Paillard himself took the proposed alliance calmly. He was not an impetuous suitor. With Widow Ducrot he agreed that Claire was still too young to marry, and to himself kept the fact that to remarry he was in no haste. In his mind doubts still lingered. With a wife, young enough to be one of his children, disorganizing the routine of his villa, would it be any more comfortable than he now found it? Would his eldest daughter and her stepmother dwell together in harmony? The eldest daughter had assured him that so far as she was concerned they would not; and, after all, in marrying a girl, no matter how charming, without a dot, and the daughter of a boarding-house keeper, no matter how respectable, was he not disposing of himself too cheaply? These doubts assailed Papa Paillard; these speculations were in his mind. And while he speculated Billy acted.

"I know that in France," Billy assured Claire, "marriages are arranged by the parents; but in *my* country they are arranged in heaven. And who are we to disregard the edicts of heaven? Ages and ages ago, before the flood, before Napoleon, even before old Paillard with his four children, it was arranged in heaven that you were to marry me. So, what little plans

BILLY AND THE BIG STICK

your good mother may make don't cut enough ice to cool a green mint. Now, we can't try to get married here," continued Billy, "without your mother and Paillard knowing it. In this town as many people have to sign the marriage contract as signed our Declaration of Independence: all the civil authorities, all the clergy, all the relatives; if every man in the telephone book isn't a witness, the marriage doesn't 'take.' So, we must elope!"

Having been brought up in a convent, where she was taught to obey her mother and forbidden to think of marriage, Claire was naturally delighed with the idea of an elopement.

"To where will we elope to?" she demanded. Her English, as she learned it from Billy, was sometimes confusing.

"To New York," said Billy. "On the voyage there I will put you in charge of the stewardess and the captain; and there isn't a captain on the Royal Dutch or the Atlas that hasn't known you since you were a baby. And as soon as we dock we'll drive straight to the city hall for a license and the mayor himself will marry us. Then I'll get back my old job from the Wilmot folks and we'll live happy ever after!"

"In New York, also," asked Claire proudly, "are you directeur of the electric lights?"

"On Broadway alone," Billy explained reprov-

BILLY AND THE BIG STICK

ingly, "there is one sign that uses more bulbs than there are in the whole of Hayti!"

"New York is a large town!" exclaimed Claire.

"It's a large sign," corrected Billy. "But," he pointed out, "with no money we'll never see it. So to-morrow I'm going to make a social call on Grandpa Ham and demand my ten thousand francs."

Claire grasped his arm.

"Be careful," she pleaded. "Remember the chicken soup. If he offers you the champagne, refuse it!"

"He won't offer me the champagne," Billy assured her. "It won't be that kind of a call."

Billy left the Café Ducrot and made his way to the water-front. He was expecting some electrical supplies by the *Prinz der Nederlanden,* and she had already come to anchor.

He was late, and save for a group of his countrymen, who with the customs officials were having troubles of their own, the customs shed was all but deserted. Billy saw his freight cleared and was going away when one of those in trouble signalled for assistance.

He was a good-looking young man in a Panama hat and his manner seemed to take it for granted that Billy knew who he was.

"They want us to pay duty on our trunks,"

BILLY AND THE BIG STICK

he explained, "and we want to leave them in bond. We'll be here only until to-night, when we're going on down the coast to Santo Domingo. But we don't speak French, and we can't make them understand that."

"You don't need to speak any language to give a man ten dollars," said Billy.

"Oh!" exclaimed the man in the Panama. "I was afraid if I tried that they might arrest us."

"They may arrest you if you don't," said Billy.

Acting both as interpreter and disbursing agent, Billy satisfied the demands of his fellow employees of the government, and his fellow countrymen he directed to the Hotel Ducrot.

As some one was sure to take their money, he thought it might as well go to his mother-in-law elect. The young man in the Panama expressed the deepest gratitude, and Billy, assuring him he would see him later, continued to the power-house, still wondering where he had seen him before.

At the power-house he found seated at his desk a large, bearded stranger whose derby hat and ready-to-wear clothes showed that he also had but just arrived on the *Prinz der Nederlanden*.

"You William Barlow?" demanded the

BILLY AND THE BIG STICK

stranger. "I understand you been threatening, unless you get your pay raised, to commit sabotage on these works?"

"Who the devil are you?" inquired Billy.

The stranger produced an impressive-looking document covered with seals.

"Contract with the president," he said. "I've taken over your job. You better get out quiet," he advised, "as they've given me a squad of nigger policemen to see that you do."

"Are you aware that these works are the property of the Wilmot Company?" asked Billy, "and that if anything went wrong here they'd hold you responsible?"

The stranger smiled complacently.

"I've run plants," he said, "that make these lights look like a stable lantern on a foggy night."

"In that case," assented Billy, "should anything happen, you'll know exactly what to do, and I can leave you in charge without feeling the least anxiety."

"That's just what you can do," the stranger agreed heartily, "and you can't do it too quick!" From the desk he took Billy's favorite pipe and loaded it from Billy's tobacco-jar. But when Billy had reached the door he called to him. "Before you go, son," he said, "you might give me a tip about this climate. I never been in the tropics. It's kind of unhealthy, ain't it?"

His expression was one of concern.

"If you hope to keep alive," began Billy, "there are two things to avoid——"

The stranger laughed knowingly.

"I got you!" he interrupted. "You're going to tell me to cut out wine and women."

"I was going to tell you," said Billy, "to cut out hoping to collect any wages and to avoid every kind of soup."

From the power-house Billy went direct to the palace. His anxiety was great. Now that Claire had consented to leave Hayti, the loss of his position did not distress him. But the possible loss of his back pay would be a catastrophe. He had hardly enough money to take them both to New York, and after they arrived none with which to keep them alive. Before the Wilmot Company could find a place for him a month might pass, and during that month they might starve. If he went alone and arranged for Claire to follow, he might lose her. Her mother might marry her to Paillard; Claire might fall ill; without him at her elbow to keep her to their purpose the voyage to an unknown land might require more courage than she possessed. Billy saw it was imperative they

BILLY AND THE BIG STICK

should depart together, and to that end he must have his two thousand dollars. The money was justly his. For it he had sweated and slaved; had given his best effort. And so, when he faced the president, he was in no conciliatory mood. Neither was the president.

By what right, he demanded, did this foreigner affront his ears with demands for money; how dared he force his way into his presence and to his face babble of back pay? It was insolent, incredible. With indignation the president set forth the position of the government. Billy had been discharged and, with the appointment of his successor, the stranger in the derby hat, had ceased to exist. The government could not pay money to some one who did not exist. All indebtedness to Billy also had ceased to exist. The account had been wiped out. Billy had been wiped out.

The big negro, with the chest and head of a gorilla, tossed his kinky white curls so violently that the ringlets danced. Billy, he declared, had been a pest; a fly that buzzed and buzzed and disturbed his slumbers. And now when the fly thought he slept he had caught and crushed it—so. President Ham clinched his great fist convulsively and, with delight in his pantomime, opened his fingers one by one, and held out his pink palm, wrinkled and crossed like the

BILLY AND THE BIG STICK

hand of a washerwoman, as though to show Billy that in it lay the fly, dead.

"*C'est une chose jugée!*" thundered the president.

He reached for his quill pen.

But Billy, with Claire in his heart, with the injustice of it rankling in his mind, did not agree.

"It is not an affair closed," shouted Billy in his best French. "It is an affair international, diplomatic; a cause for war!"

Believing he had gone mad, President Ham gazed at him speechless.

"From here I go to the cable office," shouted Billy. "I cable for a warship! If, by to-night, I am not paid my money, marines will surround our power-house, and the Wilmot people will back me up, and my government will back me up!"

It was, so Billy thought, even as he launched it, a tirade satisfying and magnificent. But in his turn the president did not agree.

He rose. He was a large man. Billy wondered he had not previously noticed how very large he was.

"To-night at nine o'clock," he said, "the German boat departs for New York." As though aiming a pistol, he raised his arm and at Billy pointed a finger. "If, after she departs,

BILLY AND THE BIG STICK

you are found in Port-au-Prince, you will be shot!"

The audience-chamber was hung with great mirrors in frames of tarnished gilt. In these Billy saw himself reproduced in a wavering line of Billies that, like the ghost of Banquo, stretched to the disappearing point. Of such images there was an army, but of the real Billy, as he was acutely conscious, there was but one. Among the black faces scowling from the doorways he felt the odds were against him. Without making a reply he passed out between the racks of rusty muskets in the anteroom, between the two Gatling guns guarding the entrance, and on the palace steps, in indecision, halted.

As Billy hesitated an officer followed him from the palace and beckoned to the guard that sat in the bare dust of the Champ de Mars playing cards for cartridges. Two abandoned the game, and, having received their orders, picked their muskets from the dust and stood looking expectantly at Billy.

They were his escort, and it was evident that until nine o'clock, when he sailed, his movements would be spied upon; his acts reported to the president.

Such being the situation, Billy determined that his first act to be reported should be of a

BILLY AND THE BIG STICK

nature to cause the president active mental anguish. With his guard at his heels he went directly to the cable station, and to the Secretary of State of the United States addressed this message: "President refuses my pay; threatens shoot; wireless nearest war-ship proceed here full speed. William Barlow."

Billy and the director of telegraphs, who out of office hours was a field-marshal, and when not in his shirt-sleeves always appeared in uniform, went over each word of the cablegram together. When Billy was assured that the field-marshal had grasped the full significance of it he took it back and added, "Love to Aunt Maria." The extra words cost four dollars and eighty cents gold, but, as they suggested ties of blood between himself and the Secretary of State, they seemed advisable. In the account-book in which he recorded his daily expenditures Billy credited the item to "life-insurance."

The revised cablegram caused the field-marshal deep concern. He frowned at Billy ferociously.

"I will forward this at once," he promised. "But, I warn you," he added, "I deliver also a copy to *my* president!"

Billy sighed hopefully.

"You might deliver the copy first," he suggested.

BILLY AND THE BIG STICK

From the cable station Billy, still accompanied by his faithful retainers, returned to the power-house. There he bade farewell to the black brothers who had been his assistants, and upon one of them pressed a sum of money.

As they parted, this one, as though giving the pass-word of a secret society, chanted solemnly:

"*A huit heures juste!*"

And Billy clasped his hand and nodded.

At the office of the Royal Dutch West India Line Billy purchased a ticket to New York and inquired were there many passengers.

"The ship is empty," said the agent.

"I am glad," said Billy, "for one of my assistants may come with me. He also is being deported."

"You can have as many cabins as you want," said the agent. "We are so sorry to see you go that we will try to make you feel you leave us on your private yacht."

The next two hours Billy spent in seeking out those acquaintances from whom he could borrow money. He found that by asking for it in homœopathic doses he was able to shame the foreign colony into loaning him all of one hundred dollars. This, with what he had in hand, would take Claire and himself to New York and for a week keep them alive. After that he must find work or they must starve.

BILLY AND THE BIG STICK

In the garden of the Café Ducrot Billy placed his guard at a table with bottles of beer between them, and at an adjoining table with Claire plotted the elopement for that night. The garden was in the rear of the hotel and a door in the lower wall opened into the rue Cambon, that led directly to the water-front.

Billy proposed that at eight o'clock Claire should be waiting in the rue Cambon outside this door. They would then make their way to one of the less frequented wharfs, where Claire would arrange to have a rowboat in readiness, and in it they would take refuge on the steamer. An hour later, before the flight of Claire could be discovered, they would have started on their voyage to the mainland.

"I warn you," said Billy, "that after we reach New York I have only enough to keep us for a week. It will be a brief honey-moon. After that we will probably starve. I'm not telling you this to discourage you," he explained; "only trying to be honest."

"I would rather starve with you in New York," said Claire, "than die here without you."

At these words Billy desired greatly to kiss Claire, but the guards were scowling at him. It was not until Claire had gone to her room to pack her bag and the chance to kiss her had

BILLY AND THE BIG STICK

passed that Billy recognized that the scowls were intended to convey the fact that the beer bottles were empty. He remedied this and remained alone at his table considering the outlook. The horizon was, indeed, gloomy, and the only light upon it, the loyalty and love of the girl, only added to his bitterness. Above all things he desired to make her content, to protect her from disquiet, to convince her that in the sacrifice she was making she also was plotting her own happiness. Had he been able to collect his ten thousand francs his world would have danced in sunshine. As it was, the heavens were gray and for the future the skies promised only rainy days. In these depressing reflections Billy was interrupted by the approach of the young man in the Panama hat. Billy would have avoided him, but the young man and his two friends would not be denied. For the service Billy had rendered them they wished to express their gratitude. It found expression in the form of Planter's punch. As they consumed this Billy explained to the strangers why the customs men had detained them.

"You told them you were leaving to-night for Santo Domingo," said Billy; "but they knew that was impossible, for there is no steamer down the coast for two weeks."

BILLY AND THE BIG STICK

The one whose features seemed familiar replied:

"Still, we *are* leaving to-night," he said; "not on a steamer, but on a war-ship."

"A war-ship?" cried Billy. His heart beat at high speed. "Then," he exclaimed, "you are a naval officer?"

The young man shook his head and, as though challenging Billy to make another guess, smiled.

"Then," Billy complied eagerly, "you are a diplomat! Are you our new minister?"

One of the other young men exclaimed reproachfully:

"You know him perfectly well!" he protested. "You've seen his picture thousands of times."

With awe and pride he placed his hand on Billy's arm and with the other pointed at the one in the Panama hat.

"It's Harry St. Clair," he announced. "Harry St. Clair, the King of the Movies!"

"The King of the Movies," repeated Billy. His disappointment was so keen as to be embarrassing.

"Oh!" he exclaimed, "I thought you—" Then he remembered his manners. "Glad to meet you," he said. "Seen you on the screen."

Again his own troubles took precedence.

BILLY AND THE BIG STICK

"Did you say," he demanded, "one of our warships is coming here *to-day*?"

"Coming to take me to Santo Domingo," explained Mr. St. Clair. He spoke airily, as though to him as a means of locomotion battleships were as trolley-cars. The Planter's punch, which was something he had never before encountered, encouraged the great young man to unbend. He explained further and fully, and Billy, his mind intent upon his own affair, pretended to listen.

The United States Government, Mr. St. Clair explained, was assisting him and the Apollo Film Company in producing the eight-reel film entitled "The Man Behind the Gun."

With it the Navy Department plotted to advertise the navy and encourage recruiting. In moving pictures, in the form of a story, with love interest, villain, comic relief, and thrills, it would show the life of American bluejackets afloat and ashore, at home and abroad. They would be seen at Yokohama playing baseball with Tokio University; in the courtyard of the Vatican receiving the blessing of the Pope; at Waikiki riding the breakers on a scrubbing-board; in the Philippines eating cocoanuts in the shade of the sheltering palm, and in Brooklyn in the Y. M. C. A. club, in the shadow of the

BILLY AND THE BIG STICK

New York sky-scrapers, playing billiards and reading the sporting extras.

As it would be illustrated on the film the life of "The Man Behind the Gun" was one of luxurious ease. In it coal-passing, standing watch in a blizzard, and washing down decks, cold and unsympathetic, held no part. But to prove that the life of Jack was not all play he would be seen fighting for the flag. That was where, as "Lieutenant Hardy, U. S. A.," the King of the Movies entered.

"Our company arrived in Santo Domingo last week," he explained. "And they're waiting for me now. I'm to lead the attack on the fortress. We land in shore boats under the guns of the ship and I take the fortress. First, we show the ship clearing for action and the men lowering the boats and pulling for shore. Then we cut back to show the gun-crews serving the guns. Then we jump to the landing-party wading through the breakers. I lead them. The man who is carrying the flag gets shot and drops in the surf. I pick him up, put him on my shoulder, and carry him *and* the flag to the beach, where I——"

Billy suddenly awoke. His tone was one of excited interest.

"You got a uniform?" he demanded.

"Three," said St. Clair impressively, "made

BILLY AND THE BIG STICK

to order according to regulations on file in the Quartermaster's Department. Each absolutely correct." Without too great a show of eagerness he inquired: "Like to see them?"

Without too great a show of eagerness Billy assured him that he would.

"I got to telephone first," he added, "but by the time you get your trunk open I'll join you in your room."

In the café, over the telephone, Billy addressed himself to the field-marshal in charge of the cable office. When Billy gave his name, the voice of that dignitary became violently agitated.

"Monsieur Barlow," he demanded, "do you know that the war-ship for which you cabled your Secretary of State makes herself to arrive?"

At the other end of the 'phone, although restrained by the confines of the booth, Billy danced joyously. But his voice was stern.

"Naturally," he replied. "Where is she now?"

An hour before, so the field-marshal informed him, the battle-ship *Louisiana* had been sighted and by telegraph reported. She was approaching under forced draft. At any moment she might anchor in the outer harbor. Of this President Ham had been informed. He was

BILLY AND THE BIG STICK

grieved, indignant; he was also at a loss to understand.

"It is very simple," explained Billy. "She probably was somewhere in the Windward Passage. When the Secretary got my message he cabled Guantanamo, and Guantanamo wirelessed the war-ship nearest Port-au-Prince."

"President Poussevain," warned the field-marshal, "is greatly disturbed."

"Tell him not to worry," said Billy. "Tell him when the bombardment begins I will see that the palace is outside the zone of fire."

As Billy entered the room of St. Clair his eyes shone with a strange light. His manner, which toward a man of his repute St. Clair had considered a little too casual, was now enthusiastic, almost affectionate.

"My dear St. Clair," cried Billy, "*I've fixed it!* But, until I was *sure*, I didn't want to raise your hopes!"

"Hopes of what?" demanded the actor.

"An audience with the president!" cried Billy. "I've just called him up and he says I'm to bring you to the palace at once. He's heard of you, of course, and he's very pleased to meet you. I told him about 'The Man Behind the Gun,' and he says you must come in your make-up as 'Lieutenant Hardy, U. S. A.,' just as he'll see you on the screen."

BILLY AND THE BIG STICK

Mr. St. Clair stammered delightedly.

"In uniform," he protested; "won't that be——"

"White, special full dress," insisted Billy. "Medals, side-arms, full-dress belt, *and* gloves. What a press story! 'The King of the Movies Meets the President of Hayti!' Of course, he's only an ignorant negro, but on Broadway they don't know that; and it will sound fine!"

St. Clair coughed nervously.

"*Don't* forget," he stammered, "I can't speak French, or understand it, either."

The eyes of Billy became as innocent as those of a china doll.

"Then I'll interpret," he said. "And, oh, yes," he added, "he's sending two of the palace soldiers to act as an escort—sort of guard of honor!"

The King of the Movies chuckled excitedly.

"Fine!" he exclaimed. "You *are* a brick!"

With trembling fingers he began to shed his outer garments.

To hide his own agitation Billy walked to the window and turned his back. Night had fallen and the electric lights, that once had been his care, sprang into life. Billy looked at his watch. It was seven o'clock. The window gave upon the harbor, and a mile from shore he saw the cargo lights of the *Prinz der Nederlanden*, and

BILLY AND THE BIG STICK

slowly approaching, as though feeling for her berth, a great battle-ship. When Billy turned from the window his voice was apparently undisturbed.

"We've got to hurry," he said. "The *Louisiana* is standing in. She'll soon be sending a launch for you. We've just time to drive to the palace and back before the launch gets here."

From his mind President Ham had dismissed all thoughts of the war-ship that had been sighted and that now had come to anchor. For the moment he was otherwise concerned. Fate could not harm him; he was about to dine.

But, for the first time in the history of his administration, that solemn ceremony was rudely halted. An excited aide, trembling at his own temerity, burst upon the president's solitary state.

In the anteroom, he announced, an officer from the battle-ship *Louisiana* demanded instant audience.

For a moment, transfixed in amazement, anger, and alarm President Ham remained seated. Such a visit, uninvited, was against all tradition; it was an affront, an insult. But that it was against all precedent argued some serious necessity. He decided it would be best

BILLY AND THE BIG STICK

to receive the officer. Besides, to continue his dinner was now out of the question. Both appetite and digestion had fled from him.

In the anteroom Billy was whispering final instructions to St. Clair.

"Whatever happens," he begged, "don't *laugh!* Don't even smile politely! He's very ignorant, you see, and he's sensitive. When he meets foreigners and can't understand their language, he's always afraid if they laugh that he's made a break and that they're laughing at *him.* So, be solemn; look grave; look haughty!"

"I got you," assented St. Clair. "I'm to 'register' pride."

"Exactly!" said Billy. "The more pride you register, the better for us."

Inwardly cold with alarm, outwardly frigidly polite, Billy presented "Lieutenant Hardy." He had come, Billy explained, in answer to the call for help sent by himself to the Secretary of State, which by wireless had been communicated to the *Louisiana.* Lieutenant Hardy begged him to say to the president that he was desolate at having to approach His Excellency so unceremoniously. But His Excellency, having threatened the life of an American citizen, the captain of the *Louisiana* was forced to act quickly.

BILLY AND THE BIG STICK

"And this officer?" demanded President Ham; "what does he want?"

"He says," Billy translated to St. Clair, "that he is very glad to meet you, and he wants to know how much you earn a week."

The actor suppressed his surprise and with pardonable pride said that his salary was six hundred dollars a week and royalties on each film.

Billy bowed to the president.

"He says," translated Billy, "he is here to see that I get my ten thousand francs, and that if I don't get them in ten minutes he will return to the ship and land marines."

To St. Clair it seemed as though the president received his statement as to the amount of his salary with a disapproval that was hardly flattering. With the heel of his giant fist the president beat upon the table, his curls shook, his gorilla-like shoulders heaved.

In an explanatory aside Billy made this clear.

"He says," he interpreted, "that you get more as an actor than he gets as president, and it makes him mad."

"I can see it does myself," whispered St. Clair. "And I don't understand French, either."

President Ham was protesting violently. It was outrageous, he exclaimed; it was inconceiv-

BILLY AND THE BIG STICK

able that a great republic should shake the Big Stick over the head of a small republic, and for a contemptible ten thousand francs.

"I will not believe," he growled, "that this officer has authority to threaten me. You have deceived him. If he knew the truth, he would apologize. Tell him," he roared suddenly, "that I *demand* that he apologize!"

Billy felt like the man who, after jauntily forcing the fighting, unexpectedly gets a jolt on the chin that drops him to the canvas.

While the referee might have counted three Billy remained upon the canvas.

Then again he forced the fighting. Eagerly he turned to St. Clair.

"He says," he translated, "you must recite something."

St. Clair exclaimed incredulously:

"Recite!" he gasped.

Than his indignant protest nothing could have been more appropriate.

"Wants to see you act out," insisted Billy. "Go on," he begged; "humor him. Do what he wants or he'll put us in jail!"

"But what shall I——"

"He wants the curse of Rome from Richelieu," explained Billy. "He knows it in French and he wants you to recite it in English. Do you know it?"

BILLY AND THE BIG STICK

The actor smiled haughtily.

"I *wrote* it!" he protested. "Richelieu's my middle name. I've done it in stock."

"Then do it now!" commanded Billy. "Give it to him hot. I'm Julie de Mortemar. He's the villain Barabas. Begin where Barabas hands you the cue, 'The country is the king!'"

In embarrassment St. Clair coughed tentatively.

"Whoever heard of Cardinal Richelieu," he protested, "in a navy uniform?"

"Begin!" begged Billy.

"What'll I do with my cap?" whispered St. Clair.

In an ecstasy of alarm Billy danced from foot to foot.

"I'll hold your cap," he cried. "Go on!"

St. Clair gave his cap of gold braid to Billy and shifted his "full-dress" sword-belt. Not without concern did President Ham observe these preparations. For the fraction of a second, in alarm, his eyes glanced to the exits. He found that the officers of his staff completely filled them. Their presence gave him confidence and his eyes returned to Lieutenant Hardy.

That gentleman heaved a deep sigh. Dejectedly, his head fell forward until his chin rested upon his chest. Much to the relief of the president, it appeared evident that Lieutenant Hardy

BILLY AND THE BIG STICK

was about to accede to his command and apologize.

St. Clair groaned heavily.

"Ay, is it so?" he muttered. His voice was deep, resonant, vibrating like a bell. His eyes no longer suggested apology. They were strange, flashing; the eyes of a religious fanatic; and balefully they were fixed upon President Ham.

"Then wakes the power," the deep voice rumbled, "that in the age of iron burst forth to curb the great and raise the low." He flung out his left arm and pointed it at Billy.

"Mark where she stands!" he commanded.

With a sweeping, protecting gesture he drew around Billy an imaginary circle. The pantomime was only too clear. To the aged negro, who feared neither God nor man, but only voodoo, there was in the voice and gesture that which caused his blood to chill.

"Around her form," shrieked St. Clair, "I draw the awful circle of our solemn church! Set but one foot within that holy ground and on thy head—" Like a semaphore the left arm dropped, and the right arm, with the forefinger pointed, shot out at President Ham. "Yea, though it wore a CROWN—I launch the CURSE OF ROME!"

No one moved. No one spoke. What ter-

BILLY AND THE BIG STICK

rible threat had hit him President Ham could not guess. He did not ask. Stiffly, like a man in a trance, he turned to the rusty iron safe behind his chair and spun the handle. When again he faced them he held a long envelope which he presented to Billy.

"There are the ten thousand francs," he said. "Ask him if he is satisfied, and demand that he go at once!"

Billy turned to St. Clair.

"He says," translated Billy, "he's very much obliged and hopes we will come again. Now," commanded Billy, "bow low and go out facing him. We don't want him to shoot us in the back!"

Bowing to the president, the actor threw at Billy a glance full of indignation.

"Was I as bad as *that?*" he demanded.

On schedule time Billy drove up to the Hotel Ducrot and relinquished St. Clair to the ensign in charge of the launch from the *Louisiana*. At sight of St. Clair in the regalia of a superior officer, that young gentleman showed his surprise.

"I've been giving a 'command' performance for the president," explained the actor modestly. "I recited for him, and, though I spoke in English, I think I made quite a hit."

"You certainly," Billy assured him gratefully, "made a terrible hit with me."

BILLY AND THE BIG STICK

As the moving-picture actors, escorted by the ensign, followed their trunks to the launch, Billy looked after them with a feeling of great loneliness. He was aware that from the palace his carriage had been followed; that drawn in a cordon around the hotel negro policemen covertly observed him. That President Ham still hoped to recover his lost prestige and his lost money was only too evident.

It was just five minutes to eight.

Billy ran to his room, and with his suit-case in his hand slipped down the back stairs and into the garden. Cautiously he made his way to the gate in the wall, and in the street outside found Claire awaiting him.

With a cry of relief she clasped his arm.

"You are safe!" she cried. "I was so frightened for you. That President Ham, he is a beast, an ogre!" Her voice sank to a whisper. "And for myself also I have been frightened. The police, they are at each corner. They watch the hotel. They watch *me!* Why? What do they want?"

"They want something of mine," said Billy. "But I can't tell you what it is until I'm sure it *is* mine. Is the boat at the wharf?"

"All is arranged," Claire assured him. "The boatmen are our friends; they will take us safely to the steamer."

BILLY AND THE BIG STICK

With a sigh of relief Billy lifted her valise and his own, but he did not move forward.

Anxiously Claire pulled at his sleeve.

"Come!" she begged. "For what it is that you wait?"

It was just eight o'clock.

Billy was looking up at the single electric-light bulb that lit the narrow street, and following the direction of his eyes, Claire saw the light grow dim, saw the tiny wires grow red, and disappear. From over all the city came shouts, and cries of consternation oaths, and laughter, and then darkness.

"I was waiting for *this!*" cried Billy.

With the delight of a mischievous child Claire laughed aloud.

"*You*—you did it!" she accused.

"I did!" said Billy. "And now—we must run like the devil!"

The *Prinz der Nederlanden* was drawing slowly out of the harbor. Shoulder to shoulder Claire and Billy leaned upon the rail. On the wharfs of Port-au-Prince they saw lanterns tossing and candles twinkling; saw the *Louisiana*, blazing like a Christmas-tree, steaming majestically south; in each other's eyes saw that all was well.

From his pocket Billy drew a long envelope.

"I can now with certainty," said Billy, "state that this is mine—*ours*."

BILLY AND THE BIG STICK

He opened the envelope, and while Claire gazed upon many mille-franc notes Billy told how he had retrieved them.

"But what danger!" cried Claire. "In time Ham would have paid. Your president at Washington would have *made* him pay. Why take such risks? You had but to wait!"

Billy smiled contentedly.

"Dear one!" he exclaimed, "the policy of watchful waiting is safer, but the Big Stick acts quicker and gets results!"

THE FRAME-UP

WHEN the voice over the telephone promised to name the man who killed Hermann Banf, District Attorney Wharton was up-town lunching at Delmonico's. This was contrary to his custom and a concession to Hamilton Cutler, his distinguished brother-in-law. That gentleman was interested in a State constabulary bill and had asked State Senator Bissell to father it. He had suggested to the senator that, in the legal points involved in the bill, his brother-in-law would undoubtedly be charmed to advise him. So that morning, to talk it over, Bissell had come from Albany and, as he was forced to return the same afternoon, had asked Wharton to lunch with him up-town near the station.

That in public life there breathed a man with soul so dead who, were he offered a chance to serve Hamilton Cutler, would not jump at the chance was outside the experience of the county chairman. And in so judging his fellow men, with the exception of one man, the senator was right. The one man was Hamilton Cutler's brother-in-law.

In the national affairs of his party Hamilton

THE FRAME-UP

Cutler was one of the four leaders. In two cabinets he had held office. At a foreign court as an ambassador his dinners, of which the diplomatic corps still spoke with emotion, had upheld the dignity of ninety million Americans. He was rich. The history of his family was the history of the State. When the Albany boats drew abreast of the old Cutler mansion on the east bank of the Hudson the passengers pointed at it with deference. Even when the searchlights pointed at it, it was with deference. And on Fifth Avenue, as the "Seeing New York" car passed his town house it slowed respectfully to half speed. When, apparently for no other reason than that she was good and beautiful, he had married the sister of a then unknown up-State lawyer, every one felt Hamilton Cutler had made his first mistake. But, like everything else into which he entered, for him matrimony also was a success. The prettiest girl in Utica showed herself worthy of her distinguished husband. She had given him children as beautiful as herself; as what Washington calls "a cabinet lady" she had kept her name out of the newspapers; as Madame l'Ambassatrice she had put archduchesses at their ease; and after ten years she was an adoring wife, a devoted mother, and a proud woman. Her pride was in believing that for every joy she

THE FRAME-UP

knew she was indebted entirely to her husband. To owe everything to him, to feel that through him the blessings flowed, was her ideal of happiness.

In this ideal her brother did not share. Her delight in a sense of obligation left him quite cold. No one better than himself knew that his rapid-fire rise in public favor was due to his own exertions, to the fact that he had worked very hard, had been independent, had kept his hands clean, and had worn no man's collar. Other people believed he owed his advancement to his brother-in-law. He knew they believed that, and it hurt him. When, at the annual dinner of the Amen Corner, they burlesqued him as singing to "Ham" Cutler, "You made me what I am to-day, I hope you're sat-isfied," he found that to laugh with the others was something of an effort. His was a difficult position. He was a party man; he had always worked inside the organization. The fact that whenever he ran for an elective office the reformers indorsed him and the best elements in the opposition parties voted for him did not shake his loyalty to his own people. And to Hamilton Cutler, as one of his party leaders, as one of the bosses of the "invisible government," he was willing to defer. But while he could give allegiance to his party leaders, and from them was willing to receive the rewards of office, from a rich brother-in-law he was not at all willing to accept anything. Still less was he willing that of the credit he deserved for years of hard work for the party, of self-denial, and of efficient public service the rich brother-in-law should rob him.

His pride was to be known as a self-made man, as the servant only of the voters. And now that he had fought his way to one of the goals of his ambition, now that he was district attorney of New York City, to have it said that the office was the gift of his brother-in-law was bitter. But he believed the injustice would soon end. In a month he was coming up for re-election, and night and day was conducting a campaign that he hoped would result in a personal victory so complete as to banish the shadow of his brother-in-law. Were he re-elected by the majority on which he counted, he would have the party leaders on their knees. Hamilton Cutler would be forced to come to him. He would be in line for promotion. He knew the leaders did not want to promote him, that they considered him too inclined to kick over the traces; but were he now re-elected, at the next election, either for mayor or governor, he would be his party's obvious and legitimate candidate.

The re-election was not to be an easy victory.

THE FRAME-UP

Outside his own party, to prevent his succeeding himself as district attorney, Tammany Hall was using every weapon in her armory. The commissioner of police was a Tammany man, and in the public prints Wharton had repeatedly declared that Banf, his star witness against the police, had been killed by the police, and that they had prevented the discovery of his murderer. For this the wigwam wanted his scalp, and to get it had raked his public and private life, had used threats and bribes, and with women had tried to trap him into a scandal. But "Big Tim" Meehan, the lieutenant the Hall had detailed to destroy Wharton, had reported back that for their purpose his record was useless, that bribes and threats only flattered him, and that the traps set for him he had smilingly side-stepped. This was the situation a month before election day when, to oblige his brother-in-law, Wharton was up-town at Delmonico's lunching with Senator Bissell.

Down-town at the office, Rumson, the assistant district attorney, was on his way to lunch when the telephone-girl halted him. Her voice was lowered and betrayed almost human interest.

From the corner of her mouth she whispered: "This man has a note for Mr. Wharton—says

THE FRAME-UP

if he don't get it quick it'll be too late—says it will tell him who killed 'Heimie' Banf!"

The young man and the girl looked at each other and smiled. Their experience had not tended to make them credulous. Had he lived, Hermann Banf would have been, for Wharton, the star witness against a ring of corrupt police officials. In consequence his murder was more than the taking off of a shady and disreputable citizen. It was a blow struck at the high office of the district attorney, at the grand jury, and the law. But, so far, whoever struck the blow had escaped punishment, and though for a month, ceaselessly, by night and day "the office" and the police had sought him, he was still at large, still "unknown." There had been hundreds of clews. They had been furnished by the detectives of the city and county and of the private agencies, by amateurs, by newspapers, by members of the underworld with a score to pay off or to gain favor. But no clew had led anywhere. When, in hoarse whispers, the last one had been confided to him by his detectives, Wharton had protested indignantly.

"Stop bringing me clews!" he exclaimed. "I want the man. I can't electrocute a clew!"

So when, after all other efforts, over the telephone a strange voice offered to deliver the murderer, Rumson was sceptical. He motioned the girl to switch to the desk telephone.

"Assistant District Attorney Rumson speaking," he said. "What can I do for you?"

Before the answer came, as though the speaker were choosing his words, there was a pause. It lasted so long that Rumson exclaimed sharply:

"Hello," he called. "Do you want to speak to me, or do you want to speak to me?"

"I've gotta letter for the district attorney," said the voice. "I'm to give it to nobody but him. It's about Banf. He must get it quick, or it'll be too late."

"Who are you?" demanded Rumson. "Where are you speaking from?"

The man at the other end of the wire ignored the questions.

"Where'll Wharton be for the next twenty minutes?"

"If I tell you," parried Rumson, "will you bring the letter at once?"

The voice exclaimed indignantly:

"Bring nothing! I'll send it by district messenger. You're wasting time trying to reach me. It's the *letter you* want. It tells"—the voice broke with an oath and instantly began again: "I can't talk over a phone. I tell you, it's life or death. If you lose out, it's your own fault. Where can I find Wharton?"

THE FRAME-UP

"At Delmonico's," answered Rumson. "He'll be there until two o'clock."

"Delmonico's! That's Forty-fort Street?"

"Right," said Rumson. "Tell the messenger——"

He heard the receiver slam upon the hook.

With the light of the hunter in his eyes, he turned to the girl.

"They can laugh," he cried, "but I believe we've hooked something. I'm going after it."

In the waiting-room he found the detectives.

"Hewitt," he ordered, "take the subway and whip up to Delmonico's. Talk to the taxi-starter till a messenger-boy brings a letter for the D. A. Let the boy deliver the note, and then trail him till he reports to the man he got it from. Bring the man here. If it's a district messenger and he doesn't report, but goes straight back to the office, find out who gave him the note; get his description. Then meet me at Delmonico's."

Rumson called up that restaurant and had Wharton come to the phone. He asked his chief to wait until a letter he believed to be of great importance was delivered to him. He explained, but, of necessity, somewhat sketchily.

"It sounds to me," commented his chief, "like a plot of yours to get a lunch up-town."

THE FRAME-UP

"Invitation!" cried Rumson. "I'll be with you in ten minutes."

After Rumson had joined Wharton and Bissell the note arrived. It was brought to the restaurant by a messenger-boy, who said that in answer to a call from a saloon on Sixth Avenue he had received it from a young man in ready-to-wear clothes and a green hat. When Hewitt, the detective, asked what the young man looked like, the boy said he looked like a young man in ready-to-wear clothes and a green hat. But when the note was read the identity of the man who delivered it ceased to be of importance. The paper on which it was written was without stamped address or monogram, and carried with it the mixed odors of the drug-store at which it had been purchased. The handwriting was that of a woman, and what she had written was: "If the district attorney will come at once, and alone, to Kessler's Café, on the Boston Post Road, near the city line, he will be told who killed Hermann Banf. If he don't come in an hour, it will be too late. If he brings anybody with him, he won't be told anything. Leave your car in the road and walk up the drive. Ida Earle."

Hewitt, who had sent away the messenger-boy and had been called in to give expert advice, was enthusiastic.

THE FRAME-UP

"Mr. District Attorney," he cried, "that's no crank letter. This Earle woman is wise. You got to take her as a serious proposition. She wouldn't make that play if she couldn't get away with it."

"Who is she?" asked Wharton.

To the police, the detective assured them, Ida Earle had been known for years. When she was young she had been under the protection of a man high in the ranks of Tammany, and, in consequence, with her different ventures the police had never interfered. She now was proprietress of the road-house in the note described as Kessler's Café. It was a place for joy-riders. There was a cabaret, a hall for public dancing, and rooms for very private suppers.

In so far as it welcomed only those who could spend money it was exclusive, but in all other respects its reputation was of the worst. In situation it was lonely, and from other houses separated by a quarter of a mile of dying trees and vacant lots.

The Boston Post Road upon which it faced was the old post road, but lately, through this back yard and dumping-ground of the city, had been relaid. It was patrolled only and infrequently by bicycle policemen.

"But this," continued the detective eagerly,

"is where we win out. The road-house is an old farmhouse built over, with the barns changed into garages. They stand on the edge of a wood. It's about as big as a city block. If we come in through the woods from the rear, the garages will hide us. Nobody in the house can see us, but we won't be a hundred yards away. You've only to blow a police whistle and we'll be with you."

"You mean I ought to go?" said Wharton.

Rumson exclaimed incredulously:

"You *got* to go!"

"It looks to me," objected Bissell, "like a plot to get you there alone and rap you on the head."

"Not with that note inviting him there," protested Hewitt, "and signed by Earle herself."

"You don't know she signed it?" objected the senator.

"I know *her*," returned the detective. "I know she's no fool. It's her place, and she wouldn't let them pull off any rough stuff there—not against the D. A., anyway."

The D. A. was rereading the note.

"Might this be it?" he asked. "Suppose it's a trick to mix me up in a scandal? You say the place is disreputable. Suppose they're planning to compromise me just before election. They've tried it already several times."

"You've still got the note," persisted Hewitt.

"It proves *why* you went there. And the senator, too. He can testify. And we won't be a hundred yards away. And," he added grudgingly, "you have Nolan."

Nolan was the spoiled child of "the office." He was the district attorney's pet. Although still young, he had scored as a detective and as a driver of racing-cars. As Wharton's chauffeur he now doubled the parts.

"What Nolan testified wouldn't be any help," said Wharton. "They would say it was just a story he invented to save me."

"Then square yourself this way," urged Rumson. "Send a note now by hand to Ham Cutler and one to your sister. Tell *them* you're going to Ida Earle's—and why—tell them you're afraid it's a frame-up, and for them to keep your notes as evidence. And enclose the one from her."

Wharton nodded in approval, and, while he wrote, Rumson and the detective planned how, without those inside the road-house being aware of their presence, they might be near it.

Kessler's Café lay in the Seventy-ninth Police Precinct. In taxi-cabs they arranged to start at once and proceed down White Plains Avenue, which parallels the Boston Road, until they were on a line with Kessler's, but from it hidden by the woods and the garages. A walk of a quarter of a mile across lots and under cover of the trees would bring them to within a hundred yards of the house.

Wharton was to give them a start of half an hour. That he might know they were on watch, they agreed, after they dismissed the taxi-cabs, to send one of them into the Boston Post Road past the road-house. When it was directly in front of the café, the chauffeur would throw away into the road an empty cigarette-case.

From the cigar-stand they selected a cigarette box of a startling yellow. At half a mile it was conspicuous.

"When you see this in the road," explained Rumson, "you'll know we're on the job. And after you're inside, if you need us, you've only to go to a rear window and wave."

"If they mean to do him up," growled Bissell, "he won't get to a rear window."

"He can always tell them we're outside," said Rumson—"and they are extremely likely to believe him. Do you want a gun?"

"No," said the D. A.

"Better have mine," urged Hewitt.

"I have my own," explained the D. A.

Rumson and Hewitt set off in taxi-cabs and, a half-hour later, Wharton followed. As he sank back against the cushions of the big touring-car he felt a pleasing thrill of excitement, and as he passed the traffic police, and they saluted mechanically, he smiled. Had they guessed his errand their interest in his progress would have been less perfunctory. In half an hour he might know that the police killed Banf; in half an hour he himself might walk into a trap they had, in turn, staged for him. As the car ran swiftly through the clean October air, and the wind and sun alternately chilled and warmed his blood, Wharton considered these possibilities.

He could not believe the woman Earle would lend herself to any plot to do him bodily harm. She was a responsible person. In her own world she was as important a figure as was the district attorney in his. Her allies were the man "higher up" in Tammany and the police of the upper ranks of the uniformed force. And of the higher office of the district attorney she possessed an intimate and respectful knowledge. It was not to be considered that against the prosecuting attorney such a woman would wage war. So the thought that upon his person any assault was meditated Wharton dismissed as unintelligent. That it was upon his reputation the attack was planned seemed much more probable. But that contingency he had foreseen and so, he believed, forestalled. There then remained only the possibility that the offer in the letter was genuine. It seemed quite too good to be true. For, as he asked himself, on the very eve of an election, why should Tammany, or a friend of Tammany, place in his possession the information that to the Tammany candidate would bring inevitable defeat. He felt that the way they were playing into his hands was too open, too generous. If their object was to lead him into a trap, of all baits they might use the promise to tell him who killed Banf was the one certain to attract him. It made their invitation to walk into the parlor almost too obvious. But were the offer not genuine, there was a condition attached to it that puzzled him. It was not the condition that stipulated he should come alone. His experience had taught him many will confess, or betray, to the district attorney who, to a deputy, will tell nothing. The condition that puzzled him was the one that insisted he should come at once or it would be "too late."

Why was haste so imperative? Why, if he delayed, would he be "too late"? Was the man he sought about to escape from his jurisdiction, was he dying, and was it his wish to make a death-bed confession; or was he so reluctant to speak that delay might cause him to reconsider and remain silent?

With these questions in his mind, the minutes quickly passed, and it was with a thrill of

THE FRAME-UP

excitement Wharton saw that Nolan had left the Zoological Gardens on the right and turned into the Boston Road. It had but lately been completed and to Wharton was unfamiliar. On either side of the unscarred roadway still lay scattered the uprooted trees and boulders that had blocked its progress, and abandoned by the contractors were empty tar-barrels, cement-sacks, tool-sheds, and forges. Nor was the surrounding landscape less raw and unlovely. Toward the Sound stretched vacant lots covered with ash heaps; to the left a few old and broken houses set among the glass-covered cold frames of truck-farms.

The district attorney felt a sudden twinge of loneliness. And when an automobile sign told him he was "10 miles from Columbus Circle," he felt that from the New York he knew he was much farther. Two miles up the road his car overhauled a bicycle policeman, and Wharton halted him.

"Is there a road-house called Kessler's beyond here?" he asked.

"On the left, farther up," the officer told him, and added: "You can't miss it, Mr. Wharton; there's no other house near it."

"You know me," said the D. A. "Then you'll understand what I want you to do. I've agreed to go to that house alone. If they see you pass

THE FRAME-UP

they may think I'm not playing fair. So stop here."

The man nodded and dismounted.

"But," added the district attorney, as the car started forward again, "if you hear shots, I don't care how fast you come."

The officer grinned.

"Better let me trail along now," he called; "that's a tough joint."

But Wharton motioned him back; and when again he turned to look the man still stood where they had parted.

Two minutes later an empty taxi-cab came swiftly toward him and, as it passed, the driver lifted his hand from the wheel, and with his thumb motioned behind him.

"That's one of the men," said Nolan, "that started with Mr. Rumson and Hewitt from Delmonico's."

Wharton nodded; and, now assured that in their plan there had been no hitch, smiled with satisfaction. A moment later, when ahead of them on the asphalt road Nolan pointed out a spot of yellow, he recognized the signal and knew that within call were friends.

The yellow cigarette-box lay directly in front of a long wooden building of two stories. It was linked to the road by a curving driveway marked on either side by whitewashed stones.

THE FRAME-UP

On verandas enclosed in glass Wharton saw white-covered tables under red candle-shades and, protruding from one end of the house and hung with electric lights in paper lanterns, a pavilion for dancing. In the rear of the house stood sheds and a thick tangle of trees on which the autumn leaves showed yellow. Painted fingers and arrows pointing, and an electric sign, proclaimed to all who passed that this was Kessler's. In spite of its reputation, the house wore the aspect of the commonplace. In evidence nothing flaunted, nothing threatened. From a dozen other inns along the Pelham Parkway and the Boston Post Road it was in no way to be distinguished.

As directed in the note, Wharton left the car in the road. "For five minutes stay where you are," he ordered Nolan; "then go to the bar and get a drink. Don't talk to any one or they'll think you're trying to get information. Work around to the back of the house. Stand where I can see you from the window. I may want you to carry a message to Mr. Rumson."

On foot Wharton walked up the curving driveway, and if from the house his approach was spied upon, there was no evidence. In the second story the blinds were drawn and on the first floor the verandas were empty. Nor, not even after he had mounted to the veranda and stepped inside the house, was there any sign that his visit was expected. He stood in a hall, and in front of him rose a broad flight of stairs that he guessed led to the private supper-rooms. On his left was the restaurant.

Swept and garnished after the revels of the night previous, and as though resting in preparation for those to come, it wore an air of peaceful inactivity. At a table a maître d'hôtel was composing the menu for the evening, against the walls three colored waiters lounged sleepily, and on a platform at a piano a pale youth with drugged eyes was with one hand picking an accompaniment. As Wharton paused uncertainly the young man, disdaining his audience, in a shrill, nasal tenor raised his voice and sang:

> "And from the time the rooster calls
>   I'll wear my overalls,
>   And you, a simple gingham gown.
>   So, if you're strong for a shower of rice,
>   We two could make a paradise
>   Of any One-Horse Town."

At sight of Wharton the head waiter reluctantly detached himself from his menu and rose. But before he could greet the visitor, Wharton heard his name spoken and, looking up, saw a woman descending the stairs. It was apparent that when young she had been beautiful, and, in spite of an expression in her eyes of hardness and distrust, which seemed habitual, she was still handsome. She was without a hat and wearing a house dress of decorous shades and in the extreme of fashion. Her black hair, built up in artificial waves, was heavy with brilliantine; her hands, covered deep with rings, and of an unnatural white, showed the most fastidious care. But her complexion was her own; and her skin, free from paint and powder, glowed with that healthy pink that is supposed to be the perquisite only of the simple life and a conscience undisturbed.

"I am Mrs. Earle," said the woman. "I wrote you that note. Will you please come this way?"

That she did not suppose he might not come that way was obvious, for, as she spoke, she turned her back on him and mounted the stairs. After an instant of hesitation, Wharton followed.

As well as his mind, his body was now acutely alive and vigilant. Both physically and mentally he moved on tiptoe. For whatever surprise, for whatever ambush might lie in wait, he was prepared. At the top of the stairs he found a wide hall along which on both sides were many doors. The one directly facing the stairs stood open. At one side of this the woman halted and with a gesture of the jewelled fingers invited him to enter.

THE FRAME-UP

"My sitting-room," she said. As Wharton remained motionless she substituted: "My office."

Peering into the room, Wharton found it suited to both titles. He saw comfortable chairs, vases filled with autumn leaves, in silver frames photographs, and between two open windows a business-like roller-top desk on which was a hand telephone. In plain sight through the windows he beheld the garage and behind it the tops of trees. To summon Rumson, to keep in touch with Nolan, he need only step to one of these windows and beckon. The strategic position of the room appealed, and with a bow of the head he passed in front of his hostess and entered it. He continued to take note of his surroundings.

He now saw that from the office in which he stood doors led to rooms adjoining. These doors were shut, and he determined swiftly that before the interview began he first must know what lay behind them. Mrs. Earle had followed and, as she entered, closed the door.

"No!" said Wharton.

It was the first time he had spoken. For an instant the woman hesitated, regarding him thoughtfully, and then without resentment pulled the door open. She came toward him swiftly, and he was conscious of the rustle of

THE FRAME-UP

silk and the stirring of perfumes. At the open door she cast a frown of disapproval and then, with her face close to his, spoke hurriedly in a whisper.

"A man brought a girl here to lunch," she said; "they've been here before. The girl claims the man told her he was going to marry her. Last night she found out he has a wife already, and she came here to-day meaning to make trouble. She brought a gun. They were in the room at the far end of the hall. George, the waiter, heard the two shots and ran down here to get me. No one else heard. These rooms are fixed to keep out noise, and the piano was going. We broke in and found them on the floor. The man was shot through the shoulder, the girl through the body. His story is that after she fired, in trying to get the gun from her, she shot herself—by accident. That's right, I guess. But the girl says they came here to die together —what the newspaper call a 'suicide pact'— because they couldn't marry, and that he first shot her, intending to kill her and then himself. That's silly. She framed it to get him. She missed him with the gun, so now she's trying to get him with this murder charge. I know her. If she'd been sober she wouldn't have shot him; she'd have blackmailed him. She's *that* sort. I know her, and——"

THE FRAME-UP

With an exclamation the district attorney broke in upon her. "And the man," he demanded eagerly; "was it *he* killed Banf?"

In amazement the woman stared. "Certainly *not!*" she said.

"Then what *has* this to do with Banf?"

"Nothing!" Her tone was annoyed, reproachful. "That was only to bring you here——"

His disappointment was so keen that it threatened to exhibit itself in anger. Recognizing this, before he spoke Wharton forced himself to pause. Then he repeated her words quietly.

"Bring me here?" he asked. "Why?"

The woman exclaimed impatiently: "So you could beat the police to it," she whispered. "So you could *hush it up!*"

The surprised laugh of the man was quite real. It bore no resentment or pose. He was genuinely amused. Then the dignity of his office, tricked and insulted, demanded to be heard. He stared at her coldly; his indignation was apparent.

"You have done extremely ill," he told her. "You know perfectly well you had no right to bring me up here; to drag me into a row in your road-house. 'Hush it up!'" he exclaimed hotly. This time his laugh was contemptuous and threatening.

THE FRAME-UP

"I'll show you how I'll hush it up!" He moved quickly to the open window.

"Stop!" commanded the woman. "You can't do that!"

She ran to the door.

Again he was conscious of the rustle of silk, of the stirring of perfumes.

He heard the key turn in the lock. It had come. It WAS a frame-up. There would be a scandal. And to save himself from it they would force him to "hush up" this other one. But, as to the outcome, in no way was he concerned. Through the window, standing directly below it, he had seen Nolan. In the sunlit yard the chauffeur, his cap on the back of his head, his cigarette drooping from his lips, was tossing the remnants of a sandwich to a circle of excited hens. He presented a picture of bored indolence, of innocent preoccupation. It was almost *too* well done.

Assured of a witness for the defense, he greeted the woman with a smile. "Why can't I do it?" he taunted.

She ran close to him and laid her hands on his arm. Her eyes were fixed steadily on his. "Because," she whispered, "the man who shot that girl—is your brother-in-law, Ham Cutler!"

For what seemed a long time Wharton stood looking down into the eyes of the woman, and the eyes never faltered. Later he recalled that in the sudden silence many noises disturbed the lazy hush of the Indian-summer afternoon: the rush of a motor-car on the Boston Road, the tinkle of the piano and the voice of the youth with the drugged eyes singing, "And you'll wear a simple gingham gown," from the yard below the cluck-cluck of the chickens and the cooing of pigeons.

His first thought was of his sister and of her children, and of what this bomb, hurled from the clouds, would mean to her. He thought of Cutler, at the height of his power and usefulness, by this one disreputable act dragged into the mire, of what disaster it might bring to the party, to himself.

If, as the woman invited, he helped to "hush it up," and Tammany learned the truth, it would make short work of him. It would say, for the murderer of Banf he had one law and for the rich brother-in-law, who had tried to kill the girl he deceived, another. But before he gave voice to his thoughts he recognized them as springing only from panic. They were of a part with the acts of men driven by sudden fear, and of which acts in their sane moments they would be incapable.

The shock of the woman's words had unsettled his traditions. Not only was he condemn-

THE FRAME-UP

ing a man unheard, but a man who, though he might dislike him, he had for years, for his private virtues, trusted and admired. The panic passed and with a confident smile he shook his head.

"I don't believe you," he said quietly.

The manner of the woman was equally calm, equally assured.

"Will you see her?" she asked.

"I'd rather see my brother-in-law," he answered.

The woman handed him a card.

"Doctor Muir took him to his private hospital," she said. "I loaned them my car because it's a limousine. The address is on that card. But," she added, "both your brother and Sammy—that's Sam Muir, the doctor—asked you wouldn't use the telephone; they're afraid of a leak."

Apparently Wharton did not hear her. As though it were "Exhibit A," presented in evidence by the defense, he was studying the card she had given him. He stuck it in his pocket.

"I'll go to him at once," he said.

To restrain or dissuade him, the woman made no sudden move. In level tones she said: "Your brother-in-law asked especially that you wouldn't do that until you'd fixed it with the girl. Your face is too well known. He's afraid

THE FRAME-UP

some one might find out where he is—and for a day or two no one must know that."

"This doctor knows it," retorted Wharton.

The suggestion seemed to strike Mrs. Earle as humorous. For the first time she laughed.

"Sammy!" she exclaimed. "He's a lobby-gow of mine. He's worked for me for years. I could send him up the river if I liked. He knows it." Her tone was convincing. "They both asked," she continued evenly, "you should keep off until the girl is out of the country, and fixed."

Wharton frowned thoughtfully.

And, observing this, the eyes of the woman showed that, so far, toward the unfortunate incident the attitude of the district attorney was to her most gratifying.

Wharton ceased frowning.

"How fixed?" he asked.

Mrs. Earle shrugged her shoulders.

"Cutler's idea is money," she said; "but, believe *me*, he's wrong. This girl is a vampire. She'll only come back to you for more. She'll keep on threatening to tell the wife, to tell the papers. The way to fix *her* is to throw a scare into her. And there's only one man can do that; there's only one man that can hush this thing up—that's you."

"When can I see her?" asked Wharton.

THE FRAME-UP

"Now," said the woman. "I'll bring her." Wharton could not suppress an involuntary start.

"Here?" he exclaimed.

For the shade of a second Mrs. Earle exhibited the slightest evidence of embarrassment.

"My room's in a mess," she explained; "and she's not hurt so much as Sammy said. He told her she was in bad just to keep her quiet until you got here."

Mrs. Earle opened one of the doors leading from the room. "I won't be a minute," she said. Quietly she closed the door behind her.

Upon her disappearance the manner of the district attorney underwent an abrupt change. He ran softly to the door opposite the one through which Mrs. Earle had passed, and pulled it open. But, if beyond it he expected to find an audience of eavesdroppers, he was disappointed. The room was empty—and bore no evidence of recent occupation. He closed the door, and, from the roller-top desk, snatching a piece of paper, scribbled upon it hastily. Wrapping the paper around a coin, and holding it exposed to view, he showed himself at the window. Below him, to an increasing circle of hens and pigeons, Nolan was still scattering crumbs. Without withdrawing his gaze from them, the chauffeur nodded. Wharton opened his hand and the note fell into the yard. Behind him he heard the murmur of voices, the sobs of a woman in pain, and the rattle of a door-knob. As from the window he turned quickly, he saw that toward the spot where his note had fallen Nolan was tossing the last remnants of his sandwich.

The girl who entered with Mrs. Earle, leaning on her and supported by her, was tall and fair. Around her shoulders her blond hair hung in disorder, and around her waist, under the kimono Mrs. Earle had thrown about her, were wrapped many layers of bandages. The girl moved unsteadily and sank into a chair.

In a hostile tone Mrs. Earle addressed her.

"Rose," she said, "this is the district attorney." To him she added: "She calls herself Rose Gerard."

One hand the girl held close against her side, with the other she brushed back the hair from her forehead. From half-closed eyes she stared at Wharton defiantly.

"Well," she challenged, "what about it?"

Wharton seated himself in front of the roller-top desk.

"Are you strong enough to tell me?" he asked.

His tone was kind, and this the girl seemed to resent.

THE FRAME-UP

"Don't you worry," she sneered, "I'm strong enough. Strong enough to tell *all* I know—to you, and to the papers, and to a jury—until I get justice." She clinched her free hand and feebly shook it at him. "*That's* what I'm going to get," she cried, her voice breaking hysterically, "justice."

From behind the arm-chair in which the girl half-reclined Mrs. Earle caught the eye of the district attorney and shrugged her shoulders.

"Just what *did* happen?" asked Wharton.

Apparently with an effort the girl pulled herself together.

"I first met your brother-in-law—" she began.

Wharton interrupted quietly.

"Wait!" he said. "You are not talking to me as anybody's brother-in-law, but as the district attorney."

The girl laughed vindictively.

"I don't wonder you're ashamed of him!" she jeered.

Again she began: "I first met Ham Cutler last May. He wanted to marry me then. He told me he was not a married man."

As her story unfolded, Wharton did not again interrupt; and speaking quickly, in abrupt, broken phrases, the girl brought her narrative to the moment when, as she claimed, Cutler had attempted to kill her. At this point a

THE FRAME-UP

knock at the locked door caused both the girl and her audience to start. Wharton looked at Mrs. Earle inquiringly, but she shook her head, and with a look at him also of inquiry, and of suspicion as well, opened the door.

With apologies her head waiter presented a letter.

"For Mr. Wharton," he explained, "from his chauffeur."

Wharton's annoyance at the interruption was most apparent. "What the devil—" he began.

He read the note rapidly, and with a frown of irritation raised his eyes to Mrs. Earle.

"He wants to go to New Rochelle for an inner tube," he said. "How long would it take him to get there and back?"

The hard and distrustful expression upon the face of Mrs. Earle, which was habitual, was now most strongly in evidence. Her eyes searched those of Wharton.

"Twenty minutes," she said.

"He can't go," snapped Wharton.

"Tell him," he directed the waiter, "to stay where he is. Tell him I may want to go back to the office any minute." He turned eagerly to the girl. "I'm sorry," he said. With impatience he crumpled the note into a ball and glanced about him. At his feet was a waste-

THE FRAME-UP

paper basket. Fixed upon him he saw, while pretending not to see, the eyes of Mrs. Earle burning with suspicion. If he destroyed the note, he knew suspicion would become certainty. Without an instant of hesitation, carelessly he tossed it intact into the waste-paper basket. Toward Rose Gerard he swung the revolving chair.

"Go on, please," he commanded.

The girl had now reached the climax of her story, but the eyes of Mrs. Earle betrayed the fact that her thoughts were elsewhere. With an intense and hungry longing, they were concentrated upon her own waste-paper basket.

The voice of the girl in anger and defiance recalled Mrs. Earle to the business of the moment.

"He tried to kill me," shouted Miss Rose. "And his shooting himself in the shoulder was a bluff. *That's* my story; that's the story I'm going to tell the judge"—her voice soared shrilly—"that's the story that's going to send your brother-in-law to Sing Sing!"

For the first time Mrs. Earle contributed to the general conversation.

"You talk like a fish," she said.

The girl turned upon her savagely.

"If he don't like the way I talk," she cried, "he can come across!"

THE FRAME-UP

Mrs. Earle exclaimed in horror. Virtuously her hands were raised in protest.

"Like hell he will!" she said. "You can't pull that under my roof!"

Wharton looked disturbed.

"'Come across'?" he asked.

"Come across?" mimicked the girl. "Send me abroad and keep me there. And I'll swear it was an accident. Twenty-five thousand, that's all I want. Cutler told me he was going to make you governor. He can't make you governor if he's in Sing Sing, can he? Ain't it worth twenty-five thousand to you to be governor? Come on," she jeered, "kick in!"

With a grave but untroubled voice Wharton addressed Mrs. Earle.

"May I use your telephone?" he asked. He did not wait for her consent, but from the desk lifted the hand telephone.

"Spring, three one hundred!" he said. He sat with his legs comfortably crossed, the stand of the instrument balanced on his knee, his eyes gazing meditatively at the yellow tree-tops.

If with apprehension both women started, if the girl thrust herself forward, and by the hand of Mrs. Earle was dragged back, he did not appear to know it.

"Police headquarters?" they heard him ask. "I want to speak to the commissioner. This is the district attorney."

THE FRAME-UP

In the pause that followed, as though to torment her, the pain in her side apparently returned, for the girl screamed sharply.

"Be still!" commanded the older woman. Breathless, across the top of the arm-chair, she was leaning forward. Upon the man at the telephone her eyes were fixed in fascination.

"Commissioner," said the district attorney, "this is Wharton speaking. A woman has made a charge of attempted murder to me against my brother-in-law, Hamilton Cutler. On account of our relationship, I want YOU to make the arrest. If there were any slip, and he got away, it might be said I arranged it. You will find him at the Winona apartments on the Southern Boulevard, in the private hospital of a Doctor Samuel Muir. Arrest them both. The girl who makes the charge is at Kessler's Café, on the Boston Post Road, just inside the city line. Arrest her too. She tried to blackmail me. I'll appear against her."

Wharton rose and addressed himself to Mrs. Earle.

"I'm sorry," he said, "but I had to do it. You might have known I could not hush it up. I am the only man who can't hush it up. The people of New York elected me to enforce the laws." Wharton's voice was raised to a loud pitch. It seemed unnecessarily loud. It was almost as though he were addressing another and more distant audience. "And," he continued, his voice still soaring, "even if my own family suffer, even if I suffer, even if I lose political promotion, those laws I will enforce!"

In the more conventional tone of every-day politeness, he added:

"May I speak to you outside, Mrs. Earle?"

But, as in silence that lady descended the stairs, the district attorney seemed to have forgotten what it was he wished to say.

It was not until he had seen his chauffeur arouse himself from apparently deep slumber and crank the car that he addressed her.

"That girl," he said, "had better go back to bed. My men are all around this house and, until the police come, will detain her."

He shook the jewelled fingers of Mrs. Earle warmly. "I thank you," he said; "I know you meant well. I know you wanted to help me, but"—he shrugged his shoulders—"my duty!"

As he walked down the driveway to his car his shoulders continued to move.

But Mrs. Earle did not wait to observe this phenomenon. Rid of his presence, she leaped, rather than ran, up the stairs and threw open the door of her office.

As she entered, two men followed her. One was a young man who held in his hand an open

THE FRAME-UP

note-book, the other was Tim Meehan, of Tammany. The latter greeted her with a shout.

"We heard everything he said!" he cried. His voice rose in torment. "An' we can't use a word of it! He acted just like we'd oughta knowed he'd act. He's HONEST! He's so damned honest he ain't human; he's a —— gilded saint!"

Mrs. Earle did not heed him. On her knees she was tossing to the floor the contents of the waste-paper basket. From them she snatched a piece of crumpled paper.

"Shut up!" she shouted. "Listen! His chauffeur brought him this." In a voice that quivered with indignation, that sobbed with anger, she read aloud:

"'As directed by your note from the window, I went to the booth and called up Mrs. Cutler's house and got herself on the phone. Your brother-in-law lunched at home to-day with her and the children and they are now going to the Hippodrome.

"'Stop, look, and listen! Back of the bar I see two men in a room, but they did not see me. One is Tim Meehan, the other is a stenographer. He is taking notes. Each of them has on the ear-muffs of a dictagraph. Looks like you'd better watch your step and not say nothing you don't want Tammany to print.'" The voice of Mrs. Earle rose in a shrill shriek.

THE FRAME-UP

"Him—a gilded saint?" she screamed; "you big stiff! He knew he was talking into a dictagraph all the time—and he double-crossed us!"

THE LOST HOUSE

The black square marks the position of the lost house

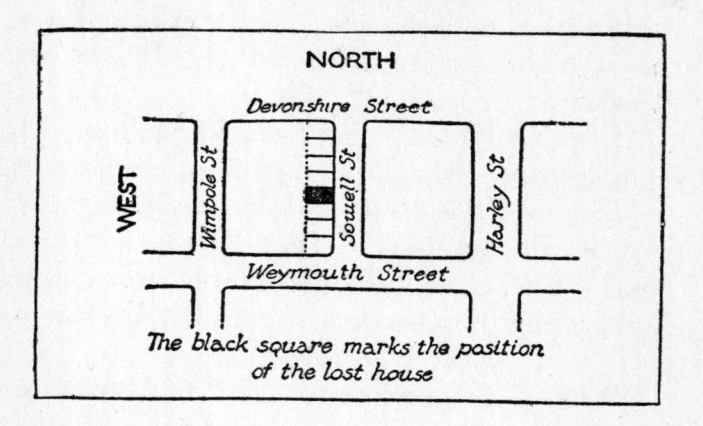

I

It was a dull day at the chancellery. His Excellency the American Ambassador was absent in Scotland, unveiling a bust to Bobby Burns, paid for by the numerous lovers of that poet in Pittsburg; the First Secretary was absent at Aldershot, observing a sham battle; the Military Attaché was absent at the Crystal Palace, watching a foot-ball match; the Naval Attaché was absent at the Duke of Deptford's, shooting pheasants; and at the Embassy, the Second Secretary, having lunched leisurely at the Ritz, was now alone, but prepared with his life to protect American interests. Accordingly, on the condition that the story should not be traced back to him, he had just confided a State secret to his young friend, Austin Ford, the London correspondent of the New York *Republic*.

"I will cable it," Ford reassured him, "as coming from a Hungarian diplomat, temporarily residing in Bloomsbury, while en route to his post in Patagonia. In that shape, not even your astute chief will suspect its real source. And further from the truth than that I refuse to go.

"What I dropped in to ask," he continued, "is whether the English are going to send over a polo team next summer to try to bring back the cup?"

"I've several other items of interest," suggested the Secretary.

"The week-end parties to which you have been invited," Ford objected, "can wait. Tell me first what chance there is for an international polo match."

"Polo," sententiously began the Second Secretary, who himself was a crackerjack at the game, "is a proposition of ponies! Men can be trained for polo. But polo ponies must be born. Without good ponies——"

THE LOST HOUSE

James, the page who guarded the outer walls of the chancellery, appeared in the doorway.

"Please, sir, a person," he announced, "with a note for the Ambassador. 'E *says* it's important."

"Tell him to leave it," said the Secretary. "Polo ponies——"

"Yes, sir," interrupted the page. "But 'e *won't* leave it, not unless he keeps the 'arf-crown."

"For Heaven's sake!" protested the Second Secretary, "then let him keep the half-crown. When I say polo ponies, I don't mean——"

James, although alarmed at his own temerity, refused to accept the dismissal.

"But, please, sir," he begged; "I think the 'arf-crown is for the Ambassador."

The astonished diplomat gazed with open eyes.

"You think—*what!*" he exclaimed.

James, upon the defensive, explained breathlessly.

"Because, sir," he stammered, "it was *inside* the note when it was thrown out of the window."

Ford had been sprawling in a soft leather chair in front of the open fire. With the privilege of an old school-fellow and college classmate, he had been jabbing the soft coal with his walking-stick, causing it to burst into tiny flames. His cigarette drooped from his lips, his hat was cocked over one eye; he was a picture of indifference, merging upon boredom. But at the words of the boy his attitude both of mind and body underwent an instant change. It was as though he were an actor, and the words "thrown from the window" were his cue. It was as though he were a dozing fox-terrier, and the voice of his master had whispered in his ear: "Sick 'em!"

For a moment, with benign reproach, the Second Secretary regarded the unhappy page, and then addressed him with laborious sarcasm.

"James," he said, "people do not communicate with ambassadors in notes wrapped around half-crowns and hurled from windows. That is the way one corresponds with an organ-grinder."

Ford sprang to his feet.

"And meanwhile," he exclaimed angrily, "the man will get away."

Without seeking permission, he ran past James, and through the empty outer offices. In two minutes he returned, herding before him an individual, seedy and soiled. In appearance the man suggested that in life his place was to support a sandwich-board. Ford reluctantly relinquished his hold upon a folded paper which he laid in front of the Secretary.

"This man," he explained, "picked that out

of the gutter in Sowell Street. It's not addressed to any one, so you read it!"

"I thought it was for the Ambassador!" said the Secretary.

The soiled person coughed deprecatingly, and pointed a dirty digit at the paper. "On the inside," he suggested. The paper was wrapped around a half-crown and folded in at each end. The diplomat opened it hesitatingly, but having read what was written, laughed.

"There's nothing in *that*," he exclaimed. He passed the note to Ford. The reporter fell upon it eagerly.

The note was written in pencil on an unruled piece of white paper. The handwriting was that of a woman. What Ford read was:

"I am a prisoner in the street on which this paper is found. The house faces east. I think I am on the top story. I was brought here three weeks ago. They are trying to kill me. My uncle, Charles Ralph Pearsall, is doing this to get my money. He is at Gerridge's Hotel in Craven Street, Strand. He will tell you I am insane. My name is Dosia Pearsall Dale. My home is at Dalesville, Kentucky, U. S. A. Everybody knows me there, and knows I am not insane. If you would save a life take this at once to the American Embassy, or to Scotland Yard. For God's sake, *help* me."

THE LOST HOUSE

When he had read the note, Ford continued to study it. Until he was quite sure his voice would not betray his interest, he did not raise his eyes.

"Why," he asked, "did you say that there's nothing in this?"

"Because," returned the diplomat conclusively, "we got a note like that, or nearly like it, a week ago, and——"

Ford could not restrain a groan. "And you never told me!"

"There wasn't anything to tell," protested the diplomat. "We handed it over to the police, and they reported there was nothing in it. They couldn't find the man at that hotel, and, of course, they couldn't find the house with no more to go on than——"

"And so," exclaimed Ford rudely, "they decided there was no man, and no house!"

"Their theory," continued the Secretary patiently, "is that the girl is confined in one of the numerous private sanatoriums in Sowell Street, that she *is* insane, that because she's under restraint she *imagines* the nurses are trying to kill her and that her relatives are after her money. Insane people are always thinking that. It's a very common delusion."

Ford's eyes were shining with a wicked joy.

THE LOST HOUSE

"So," he asked indifferently, "you don't intend to do anything further?"

"What do you *want* us to do?" cried his friend. "Ring every door-bell in Sowell Street, and ask the parlor-maid if they're murdering a lady on the top story?"

"Can I keep the paper?" demanded Ford.

"You can keep a copy of it," consented the Secretary. "But if you think you're on the track of a big newspaper sensation, I can tell you now you're not. That's the work of a crazy woman, or it's a hoax. You amateur detectives——"

Ford was already seated at the table, scribbling a copy of the message, and making marginal notes.

"Who brought the *first* paper?" he interrupted.

"A hansom-cab driver."

"What became of *him?*" snapped the amateur detective.

The Secretary looked inquiringly at James.

"'E drove away," said James.

"He drove away, did he?" roared Ford. "And that was a week ago! Ye gods! What about Dalesville, Kentucky? Did you cable any one there?"

The dignity of the diplomat was becoming ruffled.

THE LOST HOUSE

"We did not!" he answered. "If it wasn't true that her uncle was at that hotel, it was probably equally untrue that she had friends in America."

"But," retorted his friend, "you didn't forget to cable the State Department that you all went in your evening clothes to bow to the new King? You didn't neglect to cable that, did you?"

"The State Department," returned the Secretary, with withering reproof, "does not expect us to crawl over the roofs of houses and spy down chimneys to see if by any chance an American citizen is being murdered."

"Well," exclaimed Ford, leaping to his feet and placing his notes in his pocket, "fortunately, my paper expects me to do just that, and if it didn't, I'd do it anyway. And that is exactly what I am going to do now! Don't tell the others in the Embassy, and, for Heaven's sake, don't tell the police. Jimmy, get me a taxi. And you," he commanded, pointing at the one who had brought the note, "are coming with me to Sowell Street, to show me where you picked up that paper."

On the way to Sowell Street Ford stopped at a newspaper agency, and paid for the insertion that afternoon of the same advertisement in three newspapers. It read: "If hansom-cab driver who last week carried note, found in street, to American Embassy will mail his address to X. X. X., care of *Globe*, he will be rewarded."

From the nearest post-office he sent to his paper the following cable: "Query our local correspondent, Dalesville, Kentucky, concerning Dosia Pearsall Dale. Is she of sound mind, is she heiress. Who controls her money, what her business relations with her uncle, Charles Ralph Pearsall, what her present address. If any questions, say inquiries come from solicitors of Englishman who wants to marry her. Rush answer."

Sowell Street is a dark, dirty little thoroughfare, running for only one block, parallel to Harley Street. Like it, it is decorated with the brass plates of physicians and the red lamps of surgeons, but, just as the medical men in Harley Street, in keeping with that thoroughfare, are broad, open, and with nothing to conceal, so those of Sowell Street, like their hiding-place, shrink from observation, and their lives are as sombre, secret, and dark as the street itself.

Within two turns of it Ford dismissed the taxicab. Giving the soiled person a half-smoked cigarette, he told him to walk through Sowell Street, and when he reached the place where he had picked up the paper, to drop the cigarette as near that spot as possible. He

THE LOST HOUSE

then was to turn into Weymouth Street and wait until Ford joined him. At a distance of fifty feet Ford followed the man, and saw him, when in the middle of the block, without apparent hesitation, drop the cigarette. The house in front of which it fell was marked, like many others, by the brass plate of a doctor. As Ford passed it he hit the cigarette with his walking-stick, and drove it into an area. When he overtook the man, Ford handed him another cigarette. "To make sure," he said, "go back and drop this in the place you found the paper."

For a moment the man hesitated.

"I might as well tell you," Ford continued, "that I knocked that last cigarette so far from where you dropped it that you won't be able to use it as a guide. So, if you don't really know where you found the paper, you'll save my time by saying so."

Instead of being confused by the test, the man was amused by it. He laughed appreciatively.

"You've caught me out fair, governor," he admitted. "I wanted the 'arf-crown, and I dropped the cigarette as near the place as I could. But I can't do it again. It was this way," he explained. "I wasn't taking notice of the houses. I was walking along looking into the gutter for stumps. I see this paper wrapped about something round. 'It's a copper,' I thinks, 'jucked out of a winder to a organ-grinder.' I snatches it, and runs. I didn't take no time to look at the houses. But it wasn't so far from where I showed you; about the middle house in the street and on the left-'and side."

Ford had never considered the man as a serious element in the problem. He believed him to know as little of the matter as he professed to know. But it was essential he should keep that little to himself.

"No one will pay you for talking," Ford pointed out, "and I'll pay you to keep quiet. So, if you say nothing concerning that note, at the end of two weeks, I'll leave two pounds for you with James, at the Embassy."

The man, who believed Ford to be an agent of the police, was only too happy to escape on such easy terms. After Ford had given him a pound on account, they parted.

From Wimpole Street the amateur detective went to the nearest public telephone and called up Gerridge's Hotel. He considered his first step should be to discover if Mr. Pearsall was at that hotel, or had ever stopped there. When the 'phone was answered, he requested that a message be delivered to Mr. Pearsall.

THE LOST HOUSE

"Please tell him," he asked, "that the clothes he ordered are ready to try on."

He was informed that no one by that name was at the hotel. In a voice of concern Ford begged to know when Mr. Pearsall had gone away, and had he left any address.

"He was with you three weeks ago," Ford insisted. "He's an American gentleman, and there was a lady with him. She ordered a riding-habit of us: the same time he was measured for his clothes."

After a short delay, the voice from the hotel replied that no one of the name of Pearsall had been at the hotel that winter.

In apparent great disgust Ford rang off, and took a taxicab to his rooms in Jermyn Street. There he packed a suit-case and drove to Gerridge's. It was a quiet, respectable, "old-established" house in Craven Street, a thoroughfare almost entirely given over to small family hotels much frequented by Americans.

After he had registered and had left his bag in his room, Ford returned to the office, and in an assured manner asked that a card on which he had written "Henry W. Page, Dalesville, Kentucky," should be taken to Mr. Pearsall.

In a tone of obvious annoyance the proprietor returned the card, saying that there was no one of that name in the hotel, and added

THE LOST HOUSE

that no such person had ever stopped there. Ford expressed the liveliest distress.

"He *told* me I'd find him here," he protested, "he and his niece." With the garrulousness of the American abroad, he confided his troubles to the entire staff of the hotel. "We're from the same town," he explained. "That's why I *must* see him. He's the only man in London I know, and I've spent all my money. He said he'd give me some he owes me, as soon as I reached London. If I can't get it, I'll have to go home by Wednesday's steamer. And," he complained bitterly, "I haven't seen the Zoo, nor the Tower, nor Westminster Abbey."

In a moment, Ford's anxiety to meet Mr. Pearsall was apparently lost in a wave of self-pity. In his disappointment he became an appealing, pathetic figure.

Real detectives and rival newspaper men, even while they admitted Ford obtained facts that were denied them, claimed that they were given him from charity. Where they bullied, browbeat, and administered a third degree, Ford was embarrassed, deprecatory, an earnest, ingenuous, wide-eyed child. What he called his "working" smile begged of you not to be cross with him. His simplicity was apparently so hopeless, his confidence in whomever he addressed so complete, that often even the man

THE LOST HOUSE

he was pursuing felt for him a pitying contempt. Now as he stood uncertainly in the hall of the hotel, his helplessness moved the proud lady clerk to shake her cylinders of false hair sympathetically, the German waiters to regard his predicament with respect; even the proprietor, Mr. Gerridge himself, was ill at ease. Ford returned to his room, on the second floor of the hotel, and sat down on the edge of the bed.

In connecting Pearsall with Gerridge's, both the police and himself had failed. Of this there were three possible explanations: that the girl who wrote the letter was in error, that the letter was a hoax, that the proprietor of the hotel, for some reason, was protecting Pearsall, and had deceived both Ford and Scotland Yard. On the other hand, without knowing why the girl believed Pearsall would be found at Gerridge's, it was reasonable to assume that in so thinking she had been purposely misled. The question was, should he or not dismiss Gerridge's as a possible clew, and at once devote himself to finding the house in Sowell Street? He decided, for the moment at least, to leave Gerridge's out of his calculations, but, as an excuse for returning there, to still retain his room. He at once started toward Sowell Street, and in order to find out if any one from the hotel were following him, he set forth on foot. As soon as he made

THE LOST HOUSE

sure he was not spied upon, he covered the remainder of the distance in a cab.

He was acting on the supposition that the letter was no practical joke, but a genuine cry for help. Sowell Street was a scene set for such an adventure. It was narrow, mean-looking, the stucco house-fronts, soot-stained, cracked, and uncared-for, the steps broken and unwashed. As he entered it a cold rain was falling, and a yellow fog that rolled between the houses added to its dreariness.

It was now late in the afternoon, and so overcast the sky that in many rooms the gas was lit and the curtains drawn.

The girl, apparently from observing the daily progress of the sun, had written she was on the west side of the street and, she believed, in an upper story. The man who picked up the note had said he had found it opposite the houses in the middle of the block. Accordingly, Ford proceeded on the supposition that the entire east side of the street, the lower stories of the west side, and the houses at each end were eliminated. The three houses in the centre of the row were outwardly alike. They were of four stories. Each was the residence of a physician, and in each, in the upper stories, the blinds were drawn. From the front there was nothing to be learned, and in the hope that the

THE LOST HOUSE

rear might furnish some clew, Ford hastened to Wimpole Street, in which the houses to the east backed upon those to the west in Sowell Street. These houses were given over to furnished lodgings, and under the pretext of renting chambers, it was easy for Ford to enter them, and from the apartments in the rear to obtain several hasty glimpses of the backs of the three houses in Sowell Street. But neither from this view-point did he gather any fact of interest. In one of the three houses in Sowell Street iron bars were fastened across the windows of the fourth floor, but in private sanatoriums this was neither unusual nor suspicious. The bars might cover the windows of a nursery to prevent children from falling out, or the room of some timid householder with a lively fear of burglars.

In a quarter of an hour Ford was again back in Sowell Street no wiser than when he had entered it. From the outside, at least, the three houses under suspicion gave no sign. In the problem before him there was one point that Ford found difficult to explain. It was the only one that caused him to question if the letter was genuine. What puzzled him was this: Why, if the girl were free to throw *two* notes from the window, did she not throw them out by the dozen? If she were able to reach a window, opening on the street, why did she not

THE LOST HOUSE

call for help? Why did she not, by hurling out every small article the room contained, by screams, by breaking the window-panes, attract a crowd, and, through it, the police? That she had not done so seemed to show that only at rare intervals was she free from restraint, or at liberty to enter the front room that opened on the street. Would it be equally difficult, Ford asked himself, for one in the street to communicate with her? What signal could he give that would draw an answering signal from the girl?

Standing at the corner, hidden by the pillars of a portico, the water dripping from his raincoat, Ford gazed long and anxiously at the blank windows of the three houses. Like blind eyes staring into his, they told no tales, betrayed no secret. Around him the commonplace life of the neighborhood proceeded undisturbed. Somewhere concealed in the single row of houses a girl was imprisoned, her life threatened; perhaps even at that moment she was facing her death. While, on either side, shut from her by the thickness only of a brick wall, people were talking, reading, making tea, preparing the evening meal, or, in the street below, hurrying by, intent on trivial errands. Hansom cabs, prowling in search of a fare, passed through the street where a woman was being robbed of a fortune, the drivers occupied only with thoughts of a possible shilling; a housemaid with a jug in her hand and a shawl over her bare head, hastened to the near-by public-house; the postman made his rounds, and delivered comic postal-cards; a policeman, shedding water from his shining cape, halted, gazed severely at the sky, and, unconscious of the crime that was going forward within the sound of his own footsteps, continued stolidly into Wimpole Street.

A hundred plans raced through Ford's brain; he would arouse the street with a false alarm of fire and lead the firemen, with the tale of a smoking chimney, to one of the three houses; he would feign illness, and, taking refuge in one of them, at night would explore the premises; he would impersonate a detective, and insist upon his right to search for stolen property. As he rejected these and a dozen schemes as fantastic, his brain and eyes were still alert for any chance advantage that the street might offer. But the minutes passed into an hour, and no one had entered any of the three houses, no one had left them. In the lower stories, from behind the edges of the blinds, lights appeared, but of the life within there was no sign. Until he hit upon a plan of action, Ford felt there was no longer anything to be gained by remaining in Sowell Street.

Already the answer to his cable might have

THE LOST HOUSE

arrived at his rooms; at Gerridge's he might still learn something of Pearsall. He decided to revisit both these places, and, while so engaged, to send from his office one of his assistants to cover the Sowell Street houses. He cast a last, reluctant look at the closed blinds, and moved away. As he did so, two itinerant musicians dragging behind them a small street piano on wheels turned the corner, and, as the rain had now ceased, one of them pulled the oil-cloth covering from the instrument and, seating himself on a camp-stool at the curb, opened the piano. After a discouraged glance at the darkened windows, the other, in a hoarse, strident tenor, to the accompaniment of the piano, began to sing. The voice of the man was raucous, penetrating. It would have reached the recesses of a tomb.

"She sells sea-shells on the sea-shore," the vocalist wailed. "The shells she sells are sea-shells, I'm sure."

The effect was instantaneous. A window was flung open, and an indignant householder with one hand frantically waved the musicians away, and with the other threw them a copper coin.

At the same moment Ford walked quickly to the piano and laid a half-crown on top of it.

"Follow me to Harley Street," he commanded. "Don't hurry. Take your time. I want you to help me in a sort of practical joke. It's worth a sovereign to you."

He passed on quickly. When he glanced behind him, he saw the two men, fearful lest the promised fortune might escape them, pursuing him at a trot. At Harley Street they halted, breathless.

"How long," Ford demanded of the one who played the piano, "will it take you to learn the accompaniment to a new song?"

"While you're whistling it," answered the man eagerly.

"And I'm as quick at a tune as him," assured the other anxiously. "I can sing——"

"You cannot," interrupted Ford. "I'm going to do the singing myself. Where is there a public-house near here where we can hire a back room, and rehearse?"

Half an hour later, Ford and the piano-player entered Sowell Street dragging the piano behind them. The amateur detective still wore his rain-coat, but his hat he had exchanged for a cap, and, instead of a collar, he had knotted around his bare neck a dirty kerchief. At the end of the street they halted, and in some embarrassment Ford raised his voice in the chorus of a song well known in the music-halls. It was a very good voice, much too good for "open-air work," as his companion had already

THE LOST HOUSE

assured him, but, what was of chief importance to Ford, it carried as far as he wished it to go. Already in Wimpole Street four coins of the realm, flung to him from the highest windows, had testified to its power. From the end of Sowell Street Ford moved slowly from house to house until he was directly opposite the three in one of which he believed the girl to be.

"We will try the *new* songs here," he said.

Night had fallen, and, except for the gas-lamps, the street was empty, and in such darkness that even without his disguise Ford ran no risk of recognition. His plan was not new. It dated from the days of Richard the Lion-hearted. But if the prisoner were alert and intelligent, even though she could make no answer, Ford believed through his effort she would gain courage, would grasp that from the outside a friend was working toward her. All he knew of the prisoner was that she came from Kentucky. Ford fixed his eyes on the houses opposite, and cleared his throat. The man struck the opening chords, and in a high barytone, and in a cockney accent that made even the accompanist grin, Ford lifted his voice.

"The sun shines bright on my old Kentucky home," he sang; "'tis summer, and the darkies are gay."

He finished the song, but there was no sign.

THE LOST HOUSE

For all the impression he had made upon Sowell Street, he might have been singing in his chambers. "And now the other," commanded Ford. The house-fronts echoed back the cheering notes of "Dixie." Again Ford was silent, and again the silence answered him. The accompanist glared disgustedly at the darkened windows.

"They don't know them songs," he explained professionally. "Give 'em 'Mollie Married the Marquis.'"

"I'll sing the first one again," said Ford.

Once more he broke into the pathetic cadences of the "Old Kentucky Home." But there was no response. He was beginning to feel angry, absurd. He believed he had wasted precious moments, and, even as he sang, his mind was already working upon a new plan. The song ceased, unfinished.

"It's no use!" he exclaimed. Remembering himself, he added: "We'll try the next street."

But even as he spoke he leaped forward. Coming apparently from nowhere, something white sank through the semi-darkness and fell at his feet. It struck the pavement directly in front of the middle one of the three houses. Ford fell upon it and clutched it in both hands. It was a woman's glove. Ford raced back to the piano.

In a cockney accent that made even the accompanist
grin, Ford lifted his voice.

THE LOST HOUSE

"Once more," he cried, "play 'Dixie'!"

He shouted out the chorus exultantly, triumphantly. Had he spoken it in words, the message could not have carried more clearly.

Ford now believed he had found the house, found the woman, and was eager only to get rid of his companion and, in his own person, return to Sowell Street. But, lest the man might suspect there was in his actions something more serious than a practical joke, he forced himself to sing the new songs in three different streets. Then, pretending to tire of his prank, he paid the musician and left him. He was happy, exultant, tingling with excitement. Good-luck had been with him, and, hoping that Gerridge's might yet yield some clew to Pearsall, he returned there. Calling up the London office of the *Republic*, he directed that one of his assistants, an English lad named Cuthbert, should at once join him at that hotel. Cuthbert was but just out of Oxford. He wished to become a writer of fiction, and, as a means of seeing many kinds of life at first hand, was in training as a "Pressman." His admiration for Ford amounted to almost hero-worship; and he regarded an "assignment" with his chief as a joy and an honor. Full of enthusiasm, and as soon as a taxicab could bring him, he arrived at Gerridge's, where, in a corner of the deserted

THE LOST HOUSE

coffee-room, Ford explained the situation. Until he could devise a way to enter the Sowell Street house. Cuthbert was to watch over it.

"The number of the house is forty," Ford told him; "the name on the door-plate, Dr. Prothero. Find out everything you can about him without letting any one catch you at it. Better begin at the nearest chemist's. Say you are on the verge of a nervous breakdown, and ask the man to mix you a sedative, and recommend a physician. Show him Prothero's name and address on a piece of paper, and say Prothero has been recommended to you as a specialist on nervous troubles. Ask what he thinks of him. Get him to talk. Then visit the tradespeople and the public-houses in the neighborhood, and say you are from some West End shop where Prothero wants to open an account. They may talk, especially if his credit is bad. And, if you find out enough about him to give me a working basis, I'll try to get into the house to-night. Meanwhile, I'm going to make another quick search of this hotel for Pearsall. I'm not satisfied he has not been here. For why should Miss Dale, with all the hotels in London to choose from, have named this particular one, unless she had good reason for it? Now, go, and meet me in an hour in Sowell Street."

THE LOST HOUSE

Cuthbert was at the door when he remembered he had brought with him from the office Ford's mail and cablegrams. Among the latter was the one for which Ford had asked.

"Wait," he commanded. "This is about the girl. You had better know what it says."

The cable read:

"Girl orphan, Dalesville named after her family, for three generations mill-owners, father died four years ago, Pearsall brother-in-law made executor and guardian of niece until she is twenty-one, which will be in three months. Girl well known, extremely popular, lived Dalesville until last year, when went abroad with uncle, since then reports of melancholia and nervous prostration, before that health excellent—no signs insanity—none in family. Be careful how handle Pearsall, was doctor, gave up practice to look after estate, is prominent in local business and church circles, best reputation, beware libel."

For the benefit of Cuthbert, Ford had been reading the cable aloud. The last paragraph seemed especially to interest him, and he read it twice, the second time slowly, and emphasizing the word "doctor."

"A doctor!" he repeated. "Do you see where that leads us? It may explain several things. The girl was in good health until she went abroad with her uncle, and he is a medical man."

The eyes of Cuthbert grew wide with excitement.

"You mean poison!" he whispered. "Slow poison!"

"Beware libel," laughed Ford nervously, his own eyes lit with excitement. "Suppose," he exclaimed, "he has been using arsenic? He would have many opportunities, and it's colorless, tasteless; and arsenic would account for her depression and melancholia. The time when he must turn over her money is very near, and, suppose he has spent the money, speculated with it, and lost it, or that he still has it and wants to keep it? In three months she will be of age, and he must make an accounting. The arsenic does not work fast enough. So what does he do? To save himself from exposure, or to keep the money, he throws her into this private sanatorium, to make away with her."

Ford had been talking in an eager whisper. While he spoke his cigar had ceased to burn, and, to light it, from a vase on the mantel he took a spill, one of those spirals of paper that in English hotels, where the proprietor is of a frugal mind, are still used to prevent extravagance in matches. Ford lit the spill at

THE LOST HOUSE

the coal fire, and with his cigar puffed at the flame. As he did so the paper unrolled. To the astonishment of Cuthbert, Ford clasped it in both hands, blotted out the tiny flame, and, turning quickly to a table, spread out the charred paper flat. After one quick glance, Ford ran to the fireplace, and, seizing a handful of the spills, began rapidly to unroll them. Then he turned to Cuthbert and, without speaking, showed him the charred spill. It was a scrap torn from the front page of a newspaper. The half-obliterated words at which Ford pointed were *Dalesville Cour*——

"His torn paper!" said Ford. "*The Dalesville Courier.* Pearsall *has* been in this hotel!"

He handed another spill to Cuthbert.

"From that one," said Ford, "we get the date, December 3. Allowing three weeks for the newspaper to reach London, Pearsall must have seen it just three weeks ago, just when Miss Dale says he was in the hotel. The landlord has lied to me."

Ford rang for a waiter, and told him to ask Mr. Gerridge to come to the smoking-room.

As Cuthbert was leaving it, Gerridge was entering it, and Ford was saying:

"It seems you've been lying to the police and to me. Unless you desire to be an accessory to a murder, you had better talk, and talk quick!"

An hour later Ford passed slowly through Sowell Street in a taxicab, and, finding Cuthbert on guard, signalled him to follow. In Wimpole Street the cab drew up to the curb, and Cuthbert entered it.

"I have found Pearsall," said Ford. "He is in No. 40 with Prothero."

He then related to Cuthbert what had happened. Gerridge had explained that when the police called, his first thought was to protect the good name of his hotel. He had denied any knowledge of Pearsall only because he no longer was a guest, and, as he supposed Pearsall had passed out of his life, he saw no reason, why, through an arrest and a scandal, his hotel should be involved. Believing Ford to be in the secret service of the police, he was now only too anxious to clear himself of suspicion by telling all he knew. It was but little. Pearsall and his niece had been at the hotel for three days. During that time the niece, who appeared to be an invalid, remained in her room. On the evening of the third day, while Pearsall was absent, a call from him had come for her by telephone, on receiving which Miss Dale had at once left the hotel, apparently in great agitation. That night she did

THE LOST HOUSE

not return, but in the morning Pearsall came to collect his and her luggage and to settle his account. He explained that a woman relative living at the Langham Hotel had been taken suddenly ill, and had sent for him and his niece. Her condition had been so serious that they had remained with her all night, and his niece still was at her bedside. The driver of a four-wheeler, who for years had stood on the cab-rank in front of Gerridge's, had driven Pearsall to the Langham. This man was at the moment on the rank, and from him Ford learned what he most wished to know.

The cabman remembered Pearsall, and having driven him to the Langham, for the reason that immediately after setting him down there, and while "crawling" for a fare in Portland Place, a whistle from the Langham had recalled him, and the same luggage that had just been taken from the top of his cab was put back on it, and he was directed by the porter of the hotel to take it to a house in Sowell Street. There a man-servant had helped him unload the trunks and had paid him his fare. The cabman did not remember the number of the house, but knew it was on the west side of the street and in the middle of the block.

Having finished with Gerridge and the cab-

THE LOST HOUSE

man, Ford had at once gone to the Langham Hotel, where, as he anticipated, nothing was known of Pearsall or his niece, or of any invalid lady. But the hall-porter remembered the American gentleman who had driven up with many pieces of luggage, and who, although it was out of season, and many suites in the hotel were vacant, had found none to suit him. He had then set forth on foot, having left word that his trunks be sent after him. The address he gave was a house in Sowell Street.

The porter recalled the incident because he and the cabman had grumbled over the fact that in five minutes they had twice to handle the same boxes.

"It is pretty evident," said Ford, "what Pearsall had in mind, but chance was against him. He thought when he had unloaded his trunks at the Langham and dismissed the cabman he had destroyed the link connecting him with Gerridge's. He could not foresee that the same cabman would be loitering in the neighborhood. He should have known that four-wheelers are not as plentiful as they once were; and he should have given that particular one more time to get away. His idea in walking to the Sowell Street house was obviously to prevent the new cabman from seeing him enter it. But, just where he thought he was clever, was just where he tripped. If he had remained with his trunks he would have seen that the cabman was the same one who had brought them and him from Craven Street, and he would have given any other address in London than the one he did.

"And now," said Ford, "that we have Pearsall where we want him, tell me what you have learned about Prothero?"

Cuthbert smiled importantly, and produced a piece of paper scribbled over with notes.

"Prothero," he said, "seems to be *this* sort of man. If he made your coffee for you, before you tasted it, you'd like him to drink a cup of it first."

II

"Prothero," said Cuthbert, "is a man of mystery. As soon as I began asking his neighbors questions, I saw he was of interest and that I was of interest. I saw they did not believe I was an agent of a West End shop, but a detective. So they wouldn't talk at all, or else they talked freely. And from one of them, a chemist named Needham, I got all I wanted. He's had a lawsuit against Prothero, and hates him. Prothero got him to invest in a medicine to cure the cocaine habit. Need-

THE LOST HOUSE

ham found the cure was no cure, but cocaine disguised. He sued for his money, and during the trial the police brought in Prothero's record. Needham let me copy it, and it seems to embrace every crime except treason. The man is a Russian Jew. He was arrested and prosecuted in Warsaw, Vienna, Berlin, Belgrade; all over Europe, until finally the police drove him to America. There he was an editor of an anarchist paper, a blackmailer, a 'doctor' of hypnotism, a clairvoyant, and a professional bigamist. His game was to open rooms as a clairvoyant, and advise silly women how to invest their money. When he found out which of them had the *most* money, he would marry her, take over her fortune, and skip. In Chicago, he was tried for poisoning one wife, and the trial brought out the fact that two others had died under suspicious circumstances, and that there were three more unpoisoned but anxious to get back their money. He was sentenced to ten years for bigamy, but pardoned because he was supposed to be insane, and dying. Instead of dying, he opened a sanatorium in New York to cure victims of the drug habit. In reality, it was a sort of high-priced opium-den. The place was raided, and he jumped his bail and came to this country. Now he is running this private hospital

THE LOST HOUSE

in Sowell Street. Needham says it's a secret rendezvous for dope fiends. But they are very high-class dope fiends, who are willing to pay for seclusion, and the police can't get at him. I may add that he's tall and muscular, with a big black beard, and hands that could strangle a bull. In Chicago, during the poison trial, the newspapers called him 'the Modern Bluebeard.'"

For a short time Ford was silent. But, in the dark corner of the cab, Cuthbert could see that his cigar was burning briskly.

"Your friend seems a nice chap," said Ford at last. "Calling on him will be a real pleasure. I especially like what you say about his hands."

"I have a plan," began the assistant timidly, "a plan to get you into the house—if you don't mind my making suggestions?"

"Not at all!" exclaimed his chief heartily. "Get me into the house by all means; that's what we're here for. The fact that I'm to be poisoned or strangled after I get there mustn't discourage us."

"I thought," said Cuthbert, "I might stand guard outside, while you got in as a dope fiend."

Ford snorted indignantly.

"Do I *look* like a dope fiend?" he protested.

The voice of the assistant was one of discouragement.

"You certainly do not," he exclaimed regretfully. "But it's the only plan I could think of."

"It seems to me," said his chief testily, "that you are not so very healthy-looking yourself. What's the matter with *your* getting inside as a dope fiend and *my* standing guard?"

"But I wouldn't know what to do after I got inside," complained the assistant, "and you would. You are so clever."

The expression of confidence seemed to flatter Ford.

"I might do this," he said. "I might pretend I was recovering from a heavy spree, and ask to be taken care of until I am sober. Or I could be a very good imitation of a man on the edge of a nervous breakdown. I haven't been five years in the newspaper business without knowing all there is to know about nerves. That's it!" he cried. "I will do that! And if Mr. Bluebeard Svengali, the Strangler of Paris person, won't take me in as a patient, we'll come back with a couple of axes and *break* in. But we'll try the nervous breakdown first, and we'll try it now. I will be a naval officer," declared Ford. "I made

THE LOST HOUSE

the round-the-world cruise with our fleet as a correspondent, and I know enough sea slang to fool a medical man. I am a naval officer whose nerves have gone wrong. I have heard of his sanatorium through— How," asked Ford sharply, "have I heard of his sanatorium?"

"You saw his advertisement in the *Daily World*," prompted Cuthbert. "'Home of convalescents; mental and nervous troubles cured.'"

"And," continued Ford, "I have come to him for rest and treatment. My name is Lieutenant Henry Grant. I arrived in London two weeks ago on the *Mauretania*. But my name was not on the passenger-list, because I did not want the Navy Department to know I was taking my leave abroad. I have been stopping at my own address in Jermyn Street, and my references are yourself, the Embassy, and my landlord. You will telephone him at once that, if any one asks after Henry Grant, he is to say what you tell him to say. And if any one sends for Henry Grant's clothes, he is to send *my* clothes."

"But you don't expect to be in there as long as that?" exclaimed Cuthbert.

"I do not," said Ford. "But, if he takes me in, I must make a bluff of sending for my things. No; either I will be turned out in five minutes, or if he accepts me as a patient I will be there until midnight. If I cannot get the girl out of the house by midnight, it will mean that I can't get out myself, and you had better bring the police and the coroner."

"Do you mean it?" asked Cuthbert.

"I most certainly do!" exclaimed Ford. "Until twelve I want a chance to get this story exclusively for our paper. If she is not free by then it means I have fallen down on it, and you and the police are to begin to batter in the doors."

The two young men left the cab, and at some distance from each other walked to Sowell Street. At the house of Dr. Prothero, Ford stopped and rang the bell. From across the street Cuthbert saw the door open and the figure of a man of almost gigantic stature block the doorway. For a moment he stood there, and then Cuthbert saw him step to one side, saw Ford enter the house and the door close upon him. Cuthbert at once ran to a telephone, and, having instructed Ford's landlord as to the part he was to play, returned to Sowell Street. There, in a state nearly approaching a genuine nervous breakdown, he continued his vigil.

Even without his criminal record to cast a glamour over him, Ford would have found Dr. Prothero a disturbing person. His size was enormous, his eyes piercing, sinister, unblinking, and the hands that could strangle a bull, and with which, as though to control himself, he continually pulled at his black beard, were gigantic, of a deadly white, with fingers long and prehensile. In his manner he had all the suave insolence of the Oriental and the suspicious alertness of one constantly on guard, but also, as Ford at once noted, of one wholly without fear. He had not been over a moment in his presence before the reporter felt that to successfully lie to such a man might be counted as a triumph.

Prothero opened the door into a little office leading off the hall, and switched on the electric lights. For some short time, without any effort to conceal his suspicion, he stared at Ford in silence.

"Well?" he said, at last. His tone was a challenge.

Ford had already given his assumed name and profession, and he now ran glibly into the story he had planned. He opened his cardcase and looked into it doubtfully.

"I find I have no card with me," he said; "but I am, as I told you, Lieutenant Grant, of the United States Navy. I am all right physically, except for my nerves. They've played me a queer trick. If the facts get out

THE LOST HOUSE

at home, it might cost me my commission. So I've come over here for treatment."

"Why to *me?*" asked Prothero.

"I saw by your advertisement," said the reporter, "that you treated for nervous mental troubles. Mine is an illusion," he went on. "I see things, or, rather, always one thing—a battle-ship coming at us head on. For the last year I've been executive officer of the *Kearsarge*, and the responsibility has been too much for me."

"You see a battle-ship?" inquired the Jew.

"A phantom battle-ship," Ford explained, "a sort of *Flying Dutchman*. The time I saw it I was on the bridge, and I yelled and telegraphed the engine-room. I brought the ship to a full stop, and backed her. But it was dirty weather, and the error was passed over. After that, when I saw the thing coming I did nothing. But each time I think it is real." Ford shivered slightly and glanced about him. 'Some day," he added fatefully, "it *will* be real, and I will *not* signal, and the ship will sink!"

In silence, Prothero observed his visitor closely. The young man seemed sincere, genuine. His manner was direct and frank. He looked the part he had assumed, and he spoke as one used to authority.

THE LOST HOUSE

"My fees are large," said the Russian.

At this point, had Ford, regardless of terms, exhibited a hopeful eagerness to at once close with him, the Jew would have shown him the door. But Ford was on guard, and well aware that a lieutenant in the navy had but few guineas to throw away on medicines. He made a movement as though to withdraw.

"Then I am afraid," he said, "I must go somewhere else."

His reluctance apparently only partially satisfied the Jew.

Ford adopted opposite tactics. He was never without ready money. His paper saw to it that in its interests he was always able at any moment to pay for a special train across Europe, or to bribe the entire working staff of a cable office. From his breast-pocket he took a blue linen envelope, and allowed the Jew to see that it was filled with twenty-pound notes.

"I have means outside my pay," said Ford. "I would give almost any price to the man who can cure me."

The eyes of the Russian flashed avariciously.

"I will arrange the terms to suit you," he exclaimed. "Your case interests me. Do you see this—mirage only at sea?"

"In any open place," Ford assured him.

"In a park or public square, but of course most frequently at sea."

The quack waved his great hands as though brushing aside a curtain.

"I will remove the illusion," he said, "and give you others more pretty." He smiled meaningly—an evil, leering smile. "When will you come?" he asked.

Ford glanced about him nervously.

"I shall stay now," he said. "I confess, in the streets and in my lodgings I am frightened. You give me confidence. I want to stay near you. I feel safe with you. If you will give me writing-paper, I will send for my things."

For a moment the Jew hesitated, and then motioned to a desk. As Ford wrote, Prothero stood near him, and the reporter knew that over his shoulder the Jew was reading what he wrote. Ford gave him the note, unsealed, and asked that it be forwarded at once to his lodgings.

"To-morrow," he said, "I will call up our Embassy, and give my address to our Naval Attaché."

"I will attend to that," said Prothero. "From now you are in my hands, and you can communicate with the outside only through me. You are to have absolute rest—no books, no letters, no papers. And you will be fed

THE LOST HOUSE

from a spoon. I will explain my treatment later. You will now go to your room, and you will remain there until you are a well man."

Ford had no wish to be at once shut off from the rest of the house. The odor of cooking came through the hall, and seemed to offer an excuse for delay.

"I smell food," he laughed. "And I'm terrifically hungry. Can't I have a farewell dinner before you begin feeding me from a spoon?"

The Jew was about to refuse, but, with his guilty knowledge of what was going forward in the house, he could not be too sure of those he allowed to enter it. He wanted more time to spend in studying this new patient, and the dinner-table seemed to offer a place where he could do so without the other suspecting he was under observation.

"My associate and I were just about to dine," he said. "You will wait here until I have another place laid, and you can join us."

He departed, walking heavily down the hall, but almost at once Ford, whose ears were alert for any sound, heard him returning, approaching stealthily on tiptoe. If by this manœuvre the Jew had hoped to discover his patient in some indiscretion, he was unsuccessful, for he found Ford standing just where he had left him, with his back turned to the door, and gazing with apparent interest at a picture on the wall. The significance of the incident was not lost upon the intruder. It taught him he was still under surveillance, and that he must bear himself warily. Murmuring some excuse for having returned, the Jew again departed, and in a few minutes Ford heard his voice, and that of another man, engaged in low tones in what was apparently an eager argument.

Only once was the voice of the other man raised sufficiently for Ford to distinguish his words. "He is an American," protested the voice; "that makes it worse."

Ford guessed that the speaker was Pearsall, and that against his admittance to the house he was making earnest protest. A door, closing with a bang, shut off the argument, but within a few minutes it was evident the Jew had carried his point, for he reappeared to announce that dinner was waiting. It was served in a room at the farther end of the hall, and at the table, which was laid for three, Ford found a man already seated. Prothero introduced him as "my associate," but from his presence in the house, and from the fact that he was an American, Ford knew that he was Pearsall.

Pearsall was a man of fifty. He was tall, spare, with closely shaven face and gray hair, worn rather long. He spoke with the accent

THE LOST HOUSE

of a Southerner, and although to Ford he was studiously polite, he was obviously greatly ill at ease. He had the abrupt, inattentive manners, the trembling fingers and quivering lips, of one who had long been a slave to the drug habit, and who now, with difficulty, was holding himself in hand.

Throughout the dinner, speaking to him as though interested only as his medical advisers, the Jew, and occasionally the American, sharply examined and cross-examined their visitor. But they were unable to trip him in his story, or to suggest that he was not just what he claimed to be.

When the dinner was finished, the three men, for different reasons, were each more at his ease. Both Pearsall and Prothero believed from the new patient they had nothing to fear, and Ford was congratulating himself that his presence at the house was firmly secure.

"I think," said Pearsall, "we should warn Mr. Grant that there are in the house other patients who, like himself, are suffering from nervous disorders. At times some silly neurotic woman becomes hysterical, and may make an outcry or scream. He must not think——"

"Oh, that's all right!" Ford reassured him cheerfully. "I expect that. In a sanatorium it must be unavoidable."

THE LOST HOUSE

As he spoke, as though by a signal prearranged, there came from the upper portion of the house a scream, long, insistent.

It was the voice of a woman, raised in appeal, in protest, shaken with fear. Without for an instant regarding it, the two men fastened their eyes upon the visitor. The hand of the Jew dropped quickly from his beard, and slid to the inside pocket of his coat. With eyes apparently unseeing, Ford noted the movement.

"He carries a gun," was his mental comment, "and he seems perfectly willing to use it." Aloud, he said: "That, I suppose is one of them?"

Prothero nodded gravely, and turned to Pearsall.

"Will you attend her?" he asked.

As Pearsall rose and left the room, Prothero rose also.

"You will come with me," he directed, "and I will see you settle in your apartment. Your bag has arrived and is already there."

The room to which the Jew led him was the front one on the second story. It was in no way in keeping with a sanatorium, or a rest-cure. The walls were hidden by dark blue hangings, in which sparkled tiny mirrors, the floor was covered with Turkish rugs, the lights concealed inside lamps of dull brass bedecked with crimson tassels. In the air were the odors of stale tobacco-smoke, of cheap incense, and the sickly, sweet smell of opium. To Ford the place suggested a cigar-divan rather than a bedroom, and he guessed, correctly, that when Prothero had played at palmistry and clairvoyance this had been the place where he received his dupes. But the American expressed himself pleased with his surroundings, and while Prothero remained in the room, busied himself with unpacking his bag.

On leaving him the Jew halted in the door and delivered himself of a little speech. His voice was stern, sharp, menacing.

"Until you are cured," he said, "you will not put your foot outside this room. In this house are other inmates who, as you have already learned, are in a highly nervous state. The brains of some are unbalanced. With my associate and myself they are familiar, but the sight of a stranger roaming through the halls might upset them. They might attack you, might do you bodily injury. If you wish for anything, ring the electric bell beside your bed and an attendant will come. But you yourself must not leave the room."

He closed the door, and Ford, seating himself in front of the coal fire, hastily considered his position. He could not persuade himself

THE LOST HOUSE

that, strategically, it was a satisfactory one. The girl he sought was on the top or fourth floor, he on the second. To reach her he would have to pass through well-lighted halls, up two flights of stairs, and try to enter a door that would undoubtedly be locked. On the other hand, instead of wandering about in the rain outside the house, he was now established on the inside, and as an inmate. Had there been time for a siege, he would have been confident of success. But there was no time. The written call for help had been urgent. Also, the scream he had heard, while the manner of the two men had shown that to them it was a commonplace, was to him a spur to instant action. In haste he knew there was the risk of failure, but he must take that risk.

He wished first to assure himself that Cuthbert was within call, and to that end put out the lights and drew aside the curtains that covered the window. Outside, the fog was rolling between the house-fronts, both rain and snow were falling heavily, and a solitary gas-lamp showed only a deserted and dripping street. Cautiously Ford lit a match and for an instant let the flame flare. He was almost at once rewarded by the sight of an answering flame that flickered from a dark doorway. Ford closed the window, satisfied that his line of

THE LOST HOUSE

communication with the outside world was still intact. The faithful Cuthbert was on guard.

Ford rapidly reviewed each possible course of action. These were several, but to lead any one of them to success, he saw that he must possess a better acquaintance with the interior of the house. Especially was it important that he should obtain a line of escape other than the one down the stairs to the front door. The knowledge that in the rear of the house there was a means of retreat by a servants' stairway, or over the roof of an adjoining building, or by a friendly fire-escape, would at least, lend him confidence in his adventure. Accordingly, in spite of Prothero's threat, he determined at once to reconnoitre. In case of his being discovered outside his room, he would explain his electric bell was out of order, that when he rang no servant had answered, and that he had sallied forth in search of one. To make this plausible, he unscrewed the cap of the electric button in the wall, and with his knife cut off enough of the wire to prevent a proper connection. He then replaced the cap and, opening the door, stepped into the hall.

The upper part of the house was sunk in silence, but rising from the dining-room below, through the opening made by the stairs, came the voices of Prothero and Pearsall. And mixed with their voices came also the sharp hiss of water issuing from a siphon. The sound was reassuring. Apparently, over their whiskey-and-soda the two men were still lingering at the dinner-table. For the moment, then—so far, at least, as they were concerned —the coast was clear.

Stepping cautiously, and keeping close to the wall, Ford ran lightly up the stairs to the hall of the third floor. It was lit brightly by a gas-jet, but no one was in sight, and the three doors opening upon it were shut. At the rear of the hall was a window; the blind was raised, and through the panes, dripping in the rain, Ford caught a glimpse of the rigid iron rods of a fire-escape. His spirits leaped exultantly. If necessary, by means of this scaling ladder, he could work entirely from the outside. Greatly elated, he tiptoed past the closed doors and mounted to the fourth floor. This also was lit by a gas-jet that showed at one end of the hall a table on which were medicine-bottles and a tray covered by a napkin; and at the other end, piled upon each other and blocking the hall-window, were three steamer-trunks. Painted on each were the initials, "D. D." Ford breathed an exclamation.

THE LOST HOUSE

"Dosia Dale," he muttered, "I have found you!"

He was again confronted by three closed doors, one leading to a room that faced the street, another opening upon a room in the rear of the house, and opposite, across the hallway, still another door. He observed that the first two doors were each fastened from the outside by bolts and a spring lock, and that the key to each lock was in place. The fact moved him with indecision. If he took possession of the keys, he could enter the rooms at his pleasure. On the other hand, should their loss be discovered, an alarm would be raised and he would inevitably come under suspicion. The very purpose he had in view might be frustrated. He decided that where they were the keys would serve him as well as in his pocket, and turned his attention to the third door. This was not locked, and, from its position, Ford guessed it must be an entrance to a servants' stairway.

Confident of this, he opened it, and found a dark, narrow landing, a flight of steps mounting from the kitchen below, and, to his delight an iron ladder leading to a trap-door. He could hardly forego a cheer. If the trap-door were not locked, he had found a third line of retreat, a means of escape by way of the roof,

THE LOST HOUSE

far superior to any he might attempt by the main staircase and the street-door.

Ford stepped to the landing, closing the door behind him; and though this left him in complete darkness, he climbed the ladder, and with eager fingers felt for the fastenings of the trap. He had feared to find a padlock, but, to his infinite relief, his fingers closed upon two bolts. Noiselessly, and smoothly, they drew back from their sockets. Under the pressure of his hand the trap-door lifted, and through the opening swept a breath of chill night air.

Ford hooked one leg over a round of the ladder and, with hands free, moved the trap to one side. An instant later he had scrambled to the roof, and, after carefully replacing the trap, rose and looked about him. To his satisfaction, he found that the roof upon which he stood ran level with the roofs adjoining it, to as far as Devonshire Street, where they encountered the wall of an apartment house. This was of seven stories. On the fifth story a row of windows, brilliantly lighted, opened upon the roofs over which he planned to make his retreat. Ford chuckled with nervous excitement.

"Before long," he assured himself, "I will be visiting the man who owns that flat. He will think I am a burglar. He will send for the police. There is no one in the world I shall be so glad to see!"

Ford considered that running over roofs, even when their pitfalls were not concealed by a yellow fog, was an awkward exercise, and decided that before he made his dash for freedom, the part of a careful jockey would be to take a preliminary canter over the course. Accordingly, among party walls of brick, rain-pipes, chimney-pipes, and telephone wires, he felt his way to the wall of the apartment house; and then, with a clearer idea of the obstacles to be avoided, raced back to the point whence he had started.

Next, to discover the exact position of the fire-escape, he dropped to his knees and crawled to the rear edge of the roof. The light from the back windows of the fourth floor showed him an iron ladder from the edge of the roof to the platform of the fire-escape, and the platform itself, stretching below the windows the width of the building. He gave a sigh of satisfaction, but the same instant exclaimed with dismay. The windows opening upon the fire-escape were closely barred.

For a moment he was unable to grasp why a fire-escape should be placed where escape was impossible, until he recognized that the ladder must have been erected first and the iron bars

THE LOST HOUSE

later; probably only since Miss Dale had been made a prisoner.

But he now appreciated that in spite of the iron bars he was nearer that prisoner than he had ever been. Should he return to the hall below, even while he could unlock the doors, he was in danger of discovery by those inside the house. But from the fire-escape only a window-pane would separate him from the prisoner, and though the bars would keep him at arm's-length, he might at least speak with her, and assure her that her call for help had carried. He grasped the sides of the ladder and dropped to the platform. As he had already seen that the window farthest to the left was barricaded with trunks, he disregarded it, and passed quickly to the two others. Behind both of these, linen shades were lowered, but, to his relief, he found that in the middle window the lower sash, as though for ventilation, was slightly raised, leaving an opening of a few inches.

Kneeling on the gridiron platform of the fire-escape, and pressing his face against the bars, he brought his eyes level with this opening. Owing to the lowered window-blind, he could see nothing in the room, nor could he distinguish any sound until above the drip and patter of the rain there came to him the peace-

THE LOST HOUSE

ful ticking of a clock and the rattle of coal falling to the fender. But of any sound that was human there was none. That the room was empty, and that the girl was in the front of the house was possible, and the temptation to stretch his hand through the bars and lift the blind was almost compelling. If he did so, and the girl were inside, she might make an outcry, or, guarding her, there might be an attendant, who at once would sound the alarm. The risk was evident, but, encouraged by the silence, Ford determined to take the chance. Slipping one hand between the bars he caught the end of the blind, and, pulling it gently down, let the spring draw it upward. Through an opening of six inches the room lay open before him. He saw a door leading to another room, at one side an iron cot, and in front of the coal fire, facing him, a girl seated in a deep arm-chair. A book lay on her knees, and she was intently reading.

The girl was young, and her face, in spite of an unnatural pallor and an expression of deep melancholy, was one of extreme beauty. She wore over a night-dress a long loose wrapper corded at the waist, and, as though in readiness for the night, her black hair had been drawn back into smooth, heavy braids. She made so sweet and sad a picture that Ford forgot his errand, forgot his damp and chilled body, and for a moment in sheer delight knelt, with his face pressed close to the bars, and gazed at her.

A movement on the part of the girl brought him to his senses. She closed the book, and, leaning forward, rested her chin upon the hollow of her hand and stared into the fire. Her look was one of complete and hopeless misery. Ford did not hesitate. The girl was alone, but that at any moment an attendant might join her was probable, and the rare chance that now offered would be lost. He did not dare to speak, or by any sound attract her attention, but from his breast-pocket he took the glove thrown to him from the window, and, with a jerk, tossed it through the narrow opening. It fell directly at her feet. She had not seen the glove approach, but the slight sound it made in falling caused her to start and turn her eyes toward it. Through the window, breathless, and with every nerve drawn taut, Ford watched her.

For a moment, partly in alarm, partly in bewilderment, she sat motionless, regarding the glove with eyes fixed and staring. Then she lifted them to the ceiling, in quick succession to each of the closed doors, and then to the window. In his race across the roofs Ford had lacked the protection of a hat, and his hair was plastered across his forehead; his face

THE LOST HOUSE

was streaked with soot and snow, his eyes shone with excitement. But at sight of this strange apparition the girl made no sign. Her alert mind had in an instant taken in the significance of the glove, and for her what followed could have but one meaning. She knew that no matter in what guise he came the man whose face was now pressed against the bars was a friend.

With a swift, graceful movement she rose to her feet, crossed quickly to the window, and sank upon her knees.

"Speak in a whisper," she said; "and speak quickly. You are in great danger!"

That her first thought was of his safety gave Ford a thrill of shame and pleasure.

Until now Miss Dosia Dale had been only the chief feature in a newspaper story; the unknown quantity in a problem. She had meant no more to him than had the initials on her steamer-trunk. Now, through her beauty, through the distress in her eyes, through her warm and generous nature that had disclosed itself with her first words, she became a living, breathing, lovely, and lovable woman. All of the young man's chivalry leaped to the call. He had gone back several centuries. In feeling, he was a knight-errant rescuing beauty in distress from a dungeon cell.

To the girl, he was a reckless young person

THE LOST HOUSE

with a dirty face and eyes that gave confidence.

But, though a knight-errant, Ford was a modern knight-errant. He wasted no time in explanations or pretty speeches.

"In two minutes," he whispered, "I'll unlock your door. There's a ladder outside your room to the roof. Once we get to the roof the rest's easy. Should anything go wrong, I'll come back by this fire-escape. Wait at the window until you see your door open. Do you understand?"

The girl answered with an eager nod. The color had flown to her cheek. Her eyes flashed in excitement. A sudden doubt assailed Ford.

"You've no time to put on any more clothes," he commanded.

"I haven't got any!" said the girl.

The knight-errant ran up the fire-escape, pulled himself over the edge of the roof, and, crossing it, dropped through the trap to the landing of the kitchen stairs. Here he expended the greater part of the two minutes he had allowed himself in cautiously opening the door into the hall. He accomplished this without a sound, and in one step crossed the hall to the door that held Miss Dale a prisoner.

Slowly he drew back the bolts. Only the spring lock now barred him from her. With thumb and forefinger he turned the key, pushed the door gently open, and ran into the room.

At the same instant from behind him, within six feet of him, he heard the staircase creak. A bomb bursting could not have shaken him more rudely. He swung on his heel and found, blocking the door, the giant bulk of Prothero regarding him over the barrel of his pistol.

"Don't move!" said the Jew.

At the sound of his voice the girl gave a cry of warning, and sprang forward.

"Go back!" commanded Prothero. His voice was low and soft, and apparently calm, but his face showed white with rage.

Ford had recovered from the shock of the surprise. He, also, was in a rage—a rage of mortification and bitter disappointment.

"Don't point that gun at me!" he blustered.

The sound of leaping footsteps and the voice of Pearsall echoed from the floor below.

"Have you got him?" he called.

Prothero made no reply, nor did he lower his pistol. When Pearsall was at his side, without turning his head, he asked in the same steady tone:

"What shall we do with him?"

The face of Pearsall was white, and furious with fear.

THE LOST HOUSE

"I told you——" he stormed.

"Never mind what you told me," said the Jew. "What shall we do with him? He *knows!*"

Ford's mind was working swiftly. He had no real fear of personal danger for the girl or himself. The Jew, he argued, was no fool. He would not risk his neck by open murder. And, as he saw it, escape with the girl might still be possible. He had only to conceal from Prothero his knowledge of the line of retreat over the house-tops, explain his rain-soaked condition, and wait a better chance.

To this end he proceeded to lie briskly and smoothly.

"Of course I know," he taunted. He pointed to his dripping garments. "Do you know where I've been? In the street, placing my men. I have this house surrounded. I am going to walk down those stairs with this young lady. If you try to stop me I have only to blow my police-whistle——"

"And I will blow your brains out!" interrupted the Jew.

It was a most unsatisfactory climax.

"You have not been in the street," said Prothero. "You are wet because you hung out of your window signalling to your friend. Do you know *why* he did not answer your second signal? Because he is lying in an area, with a knife in him!"

"You lie!" cried Ford.

"*You* lie," retorted the Jew quietly, "when you say your men surround this house. You are alone. You are *not* in the police service, you are a busybody meddling with men who think as little of killing you as they did of killing your friend. My servant was placed to watch your window, saw your signal, reported to me. And I found your assistant and threw him into an area, with a knife in him!"

Ford felt the story was untrue. Prothero was trying to frighten him. Out of pure bravado no sane man would boast of murder. But—and at the thought Ford felt a touch of real fear—*was* the man sane? It was a most unpleasant contingency. Between a fight with an angry man and an insane man the difference was appreciable. From this new view-point Ford regarded his adversary with increased wariness; he watched him as he would a mad dog. He regretted extremely he had not brought his revolver.

With his automatic pistol still covering Ford, Prothero spoke to Pearsall.

"I found him," he recited, as though testing the story he would tell later, "prowling through my house at night. Mistaking him for a burglar, I killed him. The kitchen window will be found open, with the lock broken, showing how he gained an entrance. Why not?" he demanded.

"Because," protested Pearsall, in terror, "the man outside will tell——"

Ford shouted with genuine relief.

"Exactly!" he cried. "The man outside, who is *not* down an area with a knife in him, but who at this moment is bringing the police —*he* will tell!"

As though he had not been interrupted, Prothero continued thoughtfully:

"What they may say he expected to find here, I can explain away later. The point is that I found a strange man, hatless, dishevelled, prowling in my house. I called on him to halt; he ran, I fired, and unfortunately killed him. An Englishman's home is his castle; an English jury——"

"An English jury," said Ford briskly, "is the last thing you want to meet— It isn't a Chicago jury."

The Jew flung back his head as though Ford had struck him in the face.

"Ah!" he purred, "you know that, too, do you?" The purr increased to a snarl. "You know too much!"

For Pearsall, his tone seemed to bear an

alarming meaning. He sprang toward Prothero, and laid both hands upon his disengaged arm.

"For God's sake," he pleaded, "come away! He can't hurt you—not alive; but dead, he'll hang you—hang us both. We must go, now, this moment." He dragged impotently at the left arm of the giant. "Come!" he begged.

Whether moved by Pearsall's words or by some thought of his own, Prothero nodded in assent. He addressed himself to Ford.

"I don't know what to do with you," he said, "so I will consult with my friend outside this door. While we talk, we will lock you in. We can hear any move you make. If you raise the window or call I will open the door and kill you—you and that woman!"

With a quick gesture, he swung to the door, and the spring lock snapped. An instant later the bolts were noisily driven home.

When the second bolt shot into place, Ford turned and looked at Miss Dale.

"This is a hell of a note!" he said.

III

Outside the locked door the voices of the two men rose in fierce whispers. But Ford regarded them not at all. With the swiftness of

THE LOST HOUSE

a squirrel caught in a cage, he darted on tiptoe from side to side searching the confines of his prison. He halted close to Miss Dale and pointed at the windows.

"Have you ever tried to loosen those bars?" he whispered.

The girl nodded and, in pantomime that spoke of failure, shrugged her shoulders.

"What did you use?" demanded Ford hopefully.

The girl destroyed his hope with a shake of her head and a swift smile.

"Scissors," she said; "but they found them and took them away."

Ford pointed at the open grate.

"Where's the poker?" he demanded.

"They took that, too. I bent it trying to pry the bars. So they knew."

The man gave her a quick, pleased glance, then turned his eyes to the door that led into the room that looked upon the street.

"Is that door locked?"

"No," the girl told him. "But the door from it into the hall is fastened, like the other, with a spring lock and two bolts."

Ford cautiously opened the door into the room adjoining, and, except for a bed and wash-stand, found it empty. On tiptoe he ran to the windows. Sowell Street was deserted. He returned to Miss Dale, again closing the door between the two rooms.

"The nurse," Miss Dale whispered, "when she is on duty, leaves that door open so that she can watch me; when she goes downstairs, she locks and bolts the door from that room to the hall. It's locked now."

"What's the nurse like?"

The girl gave a shudder that seemed to Ford sufficiently descriptive. Her lips tightened in a hard, straight line.

"She's not human," she said. "I begged her to help me, appealed to her in every way; then I tried a dozen times to get past her to the stairs."

"Well?"

The girl frowned, and with a gesture signified her surroundings.

"I'm still here," she said.

She bent suddenly forward and, with her hand on his shoulder, turned the man so that he faced the cot.

"The mattress on that bed," she whispered, "rests on two iron rods. They are loose and can be lifted. I planned to smash the lock, but the noise would have brought Prothero. But you could defend yourself with one of them."

Ford had already run to the cot and dropped to his knees. He found the mattress supported

THE LOST HOUSE

on strips of iron resting loosely in sockets at the head and foot. He raised the one nearer him, and then, after a moment of hesitation, let it drop into place.

"That's fine!" he whispered. "Good as a crowbar." He shook his head in sudden indecision. "But I don't just know how to use it. His automatic could shoot six times before I could swing that thing on him once. And if I have it in my hands when he opens the door, he'll shoot, and he may hit you. But if I leave it where it is, he won't know I know it's there, and it may come in very handy later."

In complete disapproval the girl shook her head. Her eyes filled with concern.

"You must not fight him," she ordered. "I mean, not for me. You don't know the danger. The man's not sane. He won't give you a chance. He's mad. You have no right to risk your life for a stranger. I'll not permit it——"

Ford held up his hand for silence. With a jerk of his head he signified the door.

"They've stopped talking," he whispered.

Straining to hear, the two leaned forward, but from the hall there came no sound. The girl raised her eyebrows questioningly.

"Have they gone?" she breathed.

THE LOST HOUSE

"If I knew that," protested Ford, "we wouldn't be here!"

In answer to his doubt a smart rap, as though from the butt of a revolver, fell upon the door. The voice of Prothero spoke sharply:

"You, who call yourself Grant!" he shouted.

Before answering, Ford drew Miss Dale and himself away from the line of the door, and so placed the girl with her back to the wall that if the door opened she would be behind it.

"Yes," he answered.

"Pearsall and I," called Prothero, "have decided how to dispose of you—of both of you. He has gone below to make preparations. I am on guard. If you try to break out or call for help, I'll shoot you as I warned you!"

"And I warn you," shouted Ford, "if this lady and I do not instantly leave this house, or if any harm comes to her, you will hang for it!"

Prothero laughed jeeringly.

"Who will hang me?" he mocked.

"My friends," retorted Ford. "They know I am in this house. They know *why* I am here. Unless they see Miss Dale and myself walk out of it in safety, they will never let you leave it. Don't be a fool, Prothero!" he shouted. "You know I am telling the truth. You know your only chance for mercy is to open that door and let us go free."

THE LOST HOUSE

For over a minute Ford waited, but from the hall there was no answer.

After another minute of silence, Ford turned and gazed inquiringly at Miss Dale.

"Prothero!" he called.

Again for a full minute he waited and again called, and then, as there still was no reply, he struck the door sharply with his knuckles. On the instant the voice of the Jew rang forth in an angry bellow.

"Keep away from that door!" he commanded.

Ford turned to Miss Dale and bent his head close to hers.

"Now, why the devil didn't he answer?" he whispered. "Was it because he wasn't there; or is he planning to steal away and wants us to think that even if he does *not* answer, he's still outside?"

The girl nodded eagerly.

"This is it," she whispered. "My uncle is a coward, or rather he is very wise, and has left the house. And Prothero means to follow, but he wants us to think he's still on guard. If we only *knew!*" she exclaimed.

As though in answer to her thought, the voice of Prothero called to them.

"Don't speak to me again," he warned. "If you do, I'll not answer, or I'll shoot!"

THE LOST HOUSE

Flattened against the wall, close to the hinges of the door, Ford replied flippantly and defiantly:

"That makes conversation difficult, doesn't it?" he called.

There was a bursting report, and a bullet splintered the panel of the door, flattened itself against the fireplace, and fell tinkling into the grate.

"I hope I hit you!" roared the Jew.

Ford pressed his lips tightly together. Whatever happy retort may have risen to them was forever lost. For an exchange of repartee, the moment did not seem propitious.

"Perhaps now," jeered Prothero, "you'll believe I'm in earnest!"

Ford still resisted any temptation to reply. He grinned apologetically at the girl and shrugged his shoulders. Her face was white, but it was white from excitement, not from fear.

"What did I tell you?" she whispered. "He *is* mad—quite mad!"

Ford glanced at the bullet-hole in the panel of the door. It was on a line with his heart. He looked at Miss Dale; her shoulder was on a level with his own, and her eyes were following his.

"In case he does that again," said Ford, "we would be more comfortable sitting down."

THE LOST HOUSE

With their shoulders against the wall, the two young people sank to the floor. The position seemed to appeal to them as humorous, and, when their eyes met, they smiled.

"To a spectator," whispered Ford encouragingly, "we *might* appear to be getting the worst of this. But, as a matter of fact, every minute Cuthbert does not come means that the next minute may bring him."

"You don't believe he was hurt?" asked the girl.

"No," said Ford. "I believe Prothero found him, and I believe there may have been a fight. But you heard what Pearsall said: 'The man outside will tell.' *If* Cuthbert's in a position to tell, he is not down an area with a knife in him."

He was interrupted by a faint report from the lowest floor, as though the door to the street had been sharply slammed. Miss Dale showed that she also had heard it.

"My uncle," she said, "making his escape!"

"It may be," Ford answered.

The report did not suggest to him the slamming of a door, but he saw no reason for saying ing so to the girl.

With his fingers locked across his knees, Ford was leaning forward, his eyes frowning, his lips tightly shut. At his side the girl re-

THE LOST HOUSE

garded him covertly. His broad shoulders, almost touching hers, his strong jaw projecting aggressively, and the alert, observant eyes gave her confidence. For three weeks she had been making a fight single-handed. But she was now willing to cease struggling and relax. Quite happily she placed herself and her safety in the keeping of a stranger. Half to herself, half to the man, she murmured:

"It is like 'The Sieur de Maletroit's Door.'"

Without looking at her, Ford shook his head and smiled.

"No such luck," he corrected grimly. "That young man was given a choice. The moment he was willing to marry the girl he could have walked out of the room free. I do not recall Prothero's saying *I* can escape death by any such charming alternative."

The girl interrupted quickly.

"No," she said; "you are not at all like that young man. He stumbled in by chance. You came on purpose to help me. It was fine, unselfish."

"It was not," returned Ford. "My motive was absolutely selfish. It was not to help you I came, but to be able to tell about it later. It is my business to do that. And before I saw you, it was all in the day's work. But after I saw you it was no longer a part of the

THE LOST HOUSE

day's work; it became a matter of a lifetime."

The girl at his side laughed softly and lightly. "A lifetime is not long," she said, "when you are locked in a room and a madman is shooting at you. It may last only an hour."

"Whether it lasts an hour or many years," said Ford, "it can mean to me now only one thing—" He turned quickly and looked in her face boldly and steadily: "*You,*" he said.

The girl did not avoid his eyes, but returned his glance with one as steady as his own. "You are an amusing person," she said. "Do you feel it is necessary to keep up my courage with pretty speeches?"

"I made no pretty speech," said Ford. "I proclaimed a fact. You are the most charming person that ever came into my life, and whether Prothero shoots us up, or whether we live to get back to God's country, you will never leave it."

The girl pretended to consider his speech critically. "It would be almost a compliment," she said, "if it were intelligent, but when you know nothing of me—it is merely impertinent."

"I know this much of you," returned Ford, calmly; "I know you are fine and generous, for your first speech to me, in spite of your own

THE LOST HOUSE

danger, was for my safety. I know you are brave, for I see you now facing death without dismay."

He was again suddenly halted by two sharp reports. They came from the room directly below them. It was no longer possible to pretend to misinterpret their significance.

"Prothero!" exclaimed Ford, "and his pistol!"

They waited breathlessly for what might follow: an outcry, the sound of a body falling, a third pistol-shot. But throughout the house there was silence.

"If you really think we are in such danger," declared Miss Dale, "we are wasting time!"

"We are *not* wasting time," protested Ford; "we are really gaining time, for each minute Cuthbert and the police are drawing nearer, and to move about only invites a bullet. And, what is of more importance," he went on quickly, as though to turn her mind from the mysterious pistol-shots, "should we get out of this alive, I shall already have said what under ordinary conditions I might not have found the courage to tell you in many months." He waited as though hopeful of a reply, but Miss Dale remained silent. "They say," continued Ford, "when a man is drowning his whole life passes in review. We are drowning, and yet I find I can see into the past no further than the last half-hour. I find life began only then, when I looked through the bars of that window and found *you!*"

With the palm of her hand the girl struck the floor sharply. "This is neither the time," she exclaimed, "nor the place to——"

"I did not choose the place," Ford pointed out. "It was forced upon me with a gun. But the *time* is excellent. At such a time one speaks only what is true."

"You certainly have a strange sense of humor," she said, "but when you are risking your life to help me, how can I be angry?"

"Of course you can't," Ford agreed heartily; "you could not be so conventional."

"But I *am* conventional!" protested Miss Dale. "And I am not *used* to having young men tell me they have 'come into my life to stay'—certainly not young men who come into my life by way of a trap-door, and without an introduction, without a name, without even a hat! It's absurd! It's not real! It's a nightmare!"

"The whole situation is absurd!" Ford declared. "Here we are in the heart of London, surrounded by telephones, taxicabs, police—at least, hope we are surrounded by police—and yet we are crawling around the floor on our

THE LOST HOUSE

hands and knees dodging bullets. I wish it *were* a nightmare. But, as it's not"—he rose to his feet—"I think I'll try——"

He was interrupted by a sharp blow upon the door and the voice of Prothero.

"You, navy officer!" he panted. "Come to the door! Stand close to it so that I needn't shout. Come, quick!"

Ford made no answer. Motioning to Miss Dale to remain where she was, he ran noiselessly to the bed, and from beneath the mattress lifted one of the iron bars upon which it rested. Grasping it at one end, he swung the bar swiftly as a man tests the weight of a baseball bat. As a weapon it seemed to satisfy him, for he smiled. Then once more he placed himself with his back to the wall.

"Do you hear me?" roared Prothero.

"I hear you!" returned Ford. "If you want to talk to me, open the door and come inside."

"Listen to me," called Prothero. "If I open the door you may act the fool, and I will have to shoot you, and I have made up my mind to let you live. You will soon have this house to yourselves. In a few moments I will leave it, but where I am going I'll need money, and I want the bank-notes in that blue envelope."

Ford swung the iron club in short half-circles.

THE LOST HOUSE

"Come in and get them!" he called.

"Don't trifle with me!" roared the Jew, "or I may change my mind. Shove the money through the crack under the door."

"And get shot!" returned Ford. "Not a bit like it!"

"If, in one minute," shouted Prothero, "I don't see the money coming through that crack, I'll begin shooting through this door, and neither of you will live!"

Resting the bar in the crook of his elbow, Ford snatched the bank-notes from the envelope, and, sticking them in his pocket, placed the empty envelope on the floor. Still keeping out of range, and using his iron bar as a croupier uses his rake, he pushed the envelope across the carpet and under the door. When half of it had disappeared from the other side of the door, it was snatched from view.

An instant later there was a scream of anger and on a line where Ford would have been, had he knelt to shove the envelope under the door, three bullets splintered through the panel.

At the same moment the girl caught him by the wrist. Unheeding the attack upon the door, her eyes were fixed upon the windows. With her free hand she pointed at the one at which Ford had first appeared. The blind was still raised a few inches, and they saw that the night

THE LOST HOUSE

was lit with a strange and brilliant radiance. The storm had passed, and from all the houses that backed upon the one in which they were prisoners lights blazed from every window, and in each were crowded many people, and upon the roof-tops in silhouette from the glare of the street lamps below, and in the yards and clinging to the walls that separated them, were hundreds of other dark, shadowy groups changing and swaying. And from them rose the confused, inarticulate, terrifying murmur of a mob. It was as though they were on a race-track at night facing a great grandstand peopled with an army of ghosts. With the girl at his side, Ford sprang to the window and threw up the blind, and as they clung to the bars, peering into the night, the light in the room fell full upon them. And in an instant from the windows opposite, from the yards below, and from the house-tops came a savage, exultant yell of welcome, a confusion of cries, orders, entreaties, a great roar of warning. At the sound, Ford could feel the girl at his side tremble.

"What does it mean?" she cried.

"Cuthbert has raised the neighborhood!" shouted Ford jubilantly. "Or else"—he cried in sudden enlightenment—"those shots we heard——"

THE LOST HOUSE

The girl stopped him with a low cry of fear. She thrust her arms between the bars and pointed. In the yard below them was the sloping roof of the kitchen. It stretched from the house to the wall of the back yard. Above the wall from the yard beyond rose a ladder, and, face down upon the roof, awry and sprawling, were the motionless forms of two men. Their shining capes and heavy helmets proclaimed their calling.

"The police!" exclaimed Ford. "And the shots we thought were for those in the house were for *them!* This is what has happened," he whispered eagerly: "Prothero attacked Cuthbert. Cuthbert gets away and goes to the police. He tells them you are here a prisoner, that I am here probably a prisoner, and of the attack upon himself. The police try to make an entrance from the street—that was the first shot we heard—and are driven back; then they try to creep in from the yard, and those poor devils were killed."

As he spoke a sudden silence had fallen, a silence as startling as had been the shout of warning. Some fresh attack upon the house which the prisoners could not see, but which must be visible to those in the houses opposite, was going forward.

"Perhaps they are on the roof," whispered

Ford joyfully. "They'll be through the trap in a minute, and you'll be free!"

"No!" said the girl.

She also spoke in a whisper, as though she feared Prothero might hear her. And with her hand she again pointed. Cautiously above the top of the ladder appeared the head and shoulders of a man. He wore a policeman's helmet, but, warned by the fate of his comrades, he came armed. Balancing himself with his left hand on the rung of the ladder, he raised the other and pointed a revolver. It was apparently at the two prisoners, and Miss Dale sprang to one side.

"Stand still!" commanded Ford. "He knows who *you* are! You heard that yell when they saw you? They know you are the prisoner, and they are glad you're still alive. That officer is aiming at the window *below* us. He's after the men who murdered his mates."

From the window directly beneath them came the crash of a rifle, and from the top of the ladder the revolver of the police officer blazed in the darkness. Again the rifle crashed, and the man on the ladder jerked his hands above his head and pitched backward. Ford looked into the face of the girl and found her eyes filled with horror.

"Where is my uncle, Pearsall?" she faltered.

"He has two rifles—for shooting in Scotland. Was that a rifle that—" Her lips refused to finish the question.

"It was a rifle," Ford stammered, "but probably Prothero——"

Even as he spoke the voice of the Jew rose in a shriek from the floor below them, but not from the window below them. The sound was from the front room opening on Sowell Street. In the awed silence that had suddenly fallen his shrieks carried sharply. They were more like the snarls and ravings of an animal than the outcries of a man.

"Take *that!*" he shouted, with a flood of oaths, "and *that*, and *that!*"

Each word was punctuated by the report of his automatic, and, to the amazement of Ford, was instantly answered from Sowell Street by a scattered volley of rifle and pistol shots.

"This isn't a fight," he cried, "it's a battle!"

With Miss Dale at his side, he ran into the front room, and, raising the blind, appeared at the window. And instantly, as at the other end of the house, there was, at sight of the woman's figure, a tumult of cries, a shout of warning, and a great roar of welcome. From beneath them a man ran into the deserted street, and in the glare of the gas-lamp Ford saw his

THE LOST HOUSE

white, upturned face. He was without a hat and his head was circled by a bandage. But Ford recognized Cuthbert.

"That's Ford!" he cried, pointing. "And the girl's with him!" He turned to a group of men crouching in the doorway of the next house to the one in which Ford was imprisoned. "The girl's alive!" he shouted.

"The girl's alive!" The words were caught up and flung from window to window, from house-top to house-top, with savage, jubilant cheers.

Ford pushed Miss Dale forward.

"Let them see you," he said, "and you will never see a stranger sight."

Below them, Sowell Street, glistening with rain and snow, lay empty, but at either end of it, held back by an army of police, were black masses of men, and beyond them more men packed upon the tops of taxicabs and hansoms, stretching as far as the street-lamps showed, and on the roofs shadowy forms crept cautiously from chimney to chimney; and in the windows of darkened rooms opposite, from behind barricades of mattresses and upturned tables, rifles appeared stealthily, to be lost in a sudden flash of flame. And with these flashes were others that came from windows and roofs with the report of a bursting bomb, and that, on the instant, turned night into day, and then left the darkness more dark.

Ford gave a cry of delight.

"They're taking flash-light photographs!" he cried jubilantly. "Well done, you Pressmen!" The instinct of the reporter became compelling. "If they're alive to develop those photographs to-night," he exclaimed eagerly, "Cuthbert will send them by special messenger, in time to catch the *Mauretania* and the *Republic* will have them by Sunday. I mayn't be alive to see them," he added regretfully, "but what a feature for the Sunday supplement!"

As the eyes of the two prisoners became accustomed to the darkness, they saw that the street was not, as at first they had supposed, entirely empty. Directly below them in the gutter, where to approach it was to invite instant death from Prothero's pistol, lay the dead body of a policeman, and at the nearer end of the street, not fifty yards from them, were three other prostrate forms. But these forms were animate, and alive to good purpose. From a public-house on the corner a row of yellow lamps showed them clearly. Stretched on pieces of board, and mats commandeered from hallways and cabs, each of the three men lay at full length, nursing a rifle. Their belted

THE LOST HOUSE

gray overcoats, flat, visored caps, and the set of their shoulders marked them for soldiers.

"For the love of Heaven!" exclaimed Ford incredulously, "they've called out the Guards!"

As unconcernedly as though facing the butts at a rifle-range, the three sharp-shooters were firing point-blank at the windows from which Prothero and Pearsall were waging their war to the death upon the instruments of law and order. Beside them, on his knees in the snow, a young man with the silver hilt of an officer's sword showing through the slit in his greatcoat, was giving commands; and at the other end of the street, a brother officer in evening dress was directing other sharp-shooters, bending over them like the coach of a tug-of-war team, pointing with white-gloved fingers. On the side of the street from which Prothero was firing, huddled in a doorway, were a group of officials, inspectors of police, fire chiefs in brass helmets, more officers of the Guards in bearskins, and, wrapped in a fur coat, the youthful Home Secretary. Ford saw him wave his arm, and at his bidding the cordon of police broke, and slowly forcing its way through the mass of people came a huge touring-car, its two blazing eyes sending before it great shafts of light.

The driver of the car wasted no time in taking up his position. Dashing half-way down

THE LOST HOUSE

the street, he as swiftly backed the automobile over the gutter and up on the sidewalk, so that the lights in front fell full on the door of No. 40. Then, covered by the fire from the roofs, he sprang to the lamps and tilted them until they threw their shafts into the windows of the third story. Prothero's hiding-place was now as clearly exposed as though it were held in the circle of a spot-light, and at the success of the manœuvre the great mob raised an applauding cheer. But the triumph was brief. In a minute the blazing lamps had been shattered by bullets, and once more, save for the fierce flashes from rifles and pistols, Sowell Street lay in darkness.

Ford drew Miss Dale back into the room.

"Those men below," he said, "are mad. Prothero's always been mad, and your—Pearsall—is mad with drugs. And the sight of blood has made them maniacs. They know they now have no chance to live. There's no fear or hope to hold them, and one life more or less means nothing. If they should return here——"

He hesitated, but the girl nodded quickly. "I understand," she said.

"I'm going to try to break down the door and get to the roof," explained Ford. "My hope is that this attack will keep them from hearing, and——"

THE LOST HOUSE

"No," protested the girl. "They *will* hear you, and they will kill you."

"They may take it into their crazy heads to do that, anyway," protested Ford, "so the sooner I get you away, the better. I've only to smash the panels close to the bolts, put my arm through the hole, and draw the bolts back. Then, another blow on the spring lock when the firing is loudest, and we are in the hall. Should anything happen to me, you must know how to make your escape alone. Across the hall is a door leading to an iron ladder. That ladder leads to a trap-door. The trap-door is open. When you reach the roof, run westward toward a lighted building."

"I am not going without you," said Miss Dale quietly; "not after what you have done for me."

"I haven't done anything for you yet," objected Ford. "But in case I get caught I mean to make sure there will be others on hand who will."

He pulled his pencil and a letter from his pocket, and on the back of the envelope wrote rapidly: "I will try to get Miss Dale up through the trap in the roof. You can reach the roof by means of the apartment house in Devonshire Street. Send men to meet her."

In the groups of officials half hidden in the doorway farther down the street, he could make

THE LOST HOUSE

out the bandaged head of Cuthbert. "Cuthbert!" he called. Weighting the envelope with a coin, he threw it into the air. It fell in the gutter, under a lamp-post, and full in view, and at once the two madmen below splashed the street around it with bullets. But, indifferent to the bullets, a policeman sprang from a dark areaway and flung himself upon it. The next moment he staggered. Then limping, but holding himself erect, he ran heavily toward the group of officials. The Home Secretary snatched the envelope from him, and held it toward the light.

In his desire to learn if his message had reached those on the outside, Ford leaned far over the sill of the window. His imprudence was all but fatal. From the roof opposite there came a sudden yell of warning, from directly below him a flash, and a bullet grazed his forehead and shattered the window-pane above him. He was deluged with a shower of broken glass. Stunned and bleeding, he sprang back.

With a cry of concern, Miss Dale ran toward him.

"It's nothing!" stammered Ford. "It only means I must waste no more time." He balanced his iron rod as he would a pikestaff, and aimed it at the upper half of the door to the hall.

THE LOST HOUSE

"When the next volley comes," he said, "I'll smash the panel."

With the bar raised high, his muscles on a strain, he stood alert and poised, waiting for a shot from the room below to call forth an answering volley from the house-tops. But no sound came from below. And the sharpshooters, waiting for the madmen to expose themselves, held their fire.

Ford's muscles relaxed, and he lowered his weapon. He turned his eyes inquiringly to the girl. "What's *this* mean?" he demanded. Unconsciously his voice had again dropped to a whisper.

"They're short of ammunition," said the girl, in a tone as low as his own; "or they are coming *here*."

With a peremptory gesture, Ford waved her toward the room adjoining and then ran to the window.

The girl was leaning forward with her face close to the door. She held the finger of one hand to her lips. With the other hand she beckoned. Ford ran to her side.

"Some one is moving in the hall," she whispered. "Perhaps they are escaping by the roof? No," she corrected herself. "They seem to be running down the stairs again. Now they are coming back. Do you hear?" she

THE LOST HOUSE

asked. "It sounds like some one running up and down the stairs. What can it mean?"

From the direction of the staircase Ford heard a curious creaking sound as of many light footsteps. He gave a cry of relief.

"The police!" he shouted jubilantly. "They've entered through the roof, and they're going to attack in the rear. You're *safe!*" he cried.

He sprang away from the door and, with two swinging blows, smashed the broad panel. And then, with a cry, he staggered backward. Full in his face, through the break he had made, swept a hot wave of burning cinders. Through the broken panel he saw the hall choked with smoke, the steps of the staircase and the stair-rails wrapped in flame.

"The house is on fire!" he cried. "They've taken to the roof and set fire to the stairs behind them!" With the full strength of his arms and shoulders he struck and smashed the iron bar against the door. But the bolts held, and through each fresh opening he made in the panels the burning cinders, drawn by the draft from the windows, swept into the room. From the street a mighty yell of consternation told them the fire had been discovered. Miss Dale ran to the window, and the yell turned to a great cry of warning. The

THE LOST HOUSE

air was rent with frantic voices. "Jump!" cried some. "Go back!" entreated others. The fire chief ran into the street directly below her and shouted at her through his hands. "Wait for the life-net!" he commanded. "Wait for the ladders!"

"Ladders!" panted Ford. "Before they can get their engines through that mob——"

Through the jagged opening in the door he thrust his arm and jerked free the upper bolt. An instant later he had kicked the lower panel into splinters and withdrawn the second bolt, and at last, under the savage onslaught of his iron bar, the spring lock flew apart. The hall lay open before him. On one side of it the burning staircase was a well of flame; at his feet, the matting on the floor was burning fiercely. He raced into the bedroom and returned instantly, carrying a blanket and a towel dripping with water. He pressed the towel across the girl's mouth and nostrils. "Hold it there!" he commanded. Blinded by the bandage, Miss Dale could see nothing, but she felt herself suddenly wrapped in the blanket and then lifted high in Ford's arms. She gave a cry of protest, but the next instant he was running with her swiftly while the flames from the stair-well scorched her hair. She was suddenly tumbled to her feet, the towel and blanket snatched away, and she saw Ford hanging from an iron ladder holding out his hand. She clasped it, and he drew her after him, the flames and cinders pursuing and snatching hungrily.

But an instant later the cold night air smote her in the face, from hundreds of hoarse throats a yell of welcome greeted her, and she found herself on the roof, dazed and breathless, and free.

At the same moment the lifting fire-ladder reached the sill of the third-story window, and a fireman, shielding his face from the flames, peered into the blazing room. What he saw showed him there were no lives to rescue. Stretched on the floor, with their clothing in cinders and the flames licking at the flesh, were the bodies of the two murderers.

A bullet-hole in the forehead of each showed that self-destruction and cremation had seemed a better choice than the gallows and a grave of quick-lime.

On the roof above, two young people stood breathing heavily and happily, staring incredulously into each other's eyes. Running toward them across the roofs, stumbling and falling, were many blue-coated, helmeted angels of peace and law and order.

"How can I tell you?" whispered the girl

quickly. "How can I ever thank you? And I was angry," she exclaimed, with self-reproach. "I did not understand you." She gave a little sigh of content. "Now I think I do."

He took her hand, and she did not seem to know that he held it.

"And," she cried, in wonder, "*I don't even know your name!*"

The young man seemed to have lost his confidence. For a moment he was silent. "The name's all right!" he said finally. His voice was still a little shaken, a little tremulous. "I only hope you'll like it. It's got to last you a long time!"

"THE LOG OF THE 'JOLLY POLLY'"

TEMPTATION came to me when I was in the worst possible position to resist it.

It is a way temptation has. Whenever I swear off drinking invariably I am invited to an ushers' dinner. Whenever I am rich, only the highbrow publications that pay the least, want my work. But the moment I am poverty-stricken the *Manicure Girl's Magazine* and the *Rot and Spot Weekly* spring at me with offers of a dollar a word. Temptation always is on the job. When I am down and out temptation always is up and at me.

When first the Farrells tempted me my vogue had departed. On my name and "past performances" I could still dispose of what I wrote, but only to magazines that were just starting. The others knew I no longer was a best-seller. All the real editors knew it. So did the theatrical managers.

My books and plays had flourished in the dark age of the historical-romantic novel. My heroes wore gauntlets and long swords. They fought for the Cardinal or the King, and each

"THE LOG OF THE 'JOLLY POLLY'"

loved a high-born demoiselle who was a ward of the King or the Cardinal, and with feminine perversity, always of whichever one her young man was fighting. With people who had never read Guizot's "History of France," my books were popular, and for me made a great deal of money. This was fortunate, for my parents had left me nothing save expensive tastes. When the tastes became habits, the public left me. It turned to white-slave and crook plays, and to novels true to life; so true to life that one felt the author must at one time have been a masseur in a Turkish bath.

So, my heroines in black velvet, and my heroes with long swords were "scrapped." As one book reviewer put it, "To expect the public of to-day to read the novels of Fletcher Farrell is like asking people to give up the bunny hug and go back to the lancers."

And, to make it harder, I was only thirty years old.

It was at this depressing period in my career that I received a letter from Fairharbor, Massachusetts, signed Fletcher Farrell. The letter was written on the business paper of the Farrell Cotton Mills, and asked if I were related to the Farrells of Duncannon, of the County Wexford, who emigrated to Massachusetts in 1860. The writer added that he had a grand-

"THE LOG OF THE 'JOLLY POLLY'"

father named Fletcher and suggested we might be related. From the handwriting of Fletcher Farrell and from the way he ill-treated the King's English I did not feel the ties of kinship calling me very loud. I replied briefly that my people originally came from Youghal, in County Cork, that as early as 1750 they had settled in New York, and that all my relations on the Farrell side either were still at Youghal, or dead. Mine was not an encouraging letter; nor did I mean it to be; and I was greatly surprised two days later to receive a telegram reading, "Something to your advantage to communicate; wife and self calling on you Thursday at noon. Fletcher Farrell." I was annoyed, but also interested. The words "something to your advantage" always possess a certain charm. So, when the elevator boy telephoned that Mr. and Mrs. Farrell were calling, I told him to bring them up.

My first glance at the Farrells convinced me the interview was a waste of time. I was satisfied that from two such persons, nothing to my advantage could possibly emanate. On the contrary, from their lack of ease, it looked as though they had come to beg or borrow. They resembled only a butler and housekeeper applying for a new place under the disadvantage of knowing they had no reference from the last one. Of the two, I better liked the man. He was an elderly, pleasant-faced Irishman, smooth-shaven, red-cheeked, and with white hair. Although it was July, he wore a frock coat, and carried a new high hat that glistened. As though he thought at any moment it might explode, he held it from him, and eyed it fearfully. Mrs. Farrell was of a more sophisticated type. The lines in her face and hands showed that for years she might have known hard physical work. But her dress was in the latest fashion, and her fingers held more diamonds than, out of a showcase, I ever had seen.

With embarrassment old man Farrell began his speech. Evidently it had been rehearsed and as he recited it, in swift asides, his wife prompted him; but to note the effect he was making, she kept her eyes upon me. Having first compared my name, fame, and novels with those of Charles Dickens, Walter Scott, and Archibald Clavering Gunter, and to the disadvantage of those gentlemen, Farrell said the similarity of our names often had been commented upon, and that when from my letter he had learned our families both were from the South of Ireland, he had a premonition we might be related. Duncannon, where he was born, he pointed out, was but forty miles from Youghal, and the fishing boats out of Waterford

"THE LOG OF THE 'JOLLY POLLY'"

Harbor often sought shelter in Blackwater River. Had any of my forebears, he asked, followed the herring?

Alarmed, lest at this I might take offense, Mrs. Farrell interrupted him.

"The Fletchers and O'Farrells of Youghal," she exclaimed, "were gentry. What would they be doing in a trawler?"

I assured her that so far as I knew, 1750 being before my time, they might have been smugglers and pirates.

"All I ever heard of the Farrells," I told her, "begins after they settled in New York. And there is no one I can ask concerning them. My father and mother are dead; all my father's relatives are dead, and my mother's relatives are as good as dead. I mean," I added, "we don't speak!"

To my surprise, this information appeared to afford my visitors great satisfaction. They exchanged hasty glances.

"Then," exclaimed Mr. Farrell, eagerly; "if I understand you, you have no living relations at all—barring those that are dead!"

"Exactly!" I agreed.

He drew a deep sigh of relief. With apparent irrelevance but with a carelessness that was obviously assumed, he continued.

"Since I come to America," he announced,

"THE LOG OF THE 'JOLLY POLLY'"

"I have made heaps of money." As though in evidence of his prosperity, he flashed the high hat. In the sunlight it coruscated like one of his wife's diamonds. "Heaps of money," he repeated. "The mills are still in my name," he went on, "but five years since I sold them. We live on the income. We own Harbor Castle, the finest house on the whole waterfront."

"When all the windows are lit up," interjected Mrs. Farrell, "it's often took for a Fall River boat!"

"When I was building it," Farrell continued, smoothly, "they called it Farrell's Folly; but not *now*." In friendly fashion he winked at me, "Standard Oil," he explained, "offered half a million for it. They wanted my wharf for their tank steamers. But, I needed it for my yacht!"

I must have sat up rather too suddenly, for, seeing the yacht had reached home, Mr. Farrell beamed. Complacently his wife smoothed an imaginary wrinkle in her skirt.

"Eighteen men!" she protested, "with nothing to do but clean brass and eat three meals a day!"

Farrell released his death grip on the silk hat to make a sweeping gesture.

"They earn their wages," he said generously.

"THE LOG OF THE 'JOLLY POLLY'"

"Aren't they taking us this week to Cape May?"

"They're taking the yacht to Cape May!" corrected Mrs. Farrell; "not *me!*"

"The sea does not agree with her," explained Farrell; "*we're* going by auti-mobile."

Mrs. Farrell now took up the wondrous tale.

"It's a High Flyer, 1915 model," she explained; "green, with white enamel leather inside, and red wheels outside. You can see it from the window."

Somewhat dazed, I stepped to the window and found you could see it from almost anywhere. It was as large as a freight car; and was entirely surrounded by taxi-starters, bell-boys, and nurse-maids. The chauffeur, and a deputy chauffeur, in a green livery with patent-leather leggings, were frowning upon the mob. They possessed the hauteur of ambulance surgeons. I returned to my chair, and then rose hastily to ask if I could not offer Mr. Farrell some refreshment.

"Mebbe later," he said. Evidently he felt that as yet he had not sufficiently impressed me.

"Harbor Castle," he recited, "has eighteen bedrooms, billiard-room, music-room, art gallery and swimming-pool." He shook his head. "And no one to use 'em but us. We had a

"THE LOG OF THE 'JOLLY POLLY'"

boy." He stopped, and for an instant, as though asking pardon, laid his hand upon the knee of Mrs. Farrell. "But he was taken when he was four, and none came since. My wife has a niece," he added, "but——"

"But," interrupted Mrs. Farrell, "she was too high and mighty for plain folks, and now there is no one. We always took an interest in you because your name was Farrell. We were always reading of you in the papers. We have all your books, and a picture of you in the billiard-room. When folks ask me if we are any relation—sometimes I tell 'em we *are*."

As though challenging me to object, she paused.

"It's quite possible," I said hastily. And, in order to get rid of them, I added: "I'll tell you what I'll do. I'll write to Ireland and——"

Farrell shook his head firmly. "You don't need to write to Ireland," he said, "for what we want."

"What *do* you want?" I asked.

"We want a son," said Farrell; "an adopted son. We want to adopt *you!*"

"You want to *what?*" I asked.

To learn if Mrs. Farrell also was mad, I glanced toward her, but her expression was inscrutable. The face of the Irishman had grown purple.

"THE LOG OF THE 'JOLLY POLLY'"

"And why not?" he demanded. "You're a famous young man, all right, and educated. But there's nothing about me I'm ashamed of! I'm worth five million dollars and I made every cent of it myself—and I made it honest. You ask Dun or Bradstreet, ask——"

I attempted to soothe him.

"*That's* not it, sir," I explained. "It's a most generous offer, a most flattering, complimentary offer. But you don't know me. I don't know you. Choosing a son is a very——"

"I've had you looked up," announced Mrs. Farrell. "The Pinkertons give you a high rating. I hired 'em to trail you for six months."

I wanted to ask *which* six months, but decided to let sleeping dogs lie. I shook my head. Politely but firmly I delivered my ultimatum.

"It is quite impossible!" I said firmly.

Mrs. Farrell continued the debate. She talked in a businesslike manner and pronounced the arrangement one by which both sides would benefit. There were thousands of other Farrells, she pointed out, any one of whom they might have adopted. But they had selected me because in so choosing, they thought they were taking the least risk. They had decided, she was pleased to say, that I would not disgrace them, and that as a "lit-

"THE LOG OF THE 'JOLLY POLLY'"

erary author" I brought with me a certain social asset.

A clever, young businessman they did not want. Their business affairs they were quite able to manage themselves. But they would like as an adopted son one who had already added glory to the name of Farrell, which glory he was willing to share.

"We wouldn't tie you down," she urged, "but we would expect you to live at Harbor Castle a part of your time, and to call us Ma and Pa. You would have your own rooms, and your own servant, and there is a boathouse on the harbor front, where you could write your novels."

At this, knowing none wanted my novels, I may have winced, for, misreading my discontent, Farrell hastily interrupted.

"You won't have to work at all," he protested heartily. "My son can afford to live like a lord. You'll get all the spending money you want, and if you're fond of foreign parts, you can take the yacht wherever you please!"

"The farther the better," exclaimed Mrs. Farrell with heat. "And when you get it there, I hope you'll *sink* it!"

"Maybe your friends would come and visit you," suggested Farrell, I thought, a trifle wistfully. "There's bathing, tennis, eighteen bedrooms, billiard-room, art gallery——"

"You told him that!" said Mrs. Farrell.

I was greatly at a loss. Their offer was preposterous, but to them, it was apparently a perfectly possible arrangement. Nor were they acting on impulse. Mrs. Farrell had admitted that for six months she had had me "trailed." How to say "No" and not give offense, I found difficult. They were deeply in earnest and I could see that Farrell, at least, was by instinct generous, human, and kind. It was, in fact, a most generous offer. But how was I to tell them tactfully I was not for sale, that I was not looking for "ready-to-wear" parents, and that if I were in the market, they were not the parents I would choose. I had a picture of life at Harbor Castle, dependent upon the charity of the Farrells. I imagined what my friends would say to me, and worse, what they would say behind my back. But I was not forced to a refusal.

Mr. Farrell rose.

"We don't want to hurry you," he said. "We want you to think it over. Maybe if we get acquainted——"

Mrs. Farrell smiled upon me ingratiatingly.

"Why don't we get acquainted now?" she demanded. "We're motoring down to Cape

"THE LOG OF THE 'JOLLY POLLY'"

May to stay three weeks. Why don't you come along—as our guest—and see how you like us?"

I assured them, almost too hastily, that I already was deeply engaged.

As they departed, Farrell again admonished me to think it over.

"And look me up at Dun's and Bradstreet's," he advised. "Ask 'em about me at the Waldorf. Ask the head waiters and bellhops if I look twice at a five spot!"

It seemed an odd way to select a father, but I promised.

I escorted them even to the sidewalk, and not without envy watched them sweep toward the Waldorf in the High Flyer, 1915 model. I caught myself deciding, were it mine, I would paint it gray.

I was lunching at the Ritz with Curtis Spencer, and I looked forward to the delight he would take in my story of the Farrells. He would probably want to write it. He was my junior, but my great friend; and as a novelist his popularity was where five years earlier mine had been. But he belonged to the new school. His novels smelled like a beauty parlor; and his heroines, while always beautiful, were, on occasions, virtuous, but only when they thought it would pay.

"THE LOG OF THE 'JOLLY POLLY'"

Spencer himself was as modern as his novels, and I was confident his view of my adventure would be that of the great world which he described so accurately.

But to my amazement when I had finished he savagely attacked me.

"You idiot!" he roared. "Are you trying to tell me you refused five million dollars—just because you didn't like the people who wanted to force it on you? Where," he demanded, "is Cape May? We'll follow them now! We'll close this deal before they can change their minds. I'll make you sign to-night. And, then," he continued eagerly, "we'll take their yacht and escape to Newport, and you'll lend me five thousand dollars, and pay my debts, and give me back the ten you borrowed. And you might buy me a touring-car and some polo ponies and—and—oh, lots of things. I'll think of them as we go along. Meanwhile, I can't afford to give luncheons to millionaires, so you sign for this one; and then we'll start for Cape May."

"Are you mad?" I demanded; "do you think I'd sell my honor!"

"For five million dollars?" cried Spencer. "Don't make me laugh! If they want a *real* novelist for a son they can adopt me!"

I replied with dignity that I would not disgrace the memory of my parents.

"THE LOG OF THE 'JOLLY POLLY'"

"You have disgraced them!" retorted Spencer, "with your Musketeer novels for infants. You need money. To get it you may be tempted to write more novels. Here's your chance! Stop robbing the public, and lead an honest life. Think of all the money you could give to the poor, think of all the money you and I could lose at Monte Carlo!"

When he found I would not charter an automobile and at once pursue the Farrells he changed his tactics. If I would not go to Cape May, then, he begged, I would go to Fairharbor. He asked that I would, at least, find out what I was refusing. Before making their offer, for six months, the Farrells had had me "looked up," but, without knowing anything of them, after a talk of ten minutes I had turned them down. "Was that," he asked, "intelligent? Was it fair to the Farrells?" He continued to tempt me.

"They told you to think it over," he persisted. "Very well, then, think it over at Fairharbor! For the next three weeks the Farrells will be at Cape May. The coast is clear. Go to Fairharbor as somebody else and be your own detective. Find out if what they tell you is true. Get inside information. Get inside Harbor Castle. Count the eighteen bedrooms and try the beds. Never mind the art gallery, but make sure there is a wine cellar.

"THE LOG OF THE 'JOLLY POLLY'"

You can't start too soon, and *I will go with you!*"

I told him where he could go.

We then tossed to see who should pay for the lunch and who should tip the head waiter. I lost and had to tip the head waiter. We separated, and as I walked down the Avenue, it seemed as though to the proprietor of every shop I passed I owed money. Owing them the money I did not so much mind; what most distressed me was that they were so polite about it. I had always wanted to reward their patience. A favorite dream of mine was to be able to walk down Fifth Avenue, my pockets stuffed with yellow bills, paying off my debts. Compared with my steadily decreasing income, how enormous my debts appeared; but when compared with the income of a man worth— say—five million dollars, how ridiculous! I had no more than reached my apartment, than a messenger-boy arrived with an envelope. It contained a ticket for a round trip on the New Bedford Line boat leaving that afternoon a ticket for a stateroom, and a note from Curtis Spencer. The latter read: "The boat leaves at six to-night. You arrive at New Bedford seven to-morrow morning. New Bedford and Fairharbor are connected by a bridge. *Cross it!*"

"THE LOG OF THE 'JOLLY POLLY'"

I tore the note in tiny fragments, and tossed them through the open window. I was exceedingly angry. As I stood at the window adding to the name of Curtis Spencer insulting *aliases*, the street below sent up hot, stifling odors: the smoke of taxicabs, the gases of an open subway, the stale reek of thousands of perspiring, unwashed bodies. From that one side street seemed to rise the heat and smells of all New York. For relief I turned to my worktable where lay the opening chapters of my new novel, "The White Plume of Savoy." But now, in the light of Spencer's open scorn, I saw it was impudently false, childish, sentimental. My head ached, the humidity sapped my strength, at heart I felt sick, sore, discouraged. I was down and out. And seeing this, Temptation, like an obsequious floor-walker, came hurrying forward.

"And what may I show you to-day?" asked Temptation. He showed me the upper deck of the New Bedford boat feeling her way between the green banks of the Sound. A cool wind swept past me bearing clean, salty odors; on the saloon deck a band played, and from the darkness the lighthouses winked at me, and in friendly greeting the stars smiled. Temptation won. In five minutes I was feverishly packing, and at five-thirty I was on board. I

"THE LOG OF THE 'JOLLY POLLY'"

assured myself I had not listened to Temptation, that I had no interest in Fairharbor. I was taking the trip solely because it would give me a night's sleep on the Sound. I promised myself that on the morrow I would not even *look* toward Harbor Castle; but on the evening following on the same boat, return to New York. Temptation did not stop to argue, but hastened after another victim.

I turned in at nine o'clock and the coolness, and the salt air, blessed me with the first sleep I had known in weeks. And when I woke we were made fast to the company's wharf at New Bedford, and the sun was well up. I rose refreshed in body and spirit. No longer was I discouraged. Even "The White Plume of Savoy" seemed a perfectly good tale of romance and adventure. And the Farrells were a joke. Even if I were at Fairharbor, I was there only on a lark, and at the expense of Curtis Spencer, who had paid for the tickets. Distinctly the joke was on Curtis Spencer. I lowered the window screen, and looked across the harbor. It was a beautiful harbor. At ancient stone wharfs lay ancient whalers with drooping davits and squared yards, at anchor white-breasted yachts flashed in the sun, a gray man-of-war's man flaunted the week's laundry, a four-masted schooner dried her canvas, and

"THE LOG OF THE 'JOLLY POLLY'"

over the smiling surface of the harbor innumerable fishing boats darted. With delight I sniffed the odors of salt water, sun-dried herring, of oakum and tar. The shore opposite was a graceful promontory crowned with trees and decorous gray-shingled cottages set in tiny gardens that reached to the very edge of the harbor. The second officer was passing my window and I asked what the promontory was called.

"Fairharbor," he said. He answered with such proprietary pride and smiled upon Fairharbor with such approval that I ventured to guess it was his home.

"That's right," he said; "I used to live at the New York end of the run—in a flat. But never again! No place for the boy to play but in the street. I found I could rent one of those old cottages over there for the same money I paid for the flat. So I cut out New York. My boy lives in a bathing suit now, and he can handle a catboat same as me. We have a kitchen garden, and hens, and the fishermen here will give you all the fish you can carry away—fish right out of the water. I guess I've smashed the high cost of living problem all right. I wouldn't go back to living in New York now—not if they gave me the *Pilgrim!*"

As though trying to prod my memory, I

frowned. It was my conception of the part of a detective. "Hasn't Fletcher Farrell," I asked, "a house in Fairharbor?"

"Harbor Castle," said the mate promptly. "It's on the other side of the point. I'd as soon live in a jail!"

"Why?" I exclaimed.

But he was no longer listening. He pointed at the shore opposite.

"See that flag running up the staff in that garden?" he cried. "That's my boy signalling. I got to get to the boat deck and wave back!"

I felt as a detective. I had acquired important information. The mate, a man of judgment, preferred Fairharbor to New York. Also, to living in Harbor Castle, he preferred going to jail.

The boat on which I had arrived was listed to start back at six the same evening on her return trip to New York. So, at the office of the line I checked my valise, and set forth to explore New Bedford.

The whaling vessels moored to a nearby wharf, I inspected from hatches to keels, and by those on board was directed to a warehouse where were stored harpoons, whalebone, and wooden figure-heads. My pleasure in these led to my being passed on to a row of "antique" shops filled with relics of the days of whaling

"THE LOG OF THE 'JOLLY POLLY'"

and also with genuine pie-crust tables, genuine flint-lock muskets, genuine Liverpool pitchers. I coveted especially old-time engravings of the whalers, and was told at Hatchardson's bookstore on the main street others could be found in profusion.

Hatchardson's proved to be a place of great delight. As you entered there were counters for magazines and post-cards, popular music, and best-selling novels, while in the rear of the shop tables and shelves were stocked with ancient volumes, and on the wall surrounding them hung engravings, prints and woodcuts of even the eighteenth century. Just as the drug-store on the corner seemed to be a waiting station for those of New Bedford who used the trolley-cars, so for those who moved in automobiles, or still clung to the family carriage, Hatchardson's appeared to be less a shop than a public meeting-place. I noticed that the clerks, most of whom were women, were with the customers on a most friendly footing, addressing them, and by them being addressed by name. Finding I was free to wander where I pleased, I walked to the rear of the shop and from one of the tables picked up a much-worn volume. It was entitled "The Log of the *Jolly Polly*," and was illustrated with woodcuts showing square-rigged ships and whales

"THE LOG OF THE 'JOLLY POLLY'"

spouting. For five minutes, lost to my surroundings, I turned the pages; and then became conscious that across the table some one was watching me. I raised my eyes and beheld a face of most surprising charm, intelligence and beauty. It was so lovely that it made me wince. The face was the fortune, and judging from the fact that in her hand she held a salesbook, the sole fortune, of a tall young girl who apparently had approached to wait on me. She was looking toward the street, so that, with the book-shelves for a background, her face was in profile, and I determined swiftly that if she were to wait on me she would be kept waiting as long as my money lasted. I did not want "The Log of the *Jolly Polly*," but I did want to hear the lovely lady speak, and especially I desired that the one to whom she spoke should be myself.

"What is the price of this?" I asked. With magnificent self-control I kept my eyes on the book, but the lovely lady was so long silent that I raised them. To my surprise, I found on her face an expression of alarm and distress. With reluctance, and yet within her voice a certain hopefulness, she said, "Fifty dollars."

Fifty dollars was a death blow. I had planned to keep the young lady selling books throughout the entire morning, but at fifty

"THE LOG OF THE 'JOLLY POLLY'"

dollars a book, I would soon be owing her money. I attempted to gain time.

"It must be very rare!" I said. I was afraid to look at her lest my admiration should give offense, so I pretended to admire the book.

"It is the only one in existence," said the young lady. "At least, it is the only one for sale!"

We were interrupted by the approach of a tall man who, from his playing the polite host and from his not wearing a hat, I guessed was Mr. Hatchardson himself. He looked from the book in my hand to the lovely lady and said smiling, "Have you lost it?"

The girl did not smile. To her, apparently, it was no laughing matter.

"I don't know—yet," she said.

Her voice was charming, and genuinely troubled.

Mr. Hatchardson, for later I learned it was he, took the book and showed me the title-page.

"This was privately printed in 1830," he said, "by Captain Noah Briggs. He distributed a hundred presentation copies among his family and friends here in New Bedford. It is a most interesting volume."

I did not find it so. For even as he spoke the young girl, still with a troubled countenance, glided away. Inwardly I cursed Captain

"THE LOG OF THE 'JOLLY POLLY'"

Briggs and associated with him in my curse the polite Mr. Hatchardson. But, at his next words my interest returned.

Still smiling, he lowered his voice.

"Miss Briggs, the young lady who just left us," he said, is the granddaughter of Captain Briggs, and she does not want the book to go out of the family; she wants it for herself."

I interrupted eagerly.

"But it is for sale?"

Mr. Hatchardson reluctantly assented.

"Then I will take it," I said.

Fifty dollars is a great deal of money, but the face of the young lady had been very sad. Besides being sad, had it been aged, plain, and ill-tempered, that I still would have bought the book, is a question I have never determined.

To Mr. Hatchardson, of my purpose to give the book to Miss Briggs, I said nothing. Instead I planned to send it to her anonymously by mail. She would receive it the next morning when I was arriving in New York, and, as she did not know my name, she could not possibly return it. At the post-office I addressed the "Log" to "Miss Briggs, care of Hatchardson's Bookstore," and then I returned to the store. I felt I had earned that pleasure. This time, Miss Briggs was in charge of the post-card counter, and as now a post-card was the

"THE LOG OF THE 'JOLLY POLLY'"

only thing I could afford to buy, at seeing her there I was doubly pleased. But she was not pleased to see me. Evidently Mr. Hatchardson had told her I had purchased the "Log" and at her loss her very lovely face still showed disappointment. Toward me her manner was distinctly aggrieved.

But of the "Log" I said nothing, and began recklessly purchasing post-cards that pictured the show places of New Bedford. Almost the first one I picked up was labelled "Harbor Castle. Residence of Fletcher Farrell." I need not say that I studied it intently. According to the post-card, Harbor Castle stood on a rocky point with water on both sides. It was an enormous, wide-spreading structure, as large as a fort. It exuded prosperity, opulence, extravagance, great wealth. I felt suddenly a filial impulse to visit the home of my would-be forefathers.

"Is this place near here?" I asked.

Miss Briggs told me that in order to reach it I should take the ferry to Fairharbor, and then cross that town to the Buzzards Bay side.

"You can't miss it," she said. "It's a big stone house, with red and white awnings. If you see anything like a jail in ruffles, that's it."

It was evident that with the home I had rejected Miss Briggs was unimpressed; but see-

"THE LOG OF THE 'JOLLY POLLY'"

ing me add the post-card to my collection, she offered me another.

"This," she explained, "is Harbor Castle from the bay. That is their yacht in the foreground."

The post-card showed a very beautiful yacht of not less than two thousand tons. Beneath it was printed "*Harbor Lights*; steam yacht owned by Fletcher Farrell." I always had dreamed of owning a steam yacht, and seeing it stated in cold type that one *was* owned by "Fletcher Farrell," even though I was not that Fletcher Farrell, gave me a thrill of guilty pleasure. I gazed upon the post-card with envy.

"*Harbor Lights* is a strange name for a yacht," I ventured.

Miss Briggs smiled.

"Not for that yacht," she said. "She never leaves it."

I wished to learn more of my would-be parents, and I wished to keep on talking with the lovely Miss Briggs, so, as an excuse for both, I pretended I was interested in the Farrells because I had something I wanted to sell them.

"This Fletcher Farrell must be very rich," I said. "I wonder," I asked, "if I could sell him an automobile?" The moment I spoke I noticed that the manner of Miss Briggs toward

"THE LOG OF THE 'JOLLY POLLY'"

me perceptibly softened. Perhaps, from my buying offhand a fifty-dollar book she had thought me one of the idle rich, and had begun to suspect I was keeping her waiting on me only because I found her extremely easy to look at. Many times before, in a similar manner, other youths must have imposed upon her, and perhaps, also, in concealing my admiration, I had not entirely succeeded.

But, when she believed that, like herself, I was working for my living, she became more human.

"What car are you selling?" she asked.

"I am *trying* to sell," I corrected her, "the Blue Bird, six cylinder."

"I never heard of it," said Miss Briggs.

"Nor has any one else," I answered, with truth. "That is one reason why I can't sell it. I arrived here this morning, and," I added with pathos, "I haven't sold a car yet."

Miss Briggs raised her beautiful eyebrows sceptically. "Have you tried?" she said.

A brilliant idea came to me. In a side street I had passed a garage where Phœnix cars were advertised for hire. I owned a Phœnix, and I thought I saw a way by which, for a happy hour, I might secure the society of Miss Briggs.

"I am an agent and demonstrator for the

Phœnix also," I said glibly; "maybe I could show you one?"

"Show me one?" exclaimed Miss Briggs. "One sees them everywhere! They are always under your feet!"

"I mean," I explained, "might I take you for a drive in one?"

It was as though I had completely vanished. So far as the lovely Miss Briggs was concerned I had ceased to exist. She turned toward a nice old lady.

"What can I show you, Mrs. Scudder?" she asked cheerily; "and how is that wonderful baby?"

I felt as though I had been lifted by the collar, thrown out upon a hard sidewalk, and my hat tossed after me. Greatly shaken, and mentally brushing the dust from my hands and knees, I hastened to the ferry and crossed to Fairharbor. I was extremely angry. By an utter stranger I had been misjudged, snubbed and cast into outer darkness. For myself I readily found excuses. If a young woman was so attractive that at the first sight of her men could not resist buying her fifty-dollar books and hiring automobiles in which to take her driving, the fault was hers. I assured myself that girls as lovely as Miss Briggs were a menace to the public. They should not be at large.

"THE LOG OF THE 'JOLLY POLLY'"

An ordinance should require them to go masked. For Miss Briggs also I was able to make excuses. Why should she not protect herself from the advances of strange young men? If a popular novelist, and especially an ex-popular one, chose to go about disguised as a drummer for the Blue Bird automobile and behaved as such, and was treated as such, what right had he to complain? So I persuaded myself I had been punished as I deserved. But to salve my injured pride I assured myself also that any one who read my novels ought to know my attitude toward any lovely lady could be only respectful, protecting, and chivalrous. But with this consoling thought the trouble was that nobody read my novels.

In finding Harbor Castle I had no difficulty. It stood upon a rocky point that jutted into Buzzards Bay. Five acres of artificial lawn and flower-beds of the cemetery and railroad-station school of horticulture surrounded it, and from the highroad it was protected by a stone wall so low that to the passerby, of the beauties of Harbor Castle nothing was left to the imagination. Over this wall roses under conflicting banners of pink and red fought fiercely. One could almost hear the shrieks of the wounded. Upon the least thorny of these I seated myself and in tender melancholy gazed upon the home of my childhood. That is, upon the home that might—have—been.

When surveying a completed country home, to make the owner thoroughly incensed the correct thing to say is, "This place has great possibilities!"

Harbor Castle had more possibilities than any other castle I ever visited. But in five minutes I had altered it to suit myself. I had ploughed up the flower-beds, dug a sunken garden, planted a wind screen of fir, spruce, and pine, and with a huge brick wall secured warmth and privacy. So pleased was I with my changes, that when I departed I was sad and downcast. The boat-house of which Mrs. Farrell had spoken was certainly an ideal workshop, the tennis-courts made those at the Newport Casino look like a ploughed field, and the swimming-pool, guarded by white pillars and overhung with grape-vines, was a cool and refreshing picture. As, hot and perspiring, I trudged back through Fairharbor, the memory of these haunted me. That they also tempted me, it is impossible to deny. But not for long. For, after passing through the elm-shaded streets to that side of the village that faced the harbor, I came upon the cottages I had seen from the New Bedford shore. At close range they appeared even more attractive than when

"THE LOG OF THE 'JOLLY POLLY'"

pointed out to me by the mate of the steamboat. They were very old, very weather-stained and covered with honeysuckle. Flat stones in a setting of grass led from the gates to the arched doorways, hollyhocks rose above hedges of box, and from the verandas one could look out upon the busy harbor and the houses of New Bedford rising in steps up the sloping hills to a sky-line of tree-tops and church spires. The mate had told me that for what he had rented a flat in New York he had secured one of these charming old world homes. And as I passed them I began to pick out the one in which when I retired from the world I would settle down. This time I made no alterations. How much the near presence of Miss Briggs had to do with my determination to settle down in Fairharbor, I cannot now remember. But, certainly as I crossed the bridge toward New Bedford, thoughts of her entirely filled my mind. I assured myself this was so only because she was beautiful. I was sure her outward loveliness advertised a nature equally lovely, but for my sudden and extreme interest I had other excuses. Her independence in earning her living, her choice in earning it among books and pictures, her pride of family as shown by her efforts to buy the family heirloom, all these justified my admiration. And her refusing to go joy-riding with

"THE LOG OF THE 'JOLLY POLLY'"

an impertinent stranger, even though the impertinent stranger was myself, was an act I applauded. The more I thought of Miss Briggs the more was I disinclined to go away leaving with her an impression of myself so unpleasant as the one she then held. I determined to remove it. At least, until I had redeemed myself, I would remain in New Bedford. The determination gave me the greatest satisfaction. With a light heart I returned to the office of the steamboat line and retrieving my suit-case started with it toward the Parker House. It was now past five o'clock, the stores were closed, and all the people who had not gone to the baseball game with Fall River were in the streets. In consequence, as I was passing the post-office, Miss Briggs came down the steps, and we were face to face.

In her lovely eyes was an expression of mingled doubt and indignation and in her hand, freshly torn from the papers in which I had wrapped it, was "The Log of the *Jolly Polly*." In action Miss Briggs was as direct as a submarine. At sight of me she attacked.

"Did you send me this?" she asked.

I lowered my bag to the sidewalk and prepared for battle. "I didn't think of your going to the post-office," I said. "I planned you'd get it to-morrow after I'd left. When I sent it, I thought I would never see you again."

"THE LOG OF THE 'JOLLY POLLY'"

"Then you *did* send it!" exclaimed Miss Briggs. As though the book were a hot plate she dropped it into my hand. She looked straight at me, but her expression suggested she was removing a caterpillar from her pet rosebush.

"You had no right," she said. "You may not have meant to be impertinent, but you were!"

Again, as though I had disappeared from the face of the earth, Miss Briggs gazed coldly about her, and with dignity started to cross the street. Her dignity was so great that she glanced neither to the left nor right. In consequence she did not see an automobile that swung recklessly around a trolley-car and dived at her. But other people saw it and shrieked. I also shrieked, and dropping the suit-case and the "Log," jumped into the street, grabbed Miss Briggs by both arms, and flung her back to the sidewalk. That left me where she had been, and the car caught me up and slammed me head first against a telegraph pole. The pole was hard, and if any one counted me out I did not stay awake to hear him. When I came to I was conscious that I was lying on a sidewalk; but to open my eyes, I was much too tired. A voice was saying, "Do you know who he is, Miss?"

The voice that replied was the voice of the lovely Miss Briggs. But now I hardly recog-

"THE LOG OF THE 'JOLLY POLLY'"

nized it. It was full of distress, of tenderness and pity.

"No, I don't know him," it stammered. "He's a salesman—he was in the store this morning—he's selling motor-cars."

The first voice laughed.

"Motor-cars!" he exclaimed. "That's why he ain't scared of 'em. He certainly saved you from that one! I seen him, Miss Briggs, and he most certainly saved your life!"

In response to this astonishing statement I was delighted to hear a well-trained male chorus exclaim in assent.

The voices differed; some spoke in the accents of Harvard, pure and undefiled, some in a "down East" dialect, others suggested Italian peanut venders and Portuguese sailors, but all agreed that the life of Miss Briggs had been saved by myself. I had intended coming to, but on hearing the chorus working so harmoniously I decided I had better continue unconscious.

Then a new voice said importantly: "The marks on his suitcase are 'F. F., New York.'"

I appreciated instantly that to be identified as Fletcher Farrell meant humiliation and disaster. The other Fletcher Farrells would soon return to New Bedford. They would learn that in their absence I had been spying upon

"THE LOG OF THE 'JOLLY POLLY'"

the home I had haughtily rejected. Besides, one of the chorus might remember that three years back Fletcher Farrell had been a popular novelist and might recognize me, and Miss Briggs would discover I was *not* an automobile agent and that I had lied to her. I saw that I must continue to lie to her. I thought of names beginning with "F," and selected "Frederick Fitzgibbon." To christen yourself while your eyes are shut and your head rests on a curbstone is not easy, and later I was sorry I had not called myself Fairchild as being more aristocratic. But then it was too late. As Fitzgibbon I had come back to life, and as Fitzgibbon I must remain.

When I opened my eyes I found the first voice belonged to a policeman who helped me to my feet and held in check the male chorus. The object of each was to lead me to a drink. But instead I turned dizzily to Miss Briggs. She was holding my hat and she handed it to me. Her lovely eyes were filled with relief and her charming voice with remorse.

"I—I can't possibly thank you," she stammered. "Are you badly hurt?"

I felt I had never listened to words so original and well chosen. In comparison, the brilliant and graceful speeches I had placed on the lips of my heroines became flat and unconvincing.

"THE LOG OF THE 'JOLLY POLLY'"

I assured her I was not at all hurt and endeavored, jauntily, to replace my hat. But where my head had hit the telegraph pole a large bump had risen which made my hat too small. So I hung it on the bump. It gave me a rakish air. One of the chorus returned my bag and another the "Log." Not wishing to remind Miss Briggs of my past impertinences I guiltily concealed it.

Then the policeman asked my name and I gave the one I had just invented, and inquired my way to the Parker House. Half the chorus volunteered to act as my escort, and as I departed, I stole a last look at Miss Briggs. She and the policeman were taking down the pedigree of the chauffeur of the car that had hit me. He was trying to persuade them he was not intoxicated, and with each speech was furnishing evidence to the contrary.

After I had given a cold bath to the bump on my head and to the rest of my body which for the moment seemed the lesser of the two, I got into dry things and seated myself on the veranda of the hotel. With a cigar to soothe my jangling nerves, I considered the position of Miss Briggs and myself. I was happy in believing it had improved. On the morrow there was no law to prevent me from visiting Hatchardson's Bookstore, and in view of

"THE LOG OF THE 'JOLLY POLLY'"

what had happened since last I left it, I had reason to hope Miss Briggs would receive me more kindly. Of the correctness of this diagnosis I was at once assured. In front of the hotel a district messenger-boy fell off his bicycle and with unerring instinct picked me out as Mr. Fitzgibbon of New York. The note he carried was from Miss Briggs. It stated that in the presence of so many people it had been impossible for her to thank me as she wished for the service I had rendered her, and that Mrs. Cutler, with whom she boarded, and herself, would be glad if after supper I would call upon them. I gave the messenger-boy enough gold to enable him to buy a new bicycle and in my room executed a dance symbolizing joy. I then kicked my suit-case under the bed. I would not soon need it. Now that Miss Briggs had forgiven me, I was determined to live and die in New Bedford.

The home of Mrs. Cutler, where Miss Briggs lodged and boarded, was in a side street of respectable and distinguished antiquity. The street itself was arched with the branches of giant elms, and each house was an island surrounded by grass, and over the porches climbed roses. It was too warm to remain indoors, so we sat on the steps of the porch, and through the leaves of the elms the electric light globe

"THE LOG OF THE 'JOLLY POLLY'"

served us as a moon. For an automobile salesman I was very shy, very humble.

Twice before I had given offense and I was determined if it lay with me, it would not happen again. I did not hope to interest Miss Briggs in myself, nor did I let it appear how tremendously I was interested in her. For the moment I was only a stranger in a strange land making a social call. I asked Miss Briggs about New Bedford and the whaling, about the books she sold, and the books she liked. It was she who talked. When I found we looked at things in the same way and that the same things gave us pleasure I did not comment on that astonishing fact, but as an asset more precious than gold, stored it away. When I returned to the hotel I found that concerning Miss Briggs I had made important discoveries. I had learned that her name was Polly, that the *Jolly Polly* had been christened after her grandmother, that she was an orphan, that there were relatives with whom she did not "hit it off," that she was very well read, possessed of a most charming sense of humor, and that I found her the most attractive girl I had ever met.

The next morning I awoke in an exalted frame of mind. I was in love with life, with New Bedford, and with Polly Briggs. I had

"THE LOG OF THE 'JOLLY POLLY'"

been in love before, but never with a young lady who worked in a shop, and I found that loving a lady so occupied gives one a tremendous advantage. For when you call she must always be at home, nor can she plead another engagement. So, before noon, knowing she could not deny herself, I was again at Hatchardson's, purchasing more postal-cards. But Miss Briggs was not deceived. Nor apparently was any one else. The *Bedford Mercury* had told how, the previous evening, Frederick Fitzgibbon, an automobile salesman from New York, had been knocked out by an automobile while saving Miss Polly Briggs from a similar fate; and Mr. Hatchardson and all the old ladies who were in the bookstore making purchases congratulated me. It was evident that in Miss Briggs they took much more than a perfunctory interest. They were very fond of her. She was an institution; and I could see that as such to visitors she would be pointed out with pride, as was the new bronze statue of the Whaleman in Court House Square. Nor did they cease discussing her until they had made it quite clear to me that in being knocked out in her service I was a very lucky man. I did not need to be told that, especially as I noted that Miss Briggs was anxious lest I should not be properly modest. Indeed, her wish that

"THE LOG OF THE 'JOLLY POLLY'"

in the eyes of the old ladies I should appear to advantage was so evident, and her interest in me so proprietary, that I was far from unhappy.

The afternoon I spent in Fairharbor. From a real estate agent I obtained keys to those cottages on the water-front that were for rent, and I busied myself exploring them. The one I most liked I pretended I had rented, and I imagined myself at work among the flower-beds, or with my telescope scanning the shipping in the harbor, or at night seated in front of the open fire watching the green and blue flames of the driftwood. Later, irresolutely, I wandered across town to Harbor Castle, this time walking entirely around it and coming upon a sign that read, "Visitors Welcome. Do not pick the flowers."

Assuring myself that I was moved only by curiosity, I accepted the invitation, nor, though it would greatly have helped the appearance of the cemetery-like beds, did I pick the flowers. On a closer view Harbor Castle certainly possessed features calculated to make an impecunious author stop, look, and listen. I pictured it peopled with my friends. I saw them at the long mahogany table of which through the French window I got a glimpse, or dancing in the music-room, or lounging on the wicker chairs on the sweeping verandas. I could see

"THE LOG OF THE 'JOLLY POLLY'"

them in flannels at tennis, in bathing-suits diving from the spring-board of the swimming-pool, departing on excursions in the motor-cars that at the moment in front of the garage were being sponged and polished, so that they flashed like mirrors. And I thought also of the two-thousand-ton yacht and to what far countries, to what wonderful adventures it might carry me.

But all of these pictures lacked one feature. In none of them did Polly Briggs appear. For, as I very well knew, that was something the ambitions of Mrs. Farrell would not permit. That lady wanted me as a son only because she thought I was a social asset. By the same reasoning, as a daughter-in-law, she would not want a shop-girl, especially not one who as a shop-girl was known to all New Bedford. My mood as I turned my back upon the golden glories of Harbor Castle and walked to New Bedford was thoughtful.

I had telegraphed my servant to bring me more clothes and my Phœnix car; and as I did not want him inquiring for Fletcher Farrell had directed him to come by boat to Fall River. Accordingly, the next morning, I took the trolley to that city, met him at the wharf, and sent him back to New York. I gave him a check with instructions to have it cashed in that city and to send the money, and my mail, to Frederick Fitzgibbon. This *alias* I explained to him by saying I was gathering material for an article to prove one could live on fifty cents a day. He was greatly relieved to learn I did not need a valet to help me prove it.

I returned driving the Phœnix to New Bedford, and as it was a Saturday, when the store closed at noon, I had the ineffable delight of taking Polly Briggs for a drive. As chaperons she invited two young friends of hers named Lowell. They had been but very lately married, and regarded me no more than a chauffeur they had hired by the hour. This left Polly who was beside me on the front seat, and myself, to our own devices. Our devices were innocent enough. They consisted in conveying the self-centred Lowells so far from home that they could not get back for supper and were so forced to dine with me. Polly, for as Polly I now thought of her, discovered the place. It was an inn, on the edge of a lake with an Indian name. We did not get home until late, but it had been such a successful party that before we separated we planned another journey for the morrow. That one led to the Cape by way of Bourne and Wood's Hole, and back again to the North Shore to Barnstable, where we lunched. It was a grand day and the first

"THE LOG OF THE 'JOLLY POLLY'"

of others just as happy. After that every afternoon when the store closed I picked up the Lowells and then Polly, and we sought adventures. Sometimes we journeyed no farther than the baseball park, but as a rule I drove them to some inn for dinner, where later, if there were music, we danced, if not, we returned slowly through the pine woods and so home by the longest possible route. The next Saturday I invited them to Boston. We started early, dined at the Touraine and went on to a musical comedy, where I had reserved seats in the front row. This nearly led to my undoing. Late in the first act a very merry party of young people who had come up from Newport and Narragansett to the Coates-Islip wedding filled the stage boxes and at sight of me began to wave and beckon. They were so insistent that between the acts I thought it safer to visit them. They wanted to know why I had not appeared at the wedding, and who was the beautiful girl.

The next morning on our return trip to New Bedford Polly said, "I read in the papers this morning that those girls in that theatre party last night were the bridesmaids at the Coates-Islip wedding. They seemed to know you quite well."

I explained that in selling automobiles one became acquainted with many people.

"THE LOG OF THE 'JOLLY POLLY'"

Polly shook her head and laughed. Then she turned and looked at me.

"You never sold an automobile in your life," she said.

With difficulty I kept my eyes on the road; but I protested vigorously.

"Don't think I have been spying," said Polly; "I found you out quite by accident. Yesterday a young man I know asked me to persuade you to turn in your Phœnix and let him sell you one of the new model. I said you yourself were the agent for the Phœnix, and he said that, on the contrary, *he* was, and that you had no right to sell the car in his territory."

I grinned guiltily and said:

"Well, I *haven't* sold any, have I?"

"That is not the point," protested Polly. "What was your reason for telling me you were trying to earn a living selling automobiles?"

"So that I could take you driving in one," I answered.

"Oh!" exclaimed Polly.

There was a pause during which in much inward trepidation I avoided meeting her eyes. Then Polly added thoughtfully, "I think that was a very good reason."

In our many talks the name of the Fletcher Farrells had never been mentioned. I had been most careful to avoid it. As each day passed,

"THE LOG OF THE 'JOLLY POLLY'"

and their return imminent, and in consequence my need to fly grew more near, and the name was still unspoken, I was proportionately grateful. But when the name did come up I had reason to be pleased, for Polly spoke it with approval, and it was not of the owner of Harbor Castle she was speaking, but of myself. It was one evening about two weeks after we had met, and I had side-stepped the Lowells and was motoring with Polly alone. We were talking of our favorite authors, dead and alive.

"You may laugh," said Polly, and she said it defiantly, "and I don't know whether you would call him among the dead or the living, but I am very fond of Fletcher Farrell!"

My heart leaped. I was so rattled that I nearly ran the car into a stone wall. I thought I was discovered and that Polly was playing with me. But her next words showed that she was innocent. She did not know that the man to whom she was talking and of whom she was talking were the same. "Of course you will say," she went on, "that he is too romantic, that he is not true to life. But I never lived in the seventeenth century, so I don't know whether he is true to life or not. And I like romance. The life I lead in the store gives me all the reality I want. I like to read about brave men and 'great and gracious ladies.'

"THE LOG OF THE 'JOLLY POLLY'"

I never met any girls like those Farrell writes about, but it's nice to think they exist. I wish I were like them. And, his men, too—they make love better than any other man I ever read about."

"Better than I do?" I asked.

Polly gazed at the sky, frowning severely. After a pause, and as though she had dropped my remark into the road and the wheels had crushed it, she said, coldly, "Talking about books——"

"No," I corrected, "we were talking about Fletcher Farrell."

"Then," said Polly with some asperity, "don't change the subject. Do you know," she went on hurriedly, "that you look like him—like the pictures of him—as he was."

"Heavens!" I exclaimed, "the man's not dead!"

"You know what I mean," protested Polly. "As he was before he stopped writing."

"Nor has he stopped writing," I objected; "his books have stopped selling."

Polly turned upon me eagerly.

"Do you know him?" she demanded.

I answered with caution that I had met him.

"Oh!" she exclaimed, "tell me about him!"

I was extremely embarrassed. It was a bad place. About myself I could not say any-

"THE LOG OF THE 'JOLLY POLLY'"

thing pleasant, and behind my back, as it were, I certainly was not going to say anything unpleasant. But Polly relieved me of the necessity of saying anything.

"I don't know any man," she exclaimed fervently, "I would so like to meet!"

It seemed to me that after that the less I said the better. So I told her something was wrong with the engine and by the time I had pretended to fix it, I had led the conversation away from Fletcher Farrell as a novelist to myself as a chauffeur.

The next morning at the hotel, temptation was again waiting for me. This time it came in the form of a letter from my prospective father-in-law. It had been sent from Cape May to my address in New York, and by my servant forwarded in an envelope addressed to "Frederick Fitzgibbon."

It was what in the world of commerce is called a "follow-up" letter. It recalled the terms of his offer to me, and improved upon them. It made it clear that even after meeting me Mr. Farrell and his wife were still anxious to stand for me as a son. They were good enough to say they had found me a "perfect gentleman." They hoped that after considering their proposition I had come to look upon it with favor.

"THE LOG OF THE 'JOLLY POLLY'"

As his son, Mr. Farrell explained, my annual allowance would be the interest on one million dollars, and upon his death his entire fortune and property he would bequeath to me. He was willing, even anxious, to put this in writing. In a week he would return to Fairharbor when he hoped to receive a favorable answer. In the meantime he enclosed a letter to his housekeeper.

"Don't take anything for granted," he urged, "but go to Fairharbor and present this letter. See the place for yourself. Spend the week there and act like you were the owner. My housekeeper has orders to take her orders from you. Don't refuse something you have never seen!"

This part of the letter made me feel as mean and uncomfortable as a wet hen. The open, almost too open, methods of Mr. Farrell made my own methods appear contemptible. He was urging me to be his guest and I was playing the spy. But against myself my indignation did not last. A letter, bearing a special delivery stamp which arrived later in the afternoon from Mrs. Farrell, turned my indignation against her, and with bitterness. She also had been spying. Her letter read:

The Pinkerton I employed to report on you states that after losing you for a week he located you at New Bedford, that you are living under the name of Fitzgibbon, and

"THE LOG OF THE 'JOLLY POLLY'"

that you have made yourself conspicuous by attentions to a young person employed in a shop. This is for me a great blow and disappointment, and I want you to clearly understand Mr. Farrell's offer is made to you as an unmarried man. I cannot believe your attentions are serious, but whether they are serious or not, they must cease. The detective reports the pair of you are now the talk of Fairharbor. You are making me ridiculous. I do not want a shop-girl for a daughter-in-law and you will either give up her acquaintance or *give up Harbor Castle!*

I am no believer in ultimatums. In attaining one's end they seldom prove successful. I tore the note into tiny pieces, and defiantly, with Polly in the seat beside me, drove into the open country. At first we picked our way through New Bedford, from the sidewalks her friends waved to her, and my acquaintances smiled. The detective was right. We had indeed made ourselves the talk of the town, and I was determined the talk must cease.

We had reached Ruggles Point when the car developed an illness. I got out to investigate. On both sides of the road were tall hemlocks and through them to the west we could see the waters of Sippican Harbor in the last yellow rays of the sun as it sank behind Rochester. Overhead was the great harvest moon.

Polly had taken from the pocket of the car some maps and guide-books, and while I lifted the hood and was deep in the machinery she was turning them over.

"THE LOG OF THE 'JOLLY POLLY'"

"What," she asked, "is the number of this car? I forget."

As I have said, I was preoccupied and deep in the machinery; that is, with a pair of pliers I was wrestling with a recalcitrant wire. Unsuspiciously I answered:

"Eight-two-eight."

A moment later I heard a sharp cry, and raised my head. With eyes wide in terror Polly was staring at an open book. Without appreciating my danger I recognized it as "Who's Who in Automobiles." The voice of Polly rose in a cry of disbelief.

"Eight-two-eight," she read, "owned by Fletcher Farrell, Hudson Apartments, New York City." She raised her eyes to mine.

"Is that true?" she gasped. "*Are* you Fletcher Farrell?"

I leaned into the car and got hold of her hand.

"That is not important," I stammered. "What is important is this: Will you be Mrs. Fletcher Farrell?"

What she said may be guessed from the fact that before we returned to New Bedford we drove to Fairharbor and I showed her the cottage I liked best. It was the one with the oldest clapboard shingles, the oldest box hedge, the most fragrant honeysuckles, and a lawn that wet its feet in the surf. Polly liked it the best, too.

"THE LOG OF THE 'JOLLY POLLY'"

By now the daylight had gone, and on the ships the riding lights were shining, but shining sulkily, for the harvest moon filled the world with golden radiance. As we stood on the porch of the empty cottage, in the shadow of the honeysuckles, Polly asked an impossible question. It was:

"How *much* do you love me?"

"You will never know," I told her, "but I can tell you this: I love you more than a two-thousand-ton yacht, the interest on one million dollars, and Harbor Castle!"

It was a wasteful remark, for Polly instantly drew away.

"What *do* you mean?" she laughed.

"Fletcher Farrell of Harbor Castle," I explained, "offered me those things, minus you. But I wanted you."

"I see," cried Polly, "he wanted to adopt you. He always talks of that. I am sorry for him. He wants a son so badly."

She sighed softly, "Poor uncle!"

"Poor *what!*" I yelled.

"Didn't you know," exclaimed Polly, "that Mrs. Farrell was a Briggs! She was my father's sister."

"Then *you*," I said, "are the relation who was 'too high and mighty'!"

Polly shook her head.

"THE LOG OF THE 'JOLLY POLLY'"

"No," she said, "I didn't want to be dependent."

"And you gave up all that," I exclaimed, "and worked at Hatchardson's, just because you didn't want to be dependent!"

"I like my uncle-in-law very much," explained Polly, "but not my aunt. So, it was no temptation. No more," she cried, looking at me as though she were proud of me, "than it was to you!"

In guilty haste I changed the subject. In other words, I kissed her. I knew some day I would have to confess. But until we were safely married that could wait. Before confessing I would make sure of her first. The next day we announced our engagement and Polly consented that it should be a short one. For, as I pointed out, already she had kept me waiting thirty years. The newspapers dug up the fact that I had once been a popular novelist, and the pictures they published of Polly proved her so beautiful that, in congratulation, I received hundreds of telegrams. The first one to arrive came from Cape May. It read:

My dear boy—your uncle elect sends his heartiest congratulations to you and love to Polly. Don't make any plans until you hear from me—am leaving to-night.
FLETCHER FARRELL.

"THE LOG OF THE 'JOLLY POLLY'"

In terror Polly fled into my arms. Even when *not* in terror it was a practice I strongly encouraged.

"We are lost!" she cried. "They will adopt us in spite of ourselves. They will lock us up for life in Harbor Castle! I don't *want* to be adopted. I want *you!* I want my little cottage!"

I assured her she should have her little cottage; I had already bought it. And during the two weeks before the wedding, when I was not sitting around Boston while Polly bought clothes, we refurnished it. Polly furnished the library, chiefly with my own books, and "The Log of the *Jolly Polly*." I furnished the kitchen. For a man cannot live on honeysuckles alone.

My future uncle-in-law was gentle but firm.

"You can't get away from the fact," he said, "that you will be my nephew, whether you like it or not. So, be kind to an old man and let him give the bride away and let her be married from Harbor Castle."

In her white and green High Flier car and all of her diamonds, Mrs. Farrell called on Polly and begged the same boon. We were too happy to see any one else dissatisfied; so though we had planned the quietest of weddings, we gave consent. Somehow we survived it. But now we recall it only as that terrible time when we were never alone. For once in the hands of our rich relations the quiet wedding we had arranged became a royal alliance, a Field of the Cloth of Gold, the chief point of attack for the moving-picture men.

The youths who came from New York to act as my ushers informed me that the Ushers' Dinner at Harbor Castle—from which, after the fish course, I had fled—was considered by them the most successful ushers' dinner in their career of crime. My uncle-in-law also testifies to this. He ought to know. At four in the morning he was assisting the ushers in throwing the best man and the butler into the swimming-pool.

For our honeymoon he loaned us the yacht. "Take her as far as you like," he said. "After this she belongs to you and Polly. And find a better name for her than *Harbor Lights*. It sounds too much like a stay-at-home. And I want you two to see the world."

I thanked him, and suggested he might rechristen her the *Jolly Polly*.

"That was the name," I pointed out, "of the famous whaler owned by Captain Briggs, your wife's father, and it would be a compliment to Polly, too."

My uncle-in-law-elect agreed heartily; but made one condition:

"THE LOG OF THE 'JOLLY POLLY'"

"I'll christen her that," he said, "if you will promise to write a new Log of the *Jolly Polly*."
I promised.
This is it.